ICE BURN

A KATE STARK THRILLER

M. L. BUCHMAN

PRAISE FOR M. L. BUCHMAN

Tom Clancy fans open to a strong female lead will clamor for more.

— *DRONE,* PUBLISHERS WEEKLY

Superb! Miranda is utterly compelling!

— *BOOKLIST,* STARRED REVIEW

Escape Rating: A. Five Stars! OMG just start with *Drone* and be prepared for a fantastic binge-read!

— READING REALITY, MIRANDA CHASE
SERIES

The best military thriller I've read in a very long time. Love the female characters.

— *DRONE,* SHELDON MCARTHUR, FOUNDER
OF THE MYSTERY BOOKSTORE, LA

Meticulously researched, hard-hitting, and suspenseful.

— *PURE HEAT,* PUBLISHERS WEEKLY,
STARRED REVIEW

A fabulous soaring thriller.

— *TAKE OVER AT MIDNIGHT,* MIDWEST BOOK
REVIEW

Buchman has catapulted his way to the top tier of my favorite authors.

— FRESH FICTION

Nonstop action that will keep readers on the edge of their seats.

— *TAKE OVER AT MIDNIGHT,* LIBRARY
JOURNAL

M L. Buchman's ability to keep the reader right in the middle of the action is amazing.

— LONG AND SHORT REVIEWS

The only thing you'll ask yourself is, "When does the next one come out?"

— *WAIT UNTIL MIDNIGHT,* RT REVIEWS, 4
STARS

I knew the books would be good, but I didn't realize how good.

— NIGHT STALKERS SERIES, KIRKUS
REVIEWS

SIGN UP FOR M. L. BUCHMAN'S NEWSLETTER TODAY

and receive:
Release News
Free Short Stories
a Free Book

Get your free book today. Do it now.
free-book.mlbuchman.com

Other works by M. L. Buchman: *(⁴ - also in audio)*

Action-Adventure Thrillers

Kate Stark
Final Taste
Ice Burn
Knife's Edge

Miranda Chase
Drone⁺
Thunderbolt⁺
Condor⁺
Ghostrider⁺
Raider⁺
Chinook⁺
Havoc⁺
White Top⁺
Start the Chase⁺
Lightning⁺
Skibird⁺
Nightwatch⁺
Osprey⁺
Gryphon⁺
Wedgetail⁺

Science Fiction / Fantasy

Deities Anonymous
Cookbook from Hell: Reheated
Saviors 101

Contemporary Romance

Eagle Cove
Return to Eagle Cove
Recipe for Eagle Cove
Longing for Eagle Cove
Keepsake for Eagle Cove

Love Abroad
Heart of the Cotswolds: England
Path of Love: Cinque Terre, Italy

Where Dreams
Where Dreams are Born
Where Dreams Reside
Where Dreams Are of Christmas⁺
Where Dreams Unfold
Where Dreams Are Written
Where Dreams Continue

Non-Fiction

Strategies for Success
Managing Your Inner Artist/Writer
Estate Planning for Authors⁺
Character Voice
Narrate and Record Your Own Audiobook⁺
Beyond Prince Charming: One Guy's Guide to Writing Men in Romance

Short Story Series by M. L. Buchman:

Action-Adventure Thrillers

Kate Stark
Miranda Chase Stories

Romantic Suspense

Antarctic Ice Fliers

US Coast Guard

Contemporary Romance

Eagle Cove

Other

Deities Anonymous (fantasy)

Single Titles

The Emily Beale Universe
(military romantic suspense)

The Night Stalkers
MAIN FLIGHT
The Night Is Mine
I Own the Dawn
Wait Until Dark
Take Over at Midnight
Light Up the Night
Bring On the Dusk
By Break of Day
Target of the Heart
Target Lock on Love
Target of Mine
Target of One's Own
NIGHT STALKERS HOLIDAYS
Daniel's Christmas*
Frank's Independence Day*
Peter's Christmas*
Christmas at Steel Beach
Zachary's Christmas*
Roy's Independence Day*
Damien's Christmas*
Christmas at Peleliu Cove

Henderson's Ranch
Nathan's Big Sky*
Big Sky, Loyal Heart*
Big Sky Dog Whisperer*
Tales of Henderson's Ranch*

Shadow Force: Psi
At the Slightest Sound*
At the Quietest Word*
At the Merest Glance*
At the Clearest Sensation*

White House Protection Force
Off the Leash*
On Your Mark*
In the Weeds*

Firehawks
Pure Heat
Full Blaze
Hot Point*
Flash of Fire*
Wild Fire
SMOKEJUMPERS
Wildfire at Dawn*
Wildfire at Larch Creek*
Wildfire on the Skagit*

Delta Force
Target Engaged*
Heart Strike*
Wild Justice*
Midnight Trust*

Night Stalkers Reload
Guard the East Flank*

Emily Beale Universe Short Story Series
The Night Stalkers
The Night Stalkers Stories
The Night Stalkers CSAR
The Night Stalkers Wedding Stories
The Future Night Stalkers

Delta Force
Th Delta Force Shooters
The Delta Force Warriors

Firehawks
The Firehawks Lookouts
The Firehawks Hotshots
The Firebirds

White House Protection Force
Stories

Future Night Stalkers
Stories (Science Fiction)

ABOUT THIS BOOK

The head chef for the G-7 meeting at a luxury resort in the Scottish Highlands dies in the middle of a television interview. All fingers point to former Secret Service agent turned owner of Cooks Network, Kate Stark.

At the same instant, a sugar sculpture chef dies horribly on-air in her New York studio. Her failure to protect the Vice President-elect during her years as a protection detail agent does *not* improve her standing.

The FBI, the British Diplomatic Protection Group, a world-class Black Hat hacker, and an old friend from the US Secret Service all target her as Suspect Number One. Is it personal? Or is this a far more dangerous attack, perhaps targeting the Presidency itself?

Kate's ragtag team of rugged individualists must pull together once more if she wants to survive.

Previously published as Dead Chef #2, Two Chef!

About This Book

A list of characters and locations may be found at:
https://mlbuchman.com/people-places-planes#KS
And return afterward for a free bonus story
and a recipe from the book.

To the two fans who really helped me bring my vision to life: Dean and Shelly.

With special thanks to Vicki McQuillan at Inverlochy Castle Hotel for her kind assistance with "committing murder" in her hotel.

The Inverlochy Castle Hotel, the Fort William sheep race, and the Principality of Sealand are all real. The rest and what was done with them?
Well, this is a work of fiction.

TUESDAY

PROLOGUE

MAXWELL KLUGMAN ENJOYED COOKING COMPETITIONS, OR HE HAD until he'd almost died in one. He'd never found out if he won, because his competitor's dessert had killed both her and one of the judges. Poisoned. Enough to put a chef off his food.

A week later Kate Stark, the head judge and owner of the entire Cooks Network television station, had called to tell him the criminals were caught and to invite him back. He'd rather give up his grandmother's sausage recipe than ever set foot inside one of their studios again. Hell, he now considered Rockefeller Center in midtown Manhattan to be a no-man zone; especially if that man was Max Klugman.

Been kind of Ms. Stark to ask and he'd told her so, but... shit man.

Death by chocolate ganache?

Nicht. Nein. And no goddamn way.

Then Kate Stark called again, six weeks later. Not about a show she was judging—she'd be out of the country on another project—but there'd been a last-minute drop-out due to a broken leg and might he be interested?

One day.

Sugar sculpture.

He loved sculpting in sugar. Though he had no idea how she knew about that, he didn't care.

Competitions were a different kind of adrenaline rush from restaurant work—thank God. Keeping everything running smoothly night after night in a busy restaurant like his family's, well, it was both a challenge and a royal pain in the ass. Damn Pops to Hell for stroking out at fifty but not having the decency to die—instead hanging on like a dangling salami and shaming Max into taking over the business.

He'd been well down the road to making it as a sugar chef and now he was worrying about a hundred details he didn't give a rat's ass about. Crappy line cooks too drugged-out to show up. Compromising his own ideas about the menu to retain their loyal customers and not piss the fuckers off. *And* not becoming the Klugman who destroyed four generations of shining success and family tradition.

A sugar competition embodied cleanliness, purity, and it jolted the nervous system like cocaine had back when he was a younger and stupider chef.

A well-designed competition started as an adrenal high and then climbed from there—a single clear punch that left you wrung out and, hopefully, triumphant at the end.

Instant gratification.

Maxwell liked instant gratification...a lot! Nothing to do with old cocaine habits, of course.

At the highest level of sugar-work challenges, against the top competitors, the jolt climbed over a precipice he could never achieve otherwise—better than sex with his new girlfriend. It carried him into a state of simpatico with the sculpture's hard-crack architecture—a world of precise techniques, not wondering if the bloody lump on his cutting block was grass-fed beef or if the fucking merchant slipped him corn-fed instead.

He made his living with German cuisine. The towering sculptures made of glass-clear sheets of pulled sugars, swirling cones of hardened ribbon sugar, and blown-sugar figurines—they were his joy. He ran the only German restaurant in New York with an old meat locker turned into a dedicated sugar kitchen, perhaps the only one in the world.

That Kate Stark knew that about him—and thought of him when it wasn't even her show with the scheduling issue—had told him how damned impressive the woman really was. Not his type at all. He preferred his girlfriends to be...no real way to be all politically correct about it, not quite so terrifyingly competent. Kate walked into a room and made everyone want to snap to attention or bow or some such shit.

The other reason he'd agreed to do it? No taste testing during a sculpture competition. When he'd caved to Stark's ever-so-perfectly couched pleading, he figured that no one could poison him, even if he did go back to the Cooks Network studio. He'd stay focused on the competition.

He'd be fine.

Now, three hours into the competition with less than ten minutes left, he wallowed deep in the sugar-high zone. He didn't need to look at his design sketches, hadn't since the start of the competition because it radiated like shining crystal in his head. He ignored his competitors, the hot lights, the studio cameras and audience, and, most of all, the judges. Couldn't let those bastards into his head while he worked—though he couldn't keep his wheezing father out.

A slacker Klugman. Never thought I'd see the day, you overgrown fairy. That almost earned the man his death for real.

Screw the old bastard; this morning was his. He'd feed the fucking restaurant patrons later. Right now, his sous chef bore the burden.

A quick glance to either side proved that his current masterpiece existed in a far different class than his two competitors. At six feet tall, two hundred pounds of melted and re-formed sugar, Elsa's castle from Disney's *Frozen* was a shoo-in for the win.

He built towers, turrets, and battlements; he built and hung the central chandelier of spun-sugar tendrils.

The competitor to his left had chosen a similar scale, but a much simpler depiction. *WALL-E's* junk world was merely suggested—though her *pastillage* of WALL-E and EVE were damn near perfect. He wouldn't mind learning a thing or two about working soft sugars from her. Nice butt too, which he could also think of definite uses for. He'd remember that for when the current girlfriend no longer worked out.

To his right stood an elaborate and gorgeously colored sea anemone that included the weak-finned but undeniably cute Nemo and his worried looking dad, Marlin. Charming, but too small. Read as: *No victory for you, dude.*

He so had this one.

When Maxwell pulled the ball-peen hammer out of his toolkit with less than three minutes remaining on the clock, a surprised murmur rippled through the studio audience.

His ice castle looked complete.

And it was.

It only needed one final touch.

Time to kick serious sugar ass.

He kept his face carefully neutral as he waved a cameraman in for a close-up. When he positioned the lens to spy through the largest castle window, he made the move he'd practiced a hundred times in private.

The other two competitors stopped to watch what in the hell he was doing despite the last moments of the competition clock ticking down. *Hang on to your silicone mats, you're gonna need 'em to shit on after you see this move. You two can pack it up and go home now!*

Reaching into the grand entrance hall through the towering

double doors of his sugar castle, he lightly tapped the hammer in a circle around the edges of the main floor of inch-thick pressed sugar.

It was so retro to use pressed sugar, hardly any chef did anymore. It took an application of pressure and patience, waiting much longer than with other sugars for it to set. In a competition where every second was precious, it was considered a waste of time...by most. Pressed sugar was also cloudy and not a terribly aesthetic look at.

However...

He made sure the camera was in the right position, then he rapped the exact center of the sheet with his hammer.

Hard!

The judges gasped as the sugar shattered with an audible crack—normally a disastrous sound in a sugar sculpture.

A number of people in the studio audience cried out.

His petite girlfriend, who had watched him do this again and again, held her hands over her mouth; her pretty blonde hair covering half her face didn't hide the anticipation and excitement. Oh, it was gonna be good with her tonight. She always did something extra special after a competition and her imagination was amazing.

Maxwell withdrew the hammer. He picked up the tiny figurine of Elsa made of blown sugar in pale blue, white, and blonde, and tacked her to the center of the crack with a bit of dampened paste. Then he stepped back and let the camera drink its fill.

The pressed sugar base had shattered. The center of the break burst outward from the struck center to terminate at each of the tiny dents he'd made around the edges.

With that final stroke, he'd created a snowflake pattern in the sugar floor nearly identical to the one Elsa had created in the floor of her castle with a stomp of her heel—where the figurine's extended heel now rested, covering the shatter point left by the hammer. The pressed sugar's cloudiness looked exactly like ice and snow.

As people saw what he'd done on the studio monitors, they roared to their feet. The judges were standing and applauding. *Eat that, Pops!* The entire television studio rang with shouts, wolf whistles, and applause. He could only hope the old bastard was watching from what ever pit of hell he occupied.

Unknown to anyone in the studio, a ten-thousand-dollar Svantek SVAN 979 sound-and-vibration analyzer mounted beneath the sculpture's display table measured this unusually loud volume.

The applause and cheering peaked, sending vibrations through the structure of the metal table itself.

The levels exceeded the preset threshold.

The Svantek emitted an electronic error signal.

Two tiny explosive charges interpreted the Svantek's error signal as a firing charge and sheared off both legs of Maxwell Klugman's worktable on the side closest to him.

In slow motion, the legs buckled.

The table tilted.

Then collapsed.

Two hundred pounds of razor-sharp towers, spires, and buttresses slowly tilted...then tumbled.

Elsa's ice palace of sugar crashed into Maxwell Klugman's body with a hammer blow of force that drove him to the floor and spiked him there.

His last thought ever was that he'd been done in by a Disney movie.

Shit man.

1

TIM ROCKETED TO HIS FEET FROM HIS CHAIR IN THE TELEVISION studio audience and stared in horror.

Someone had anonymously given him a ticket to the sugar competition show, a thousand dollars, a fake beard, and a Yankees ball cap. The note with it had been simple: *Stay until the end. Don't look away. Get a thousand more.*

And he'd done it despite the show's early hour and his total disinterest. *Sugar sculpture? People cared shit about sugar sculpture?* But he needed the money bad for tuition and rent.

Now he couldn't look away if he wanted to.

The blood splattered across the television studio.

The chef's gaping wounds, cut deep by knifepoints of sugar towers, pumped and spewed.

One competitor screamed and ran. The other stumbled back against his workstation to vomit out his guts and knocked the crystalline reproduction of *Nemo* to the floor.

The massive sugar-built anemone hit the concrete and shattered like a bomb. Bits and pieces scattered all the way to Tim's second row seat.

The judges, now peppered with shards, were trying to take

cover behind their table. The tall brunette in the center offered the audience a major thonged full moon as she dove under the table. Certain people shouldn't try to wear things like that— definitely including her fat ass.

Most of the audience screamed and stampeded to the exit doors.

Except one.

A seriously cute blonde in the first row jumped to her feet and rushed toward the bleeding man.

Tim had watched enough CSI—when he should have been working on the fashion design portfolio that was his college senior project—to know the man was past helping and no one should disturb the crime scene.

He leapt over the seats and managed to catch the woman three steps before she reached the dying chef.

She cried out one last time as Tim turned her away from the pumping blood and into his arms. She buried her face against his shoulder and wept hysterically.

He held her and watched the last of the life drain out of the chef's straining eyes as the studio's staff rushed to help.

Holy fuck! Death was so...so...real!

Tim had never expected to see violent death any closer than his television screen.

The guy didn't look all that old, and he sported a total babe for a girlfriend, and now the dude had gone down hard. He'd never really thought about it, but always kinda figured death happened to old people.

Shit, Tim! You wanna be a Page Six designer, you better get your shit together. Might have less time than you think.

His designs always lacked something. Some zing or hook. And now, as the dead-man's blood flowed out slower and slower, Tim could see that his designs were no more than a television image of a much harsher, more vibrant reality. A month left and he'd have to redo his whole portfolio, but it would be total shit-ticket awesome.

For now, he watched reality unfold—rather *leak*—out of the chef's multiple wounds visible over the shoulder of the weeping woman he held. He shifted so that she wouldn't notice his body's inevitable reaction to holding her.

Inside Tim's baseball hat, a small camera peeked out at the base of the K in Yankees. He'd trailed the wire down through his hair, inside the back of his shirt, and to the phone in his pocket that, per instructions, he'd turned on at the start of the show. He knew enough to see that the icon on the phone screen logged onto an account in the data cloud, though he couldn't see which one. Since the beginning of the show, he'd been streaming the video from the camera.

And now he understood why he was here. In minutes, the video would be gone from the cloud. The online account deleted. So, he waited until the dude bled all the way out and the pool of blood flowed toward them.

Man! So much blood.

He noted the attributes: shine, richness of tone, flow and movement...

Waiting it out churned his stomach, but his unknown benefactor had to get full value. Besides, he needed that second thousand dollars to redo his entire line more than the need to keep his apartment.

When there was truly no more to see, he guided the sobbing blonde out of the studio without letting her turn toward the dead man.

In the hallway, she thanked him and apologized for getting his t-shirt all wet and snotty.

He mumbled something sensational like, "S'okay. Needs washing anyway." So did most of his clothes.

She dropped into a hallway chair as if leaving the studio pulled the plug on her nervous system. A network assistant rushed up to her and soon she was weeping again in that woman's arms.

Tim almost stayed with her, then considered the equipment currently hanging on his body, the fake beard and mustache he wore, and that the police would be here soon. He definitely needed to *not* be in jail as an accomplice to murder, though an unwitting one.

So, he opted for a discreet exit and headed down in the elevator. When he reached the lobby, he could see the police already blocking a few of the exit doors.

He stayed on the elevator and rode down to the Concourse Level. As casually as he could, he strolled out the long way, past Banana Republic and Ann Taylor. He couldn't help but window shop there a bit. Her designs looked impossibly simple but were so urban chic. He wished he could have an Ann Taylor girlfriend; they always looked so casual and perfect. *Not gonna happen. In your dreams, Tim.* His last girlfriend had been a goth, with habits less sanitary than his own.

Holding that weeping blonde for a moment—who would be like the perfect Ann Taylor model—was as close as he'd ever been. Probably ever would be.

At his apartment, he found a thin envelope slid under the door; the second thousand and another simple instruction: *Dump the gear.* He considered hocking it, had to be worth at least a grand retail, but that could lead to awkward questions.

Using his fan-of-CSI experience, he waited until after dark to diminish what the street cameras could see. He walked a few blocks downtown wearing his roommate's oversized Disneyland hoodie and dumped it all in a public trashcan outside the Chrysler Building wrapped up with half of a sandwich that his other roommate had left in the fridge until it was gone too green to eat.

Nowhere near his apartment or the studio.

Not a heavy tourist attraction, mostly a lot of office space.

So, the outside cans would catch a lot of garbage, but like there was no real reason to have a whole lotta cop patrols nosing around here to protect the dumbass tourists who couldn't find shit in this town. Always looking lost, always asking directions. Easy marks he'd tapped a time or two when tuition got tight.

This was now a job done clean, and he'd get bonus points from his roommates for braving the disposal of the rotting food.

Back at his apartment, he started a badly overdue load of laundry and took a shower to remove any traces of whatever. Beneath the hot water he fantasized that the pretty blonde peeled off an Ann Taylor, deep-cleavage cashmere dress in blush pink, slid into the shower with him, and held him like the world was beginning rather than ending.

2

STEPHANIE WATCHED THE LIVE BROADCAST OF THE COOKS Network *High on Sugar* in the office of her Upper East Side condo. Daddy gave it to her when she turned eighteen. She'd always appreciated the commanding view out over the Central Park Reservoir and the north end of the Metropolitan Museum of Art. She donated to the Met regularly enough to guarantee her invites to the most select of their soirees.

Her office was part corporate magnate—she'd purchased a whole set of rosewood furniture that matched Teddy Roosevelt's personal furniture; it commanded respect. It made an exceptional backdrop when she video conferenced into board meetings at the major New York newspaper that Daddy had been wise enough to leave to her.

Mom had extended clutching fingers—miraculously unwrapped from a martini glass for a moment—after Daddy's heart attack with his mistress in the Caymans. But Stephanie had crushed her feeble efforts easily.

The other part of her office constituted a fitness center—the best equipment and a floor-to-ceiling mirror; she used it diligently. Rich oriental carpets on the oak parquet tied the two halves of the room and her life together into a seamless whole. The few who entered here could never doubt the power of the woman who sat at the center of it and spun her plans.

The Cooks broadcast of *High on Sugar* condensed the first two hours and forty minutes of the three-hour competition into the show's opening forty minutes—and then run the last twenty minutes live. An extremely tough editing challenge, doing a collapsing timeline like that and yet keeping it suspenseful. She'd have to make sure to keep Kate Stark's floor manager and control-room director after she'd grabbed possession of the network; they made a clean and exciting product.

Perhaps more exciting this time than they'd anticipated. Though their cutaway was fast—done before the death became too graphic—it wasn't fast enough to disguise the *tragedy* or that initial splash of blood.

Pity that they weren't a touch slower to react. She'd have enjoyed seeing the aftermath on the live television broadcast.

But it didn't ultimately matter. That's why she'd paid the kid —the deadbeat son of a hedge fund manager she'd been having an affair with to fix her portfolio. The kid made sure she had the whole show, including after they shut down the cameras. The full three hours of the show from the kid's hidden camera feed, including the full bloody aftermath, now rested on her computer.

Stephanie had missed the first hour of the hidden camera feed while waking George in a proper fashion. She loved how men so easily believed that they were a woman's best time ever. A few well-timed moans, a shudder, a toss of long red hair, and dragging him against her bountiful breasts (she was years from needing another round of work there) at the right moment and they didn't just believe—they *believed!*

Poor George didn't even make her top third as a lover.

Her golf pro was ten times the man. When handicapped by

the thicket off the tenth green, he'd found amazing things to do with gloved hands, a five iron, and her short golf skirt while they were looking for her ball in the rough. Very rough. She drove hard for that small clump of trees every Thursday morning after that. He'd taught her well; she rarely missed.

Her personal trainer did more than keep her body perfectly toned when he visited three times a week. He liked taking her from behind, sometimes all the way behind, which was fine as his face wasn't the prettiest, but God had hung him like a horse.

George didn't make the top two-thirds now that she considered it. Frankly, her naïve housemaid at the house out in Greenwich with her dildo-for-two—shimmying away and fantasizing of her someday-green card—could out-sex George on her worst day.

But he possessed one thing going for him that no one else could deliver. What she needed most of all.

George Madsen was the Majority Whip—making him the Number Two man in the US Senate. He was the *everyone's-friend* US Senator from New York with good relations on both sides of the aisle. And, most importantly, Vice President Morgan's closest friend.

Exactly the man...if only he was more of a man. Well, nothing was perfect.

He'd set off to fill his day with what he surely thought were constructive things. That left her a chance to tip back in her office chair, sip her wheat grass-banana-soy smoothie, and watch the disaster unroll at Cooks Network.

The setup was too good to be true. It had been a long shot. She'd seen Max losing on that fatal show a few months ago. It had required some poking around to discover his weakness: sugar sculpture. Her hacker had zipped into Klugman's personal photo collection. She'd built a brochure for him and sent it to Kate Stark with Klugman's return address.

And now, he was going to become the victim. Anyone with half a brain would see that Stark wanted Klugman dead.

From the explosion on, the end result was spectacular beyond her wildest dreams.

The collapse rolled over on him with a ponderous, majestic grace. She'd hoped for a wounding, but the utter evisceration proved to be pure theater.

The kid had chased a pretty vixen—fuck buddy of the dying man by the way she acted—and gone in close to stare down at the corpse. Even crystal-clear audio. He'd captured all the initial screams as the studio emptied, as well as the quiet weepy bits muffled against his shoulder.

The kid watched it all, every last pumping spurt of red. Stayed focused on it to the bitter end—must be the way he got off. Serial killer in the making.

He'd been smart, ending the call on the phone before exiting the building. No way to tell from the video which way he turned from the exit, though Stephanie knew where to find him if she needed him again; not that he'd ever know who she was. She'd go slumming on occasion, but there were some depths she certainly wasn't going to stoop to.

And she had what she needed.

Stephanie opened a new file and started the video clip at the drama moment of Klugman cracking the crystalline floor of his sculpture and the crowd going wild. Let it run through the explosion set up by the ex-con she'd hired down in Chinatown. She ended it the moment before the kid turned away from filming the close-up of all the blood, backgrounded by the sound of wracking sobs and the kid's whispered, "Holy shit."

Simply too too perfect.

She hit send on the video clip. Her tame hacker would make sure it was sent out and went viral with no trace back to her.

She wished her personal trainer would arrive early. Today

she planned to tie him to the workout bench and fuck the shit out of him. If he recovered fast enough, she'd leave him tied there while she did her workout, then do him again. If she had her maid's double-ender here in the city, she'd take *him* right up the backside. That would be an education for him.

After months of preparation, Step One of her plan—the on-screen murder of Maxwell Klugman in Kate Stark's Cooks Network television studio—was complete. Finally, everything would start moving fast now.

3

DINO WATCHED THE CLIP.

Kinky.

His client hadn't told him what was going down but offered enough teasing tidbits and a large enough sum of cash to capture his attention. He could always hack a bank if he needed cash, but shit, she'd offered a pile. Proof that she'd be producing something fun if she lived up to her own hype.

And now this.

Make it viral! was all she'd said in the secure drop box he'd set up for her. She'd been oh so carefully anonymous, but no such thing. Not from him, anyway.

A sugar sculpture bloodbath.

A serious easy-peasy no-brainer. This vid would rock big time. He considered a theme song from Corrosion of Conformity or Dog Fashion Disco. Or go really retro with Metallica's *Sad But True*. Ultimately, he decided that the original soundtrack gave it a real-world grittiness that rocked all on its own.

She'd also been adamant about the video's title: *Kate Stark*

Nails Another. Perhaps *Another One Bites the Dust* for the soundtrack. Nah, Queen was way too mellow.

He did a quick search and scared up a video entitled *Death-by-Poisoning Double Header at Cooks Network!* It earned well over fifty million views before censors deleted it. It continued to kick around on a lot of the smaller, edgier channels, clocking a strong following.

The Stark lady sitting chill as people dropped dead all around her. Her composed jet-black hair and mystic blue-eyed beauty made a total contrast to his client's frenetic redhead. Stark was like Betty Rubble, the classiest of the whole crowd in the original cartoon. Dino always found Betty kind of sexy for that reason—until the live film put a kibosh on that. Rosie O'Donnell for a sex symbol? Who was Hollywood kidding.

He set about building the layers so that the video's point of upload wouldn't be traceable. Better yet, he laid down traces that would lead to both Iran and Israel simultaneously—which would make everyone bug-shit crazy, as a bonus.

Dino started humming the theme to *The Flintstones*.

He couldn't wait to see what came next from this client. Whatever, sure wouldn't be a moment of dullsville.

While he worked on the launch, he pulled up the montage of all her computer cameras. Bless her for wanting the convenience of computer access in every room and not knowing to put tape over the built-in webcams.

Most clients, such results weren't too interesting, but he could always count on this one for a good show. And she liked to do it with the lights on, which meant he never missed a thing, including this morning's wake-up call.

He'd built a chunk of video parsing code that always captured the segments when people were *active,* then looped those to his desktop. Oddly, she never did it solo—no self-gratification or electronic devices for her fit, full, and feisty frame. Four Fs for how much the woman liked to fuck.

Though she was never completely naked. Scarlet teddies, midnight negligees, or, at the moment, the sports bra and Lycra top, but nothing between there and her tenny trainers—natural red all the way.

She had Mr. Fitness Mexican stud strapped down, lying on a weight bench—which he didn't look too happy about, though his body didn't appear to harbor any complaints. Damn, who knew there were guys built like that? You could fly a surrender flag from that sucker.

Dino watched in fascination as she proved that she knew exactly what to do with it to get a workout.

He yelled out Fred Flintstone's trademark cheer to egg her on.

Not that she could hear him or needed the encouragement.

Yabba-dabba-doo indeed! Go girl!

4

KATE STARK WISHED SHE'D SLEPT ON THE RED-EYE FROM NEW York to Edinburgh, Scotland, yet she couldn't regret the missed night's sleep. She truly enjoyed Rikka Albert's friendship, and the woman possessed a direct line to Kate's funny bone. Throughout the flight, they were the obnoxious pair giggling like schoolgirls, keeping everyone in First Class awake.

That Kate had at one time arrested Rikka and ruined her career as a money launderer had started their friendship. After five years with no more than occasional social contact—and a minor disaster of Rikka's first cover in the Witness Protection Program getting blown and Kate hauling her out—they'd been brought back together only two months ago when they were both kidnapped by the North Koreans.

Rikka was five-foot-nothing of intensely brilliant Eurasian hacker turned sushi chef. In the last few months, she'd consumed the knowledge and skills necessary to become a fine television camera operator. Kate would have to wait to see how long that maintained her friend's insatiable energy.

When Kate chose the upcoming visit to the kitchen of the Inverlochy Castle Hotel as Rikka's first field solo, the woman offered to marry her and have her children. The fact that her boyfriend had been present neither inhibited Rikka nor fazed Sam Fierro. Of course, nothing fazed him.

At least Kate *thought* they were an item. Rikka tended to speak in circles and never on the subject where the conversation began. As to Sam Fierro—he didn't speak at all.

They were Scotland bound to do a kitchen shoot during the upcoming G-7 summit meeting. Security allowed Kate one assistant and Rikka seemed the obvious choice. Kate figured if they focused on having fun during the shoot, it should all come out well enough. But she did wish she'd had a chance to sleep on the flight before facing the DPG.

The moment they exited UK Customs, they'd been toted off to a nondescript waterfront warehouse by the British Diplomatic Protection Group in a bright red police car manned by officers who surprisingly carried firearms. They were one of the few groups in the UK domestic forces to be Authorized Firearms Officers; AFOs they'd informed her when she'd been so American as to inquire.

Once she, Rikka, and their camera equipment were deemed clear of evil intent, the security system that surrounded a meeting like the G-7 swept them into its clutches.

Kate's six years serving as an agent in the Secret Service inured her to all except the worst bureaucracy. Overly polite Brits, armed or not, counted as an easy ride.

After being the head of the Vice President-elect's Protection Detail—the detail that failed to stop his assassination by an ex-mistress—she'd retired. Not long after, she'd inherited half-control of America's Number One cooking television network. Her twin brother didn't care about his half, granting her complete creative control. It worked out fine for both of them. She made him a great deal of money, and she exercised a free hand to focus on the cooking that she loved.

Moments like this one, a trip to interview the *chef d'cuisine* responsible for the G-7 meeting, reminded Kate of that. It was a connection she sometimes lost in her world of corporate finance, network programming, and a thousand other meetings. Her happiest moments had been on the show with her mom: *Mother-Daughter Cooking*, learning a new technique, or running a cook-off between the latest James Beard Award Nominees.

"It's not working," she whispered to Rikka as they were conducted out of the interrogation rooms and told to wait in the middle of the warehouse that the DPG had commandeered.

"What isn't?"

"Your attempts to look casual."

"Well...pooh!" She used Pooh Bear's favorite curse and Kate couldn't help laughing again.

That attracted an uncertain glance from five agents, who turned away too fast for her to assess their expressions. One of them might have smiled.

"How?" Rikka asked.

"Easy guess. You're standing perfectly still. The Erika Albert I know never sat completely still in her life." Also, her green eyes were so wide that Kate wondered if Rikka would ever blink again. It was never easy to tell what caught the woman's attention, because it was often the oddest aspect of something. But the DPG's command center certainly caught it.

Kate had tried to expose her to cooking. Instead, she'd turned into a world-class sushi *itamae*—unheard of for a woman who also didn't live in Japan. It involved immense skill, but no cooking other than rice. A tour of Kate's television studio hadn't turned her into a console operator despite her massive computer background, but rather into a camera operator.

What captured Rikka about the DPG's digs in the warehouse was beyond Kate. To her, it looked like any overworked pop-up security station right down to the semi-truck pulled inside the warehouse and opened to reveal a vast array of communications gear. Maybe that was it.

The G-7 meeting of the world's leaders would convene in Scotland this year. Security had cranked up at a maximum, possibly the highest in the history of Edinburgh since the Jacobite Uprising of 1745 that had ended so abruptly on the bloodied plains at Culloden. The meeting was farther north, but Edinburgh was the common point of entry.

"I've never seen so few guns in my life," Rikka finally whispered. "How does that work?"

Rikka came out of the Chinese tong gangs working the drug and money-laundering trade in Boston. Kate had removed her, rather abruptly. So, Rikka's frame of reference about weapons was that of course everyone carried one—or two or three—at all times. Kate rather enjoyed the kinder, gentler atmosphere mandated by the British firearms policies.

Once fully cleared by the DPG, their pair of armed guards escorted them to a helicopter. It waited on the pier that stuck out into the Firth of Forth. It was a quiet July day on the Firth, mostly left to container ships and pleasure boats. The three massive red latticework sections of the Forth Rail Bridge arced with a stately dignity.

The DPG officers were hovering close, perhaps to make sure Kate and Rikka didn't decide to escape by leaping overboard and swimming across the frigid estuary. Or perhaps the DPG wanted to be sure that she didn't bend down and trigger a random bomb that happened to be hidden in plain sight on the wharf lined with officers and a pair of roving sniffer dogs.

Though in all honesty, if she were running the protection detail for the G-7, she'd be escorting herself equally closely.

Whatever their reasons, the pretty brown-and-white Eurocopter EC135 Hermes VIP-version was indeed as smooth and lush a ride as the rust-red Hermes wool blazer that Kate had, by chance, dug out of her closet against the cool July weather here in Scotland. A smooth takeoff and the midday sunshine radiant on the Firth made her think of humming Pooh's happy song.

During the hour-long flight to the helipad at the Inverlochy Castle Hotel, two interpreters also headed for the meeting discreetly ensured that she had their phone numbers, just in case. They were so identically dull that she wasn't sure whose number was which. When they found out she owned Cooks Network, they redoubled their efforts, which escalated from dull to boring.

She and Rikka traded eye rolls at how hopelessly obvious the two men were and Rikka burst into giggles, much to the men's consternation. Then Rikka leaned over, gave her a wink, followed closely by a smacking kiss. Kate barely managed to suppress her own set of giggles.

She tried to remember the last time she'd so much as laughed, never mind giggled. It felt like years since she'd unbent this much. Spending more time with Rikka Albert moved high on her personal priorities list.

5

IT WAS EARLY AFTERNOON AS THE HELICOPTER SOARED FROM THE Lowlands into the Highlands. The terrain made an abrupt shift from rolling hills covered in trees to steep hills covered in low heath, long narrow slices of water filling the valleys, and the occasional barren peak soaring several thousand feet above.

The approach to Inverlochy Castle Hotel followed a flowing river, small fields surrounded by hedgerows and old stone walls, and ancient peaks to the sides. Except Kate was on the wrong side of the helicopter and couldn't look at the hotel without one of the interpreters thinking it was a come-on, because maybe she was bi despite Rikka's kiss. Since she'd forgotten his name somewhere back around Falkirk or Stirling, she instead admired the steep hills out her side of the helicopter.

The pilot landed without any clear moment of contact, and the rotors spun down to a slow thud without stopping. He'd be gone the moment he rid himself of his human cargo to race back to Edinburgh for more.

For the hundred meters from the hotel's helipad to the back entrance of the kitchen, security tried to bundle them into a

Rolls Royce. Their refusal earned them a Protection Branch escort to the kitchen door.

As they walked, Kate was finally able to inspect the Inverlochy Castle Hotel. It was her first visit here, and it didn't disappoint.

The aesthetics utterly captivated her television producer side.

It was a three-story building built in the late nineteenth century after castles had long since become meaningless except as a statement of status. And Inverlochy stated that with a passion. Built of heavy stone, but with generous windows. Bays and turrets boasted of defense, but defense against the busy world rather than Scottish clan leaders wielding trebuchets.

Kate the woman appreciated that the perfectly groomed walkways and gardens told her of the elegance she could anticipate within. The castle faced its own private lake. It glittered beneath the midday sun that warmed the gray stone edifice isolated upon the rolling hills of Scotland.

The former United States Secret Service agent part of her noted patrol positions, spotted the snipers on the hotel's roof, and picked out the communications-and-command van tucked back in the trees to the north. She picked out three outposts perched on nearby hillsides offering a wide field of view and targeting; and could see where two others should be. They must be there, but too well hidden to spot at this distance.

Though the kitchen stood at the north end of the building, the officers walked them around the south side. Something about not wanting to *be shot up a bit*. Kate decided not to find out whether that was British humor or British understatement and went along with the slightly longer route the agents required. They'd impounded her luggage, again, so her burdens were light.

All they'd managed to keep from the agents was Rikka's camera case, and that only after careful inspection. Discovering that its contents were worth over seventy thousand pounds, if they were the ones to drop or damage it, might have been a contributing factor to its rapid release.

They circled by the main entrance out front. Halfway across the lawn to a patch of friendly looking woods stood a chess game. Most of the pieces were thigh-high, the king reaching to her waist. They were so orderly on their black-and-white stone chessboard. It would be easy to spend a great deal of time here.

"Want to play?" Rikka made a move toward one of the pawns.

"Not against you." Kate had made that mistake before and learned her lesson.

"Bawk-bawk-bawk-ba-caw!" Rikka danced in circles, making triumphant chicken noises, if there was such a thing, and flapping her elbows with her thumbs tucked under her arms. The action had both of the interpreters as well as the Protection Group agents edging away from her.

"Stop gloating."

Rikka didn't.

Kate ignored her, as well as she could ever ignore Rikka, and looked across the chessboard to the front of Inverlochy Castle. It was as impressive as the back, again the curious mixture of daunting and welcoming.

"Damn!" Rikka whispered, thankfully done with her crowing for the moment. "No wonder Queen Victoria was nuts about this place."

Kate couldn't agree more. She felt like a poor supplicant approaching grandeur. It wasn't massive, like Balmoral Castle or even Highclere where they filmed *Downton Abbey*. Stout stone, a pair of three-story bay windows, a four-story square keep, and two tiny octagonal turrets. Formal yet inviting.

She had trouble looking away as the agents led them around to the kitchen entrance.

Chef de cuisine Vivienne Jacquard greeted them warmly and

then was immediately called away to taste a sauce. Her thick Scottish brogue carried throughout the kitchen, no matter what other noise filled the air. Her manners sounded as chaotic as her wild red hair; cajoling one moment, berating the next, complimentary on only the rarest occasion.

Kate had done a lot of kitchen interviews and turned them into a successful series. *Kate's Kitchen Raids* ranked as a top show and allowed her to spend a couple of days a month working with many of the world's best chefs. That she always raided kitchens tied to major events—Hollywood premieres, the Super Bowl executive box's kitchen, key corporate retreats in foreign luxury, and the like—which certainly added to the show's high profile. It offered the added bonus of a sneak peek into the meals of the famous and powerful.

The G-7 meeting ranked as something of a hard-won coup, so to speak.

Delegates would be gathering tonight before two days of meetings, turning Vivienne Jacquard's kitchen into the center of a hot universe. The Presidents and Prime Ministers of the eight largest economies in the world, at least by someone's form of measure that always precluded the People's Republic of China, were in attendance and expecting the ultimate food experience. Russia had been a member but was booted for invading Crimea back in 2014. The EU attended; though they didn't count for reasons Kate couldn't care less about.

Give her the food and, please Lord—she didn't care if the Lord was a British, Jewish, or a buddy of the Buddha—keep the politics away from her.

Vivienne certainly ranked in the best chefs' category. She had taken a small seventeen-room luxury hotel in the Scottish Highlands and earned a Michelin star and three rosettes from the British Automobile Association. Those were big league levels that helped the hotel garner *Travel + Leisure's* Best Luxury Hotel in Europe award a few years back.

Kate sat at the small wood-surfaced prep station where Vivienne plunked them down. It was the only horizontal surface not in use. A long steel counter sported iced trays of half-meter across turbot, a grotesquely ugly but delicately flavored flatfish. A chef was working them into individual fillets, four per fish.

In a large wash sink, another chef was processing radishes, dandelion greens, and young white asparagus—Scotland was far enough north for it still to be in season in late July.

Tall windows faced a stand of trees trimmed back far enough to shed a gentle northerly light over the tidy, white-tiled workspace. The cookware had seen a thousand meals, and their scrubbed surfaces looked it, but the steel counters were generous and a chef could travel down the cook line without having to squeeze past others.

It was only mid-afternoon in Scotland, about the time she'd normally get to the office in New York, and nothing had hit the cook line yet except for sauces and tasting samples. Each breath she took tasted lush with herbs and wine reductions. Vanilla bean and lemon radiated from the baking ovens. The air in the kitchen could be a consumable delicacy all its own.

Vivienne worked down one side of the line, tasting as she went, disappeared briefly into the storerooms and her office, then back up the other side of the kitchen directing various preparations.

Rikka booted her Panasonic P2HD Varicam to life and followed Vivienne down and back. That was one of Rikka's skills. In addition to being physically small, a highly technical computer geek, and a wizard with a chef's knife, she was also the naturally stealthiest individual Kate had ever met. Rikka was constantly surprising Kate by being at her elbow when she least expected it. It was a significant advantage for a camera operator and a great combination of skills for Cooks Network.

As Vivienne came closer, she aimed a smile at Kate, but it slid strangely off her face. Not as if she was upset, rather, as if...

Rikka managed to slip through the kitchen to be again at Kate's side to film the *first meeting* of the two chefs.

Kate could see the composition in her head from Rikka's angle. Yep, a good shot. Both she and Vivienne were tall, one redhead, one jet-black haired, and both with bright blue eyes.

This would be the show's opening moment.

Between them, Vivienne and Kate would easily engage the male audience sitting on the couch beside their wives, though it was a cooking show.

Vivienne staggered, running into the chef wielding the deboning knife on the turbot. He hacked a fillet too badly to use.

"Too 'arly to be so daft clumsy, t'isn't it?" Vivienne regained her balance. "Should na be doing such until this lot are fed and I've had me a wee whisky as an excuse."

Then whatever momentarily sustained her was spent and Vivienne Jacquard collapsed forward into Kate's arms.

By the time Kate eased her to the floor, the looseness of her body told Kate that it was too late.

Vivienne's eyes were open when Kate rolled the chef onto her back on the rubber matting. Her neck flopped loose and her jaw sagged.

The nearest prep chef turned and screamed.

The release of the *chef de cuisine's* bladder added a final seasoning to the burgeoning kitchen panic.

6

KATE WASN'T SURE HOW IT HAD HAPPENED, BUT SHE HAD A MEAL to produce for eight of the world's leaders and she didn't have time to think about it.

The *sous-chef de cuisine* had panicked and run, shattering his hip when a Secret Service agent hit him with a linebacker tackle that drove him into a granite archway at the kitchen's exit. Kate initially wondered if it was a case of the *sous chef* murdering the *chef de cuisine* for advancement. Between cries of pain, the man kept babbling about never taking the job last week if he knew it could kill him.

Okay, new and panicky.

Whatever his issue, the kitchen fell into immediate disarray.

Her call for their attention had worked, and as suddenly as that, she was in charge.

The *saucier,* master of the cook top, knew squat of what the *rôtisseur* kept stashed in his ovens and fryers, and much less about the delicacies created by the top-level *pâtissier* hovering over each strawberry and flutter of powdered sugar.

As odd as it seemed, Kate knew more about all of their jobs

than anyone else did, though they'd been working side-by-side for months or longer, and she'd climbed off the helicopter less than twenty minutes ago.

Kate dropped Rikka into food prep and pulled the fish cutter up to help on the line. Rikka's last all-consuming passion prior to television camera work was making herself a premier sushi and sashimi chef, so the fish would present no problems there. Kate promoted the *saucier* to *sous chef* and then called for everyone in the kitchen—to stop. She waited until she had their full attention.

"Every sauce, fruit, vegetable that Vivienne ate, but none of you tasted, throw it out now."

"No!"

Kate looked up at the commanding voice, "Terry! Thank God!"

Terrance Tyrell was *the* person she wanted to see at this moment, all six-foot-one of him. He was the baddest and handsomest member of the Secret Service she'd ever met. Get him out of the suit and into a floppy hat and he'd make a more than fair Indiana Jones.

He was also the one who'd made the ill-advised decision five years ago to recruit Kate from the counterfeiting division over to the Protection Detail side of the Service. A decision that had cost the country a newly elected Vice President.

"Hey, stranger. Long time. You in charge all of a sudden?"

Her shrug gained his smile. It was brief, but she appreciated it nonetheless amidst the looming chaos.

"I want," Terry turned to face the other cooks, "every item that you don't trust per Kate's instructions to be preserved. Agents will come around and label the container and note the exact location of each questionable item before it is gathered for testing."

"I—" Rikka started.

"Who are you?" Terry spun to face her.

Rikka immediately stood toe-to-toe with him though he stood a foot taller. Before Rikka could start in on Terry—a battle in which Kate would not be placing any bets in favor of the United States Secret Service—Kate pulled her back.

"Terry, this is my right hand, Rikka Albert. I wouldn't suggest messing with her." It seemed only fair to give him warning, not that anyone who looked at her small Asian friend with long dark hair and angry green eyes was going to heed the warning. Rikka came across cute and pixie-like; which was right on both accounts—especially her contrary and mischievous parts.

Kate could see him preparing to ignore her warning. He'd learn soon enough.

Terry grunted in that manly, I'm-still-the-one-in-charge way that she'd always found so cute. Calling the Number Two man on the President's Protection Detail cute rested oddly on his broad shoulders, but she liked the way it fit.

"Rikka?" Kate prompted her to continue speaking.

"No, I'm not gonna help Mr. Tall-and-nasty. And he'd better call me Erika. Or better yet, Ms. Albert or I won't deign to notice him."

Terry glared down at her and she stuck her tongue out at him.

"He's rude. Why should I help Mr. Muckety-muck?"

He opened his mouth, but Kate cut him off.

"Because if things go like last time, he's our best chance for staying alive through this one."

Terry's eyes widened somewhat at that, "What last t—"

"I already texted Sam," Rikka rolled right over him. "He's on his way."

Kate figured it would take him most of a day to get here. Good. She couldn't deal with any of that at the moment. Sam might be Rikka's boyfriend, *might* be. And he had helped Kate with the North Koreans. However, he'd never forgiven Kate for the assassination of the newly elected Vice President while she'd been heading up his Protection Detail. She'd taken down the shooter, and she'd resigned despite being exonerated of any errors.

Sam wouldn't ever be satisfied.

Every attempt to talk to him about it met with his silent stonewall until Kate had subsided. It was either that or beat the crap out of him. The latter probably wasn't a smart choice as she might have been Secret Service, but he'd spent most of his two decades in the service with Marine Force Recon. Still, the temptation remained.

She'd decided that backing off in this one case indicated a healthy dose of self-preservation. Sadly, that had never been her specialty. But she wasn't going to put Rikka in the middle of it. No time for that now anyway.

The entire kitchen, packed with staff and agents, waited on their *tête-à-tête*. It was time to get the lead out.

"I told Paul to pick him up," Rikka continued.

That reduced their arrival from a day to eight hours, okay. Then she pictured the silent Sam Fierro and her never silent twin brother together on their small private jet—that was never around when Kate needed it. Maybe she should buy a second one for her own use. Again, later.

Sam was going to murder Paul before they passed the Mid-Atlantic ridge. Now if she could decide if that was a good thing or—

"Who are Sam and—"

"Later, Terry," Rikka was obviously enjoying herself at the Secret Service's expense. "What you want to know, though you don't think you do—but I'm gonna tell you anyway because Kate is a way nicer person than you are—is that I filmed Vivienne's final fifteen minutes. Didn't miss a gesture. Every dish she tasted and what she said about it." She tapped the camera once again resting on the counter beside her.

"Really? Excellent." He reached for the camera, and she slapped his hand so fast he had no chance of avoiding the hit.

"Sorry, Terry," Kate apologized, she wasn't sorry at all, but it was the only way to not laugh at him. "Forgot to warn you. She's quick. Her whole nervous system is wired faster than most humans, including yours." Kate had proven many times in the Secret Service gym that she too was one of the few people faster than Terry Tyrell, and yet she was no contest against Rikka.

"You touch my camera and break something, Mr. Secret Service, that's gonna cost you about seventy thousand pounds. Eighty grand USD to you Yank."

"And what are you?"

"I'm special!" Rikka shot back without missing a beat. "Do you have that much in your wallet? Hell, I can always hack your bank account, but I doubt if you have that much. You look like a fifteen thousand in savings kind of guy."

"Eighteen," he ground out then clamped down on his tongue.

"Tell you what, Mr. Secret Service Man. This camera records 8K at 17:9 running 120 fps capturing 8192 x 4320. If you can tell me what that means, *maybe* I'll let you touch it. Come on, even one of those?"

Terry growled once, planted a hand atop Rikka's head and straightened his arm to keep her outside kicking range as he took the camera. She swung at his arm but jerked back her hand and hissed in pain as she thudded against the knife that Kate knew he kept sheathed up the sleeve of his charcoal gray suit jacket. Not quite regulation, but no protectee ever complained about having an over-armed Service agent at their side.

Terry released her with a slight shove back that seated Rikka abruptly on a kitchen stool.

"Later, Kate. Several of the old crew are along for the ride on this one, they'll be glad to see you. A pleasure, Ms. Albert." Then he strode down the length of the silent kitchen carrying the camera.

"He's pretty," Rikka was looking at her sideways.

"I've known him since forever."

"What does that have to do with it, Kate? You've been at loose ends ever since Chicago Harold started getting down on his pastry chef."

"Don't remind me." In reality, she'd become bored with him anyway. His neediness required his woman to be nearby all the time. First off, different cities. Second, not her style in the first place. Yet, he'd been fun and...

"His loss, honey. And Mr. Agent Man is pretty."

"Let's get to work, Rikka."

They turned to figure out how to salvage the meal.

Kate cast one last look after Terry as he exited the far end of the kitchen. He wasn't pretty. He was gorgeous in every way a man should be.

And married. Surprisingly, that kind of sucked.

7

WHEN THE TEXT ARRIVED, PAUL STARK WAS HAPPILY TANGLED UP with a woman nearly twice his years who had offered to demonstrate that certain things did improve with age. She'd supported her argument impressively and repeatedly through the night, leaving him more light-headed than justified by the rarefied air of where they lay: a mountain meadow way upslope from Aspen, Colorado.

He'd thought they'd be stopping at her ranch overlooking the town, but he'd been wrong. Though it was July—early in the season to be making love out-of-doors high in the Colorado Rockies—that's precisely where she'd guided him.

Maroon Bells Lake pooled at ten thousand feet above sea level, surrounded by moonlit fourteen-thousander peaks. One hell of a setting.

An exceptionally well-maintained woman twenty years his senior, with flowing chestnut dark hair to her waist and worth a few billion on her own definitely enhanced the experience. Knowing she wasn't after his money, nor he after hers, let them simply enjoy.

And man oh man had they ever.

At some point, they'd so overheated each other that a plunge into the lake sounded like a good idea. He grimaced at the memory of his own high-pitched scream as he'd plunged into the water, unaware that it was glacier-fed. She'd laughed, made him dance naked in the moonlight to dry off and warm up, then dragged him back between the blankets she'd brought along. Once more warmth turned into heat.

Without waking her, he fished out his phone and read the text by the light of the dawn skittering golden across the maroon crags that encircled them.

Your sister in trouble again. Pick up Sam. BTW, don't fuck this up! She followed it with an emoticon that screamed at him. Easy enough to imagine coming from Rikka Albert.

Moments later a message arrived from Sam. *Noon. La Guardia.* was all it said. Not a whole lot of warm fuzzies in either message.

Shit! Kate in trouble. Last time she'd nearly gotten them all killed.

Noon in New York. Barely time if he left this instant. Not even time to kiss and run.

Well, maybe if they were quick.

8

ONE-FIFTEEN.

Sam Fierro was going to take the guy out. If he wasn't Kate's brother, he swore to God he would.

"Bad headwinds the whole way, man," Paul greeted him as he lowered the stairs on the Stark's neat Gulfstream G280 passenger jet.

Sam's years in Marine Force Recon made him expect that his ride in or out of a zone would hit the mark within thirty seconds of plan and they'd do it every time no matter where the hell you'd come down. The insert and extract teams were that accurate because the ground conditions were often tight enough that if they were forty-five seconds off the mark, the Recon team would be made up of dead men.

He knew where Paul and the Stark's plane had been. He knew the jet's capabilities, and he knew the winds aloft. The man was such a goddamn civilian, but Rikka said to bring Paul —so he'd waited.

"Let's go get lunch, buddy," Paul came clambering down the five steps. His blond hair, always looking a few weeks past when it should have been cut, lent him an air that women read as rakish and Sam read as sloppy. Paul appeared particularly proud of it.

The impossibly blue eyes that he shared with his black-haired twin sister apparently added to the charm, not that Sam could see it. Except the eyes, there was no way these two were related. Useless playboy high-rolling con-man, and kick-ass television executive who out-classed her most elegant guest stars but was nice enough to not scrub their faces with it.

Sam placed a palm in the center of Paul's chest and lifted enough of his weight that Paul had no choice except to walk backwards up the stairs and return to the small cabin. With his other hand Sam pulled up the stairs behind him.

One glance at the pilots told them it was time for takeoff. As he dropped Paul into the first seat, he heard the fuel truck—that he'd paid extra to sit and wait—finish topping off the tanks.

By the time he buckled in for flight, the engines were already winding back up.

"When you called I was with this chestnut brunette. Hair down to her butt and built to last. Has a horse ranch and rides every day. Did you know that fifty-five is like the new thirty-five or something because let me tell you..."

Sam tuned him out and watched the Brooklyn Bridge slip by far below.

He and Erika had been doing okay, hadn't they?

They got together a couple times a week and cooked together or went to a movie. They'd discovered a common taste for comfort food over fine cooking, beer over wine, and films.

He'd offered her a choice of those romantic comedies that girls liked so much, figuring he could always shoot himself later.

Instead, she'd dragged him into the latest Tom Cruise thriller. The man wasn't Van Damme, but it wasn't his fault he was such a shrimp—not much taller than Erika. Did okay for an actor though, and the film's babe was way cute. Emily Blunt kicked serious sci-fi ass.

Her choice made him like Erika a bit more, if that was possible.

She was taking it slow, and that was the girl's call, though it was killing him. One of these days he was going to lose control and kiss the shit out of her, then she'd either boot his sorry behind or they'd see where that led.

But for now he'd thought they were doing okay.

Then she'd gone and stuck him in a tiny jet with Paul Stark —a man way too convinced by the evidence of his inherited wealth and good looks of his own awesomeness. Now he was talking about sex in what he seemed to think was a guy-bonding tone.

All it did was make Sam think more about how Erika might look out of those form-fitting black clothes she always wore.

She must have it in for him to trap him alone with Paul for a five-hour flight from New York to Edinburgh.

Did she honestly expect Sam *not* to dump Paul's body from forty thousand feet?

9

KATE KNEW SHE WAS ABOUT TO WORK AS HARD AS SHE EVER HAD in her life.

"This is gonna be a challenge."

Rikka stood by her side surveying the kitchen as the last of the evidence containers were labeled and whisked away. "Yeah, but by the end of it, we'll all look like crap, and you'll be your usual fresh and perfect self."

Kate scoffed at her.

Rikka whispered, "Check out Mr. Agent Man checking you out."

Terry Tyrell returned to the kitchen and handed the camera to Rikka. Kate wouldn't have noticed if Rikka hadn't pointed it out, but Terry was definitely giving her the eye. Odd under the circumstances.

She didn't have time for this.

Terry turned to the kitchen staff and raised his voice.

"I've assigned one of my agents or one of the Brit's to every cook, waiter, or dishwasher. They'll be at your elbows for food security considerations," Terry held up his hand. "Don't bother protesting, it won't change a thing."

"Hey Mr. Agent Man?" Rikka put the camera away on a safe shelf, pulled out her long slender de-boning knife, and began running it along a honing steel with a sharp snick-snick.

Kate was glad Rikka had brought along her knife case despite all the consternation it had caused the Diplomatic Protection Group officers at the Scotland Yard mobile office. What that woman could do with a blade was desperately needed at the moment.

"What do you want, twerp?"

Kate blinked in surprise when Rikka didn't fillet him where he stood.

"Terry Tyrell? T-2? Your parents conceived you while watching the second *Terminator* movie or what? Let me guess. You and Arnold. Bet we're talking about a bromance made in heaven, right?"

"No wonder you're the height you are," he growled in a deep voice. "People have to keep hacking you back to size 'cause of your overinflated sense that you're funny. Am I right, short stuff?"

No one ever teased Rikka about being five feet tall and survived unscathed. But Terry was and not being harassed for it the least bit. What was Rikka up to?

Knowing she wasn't going to find the answer to that until Rikka was good and ready to tell her, Kate turned back to face the kitchen.

Chef Vivienne's insistence that she was the only one to handle the seasoning for this momentous dinner meant that everything had been tasted by her and her alone. So, they'd snapped it all into containers and the Specialist Protection Branch rushed it all out to the lab van that roared onto the estate from Edinburgh.

Some of those sauces had been simmering for days.

Now they were gone.

Kate had a bare cook line holding nothing but seafood and vegetables.

She checked the wall clock. Three hours until service to the G-7.

"Well," she addressed the waiting staff, "I remember when I was fourteen and cooking on one of my mom's programs with Julia Child. I was so worried about screwing up the meal in front of the *grande dame* of television cooking that I was barely functional. She leaned down and said to me in one of her room-filling whispers moments before the floor director finished the countdown to action, 'If we make a mess, dearie, we can always make scrambled eggs'." She'd started the filming with a laugh and a smile. Julia truly had been the Goddess of the small screen.

"Scrambled eggs?" the *saucier* who she'd promoted to *sous chef* protested. "You canna be feeding scrambled eggs to the G-7, it does na matter if they be buggers or na." His name was Dirk Cameron which fit his thick Scottish accent and grizzled mien.

"No? Watch me."

And that was the last breath that Kate had time to be aware of taking in the next several hours.

She sent members of the kitchen staff running to the Inverlochy Castle Hotel's gardens for fresh herbs and more vegetables.

Agents of the British Protection Branch were sent down to the local farm with a long list of meats and dairy.

A Secret Service agent headed to a bakery in Fort William for breads.

By the time the signal came down that the leaders were headed to the dinner in the Red Dining Room, they had the appetizers ready. By seconds.

Thin sliced toasted baguette brushed with garlic-infused olive oil and graced with a paper-thin slice of green tomato, tiny omelets each from a single quail's egg stuffed with slivers of local sheep cheese. She topped it off with a chiffonade of chives and a delicate dusting of scallop pan-fried in white wine, flash frozen, and grated with a nutmeg rasp.

She followed it with Loch Linnhe langoustines with a lime emulsion and roasted-chili foam. The turbot main course—with a killer chocolate *mole* sauce that she'd picked up from Marianne Rimaldi moments before her death—she served with a heart of purple artichoke and white asparagus side.

The kitchen was running like a pinball game: chefs, servers, and agents all jostling about frantically.

Then the ball would fall, and the next course hit the plates. The whole room fell dead silent each time, except perhaps for a spatter of oil or the jarring alarm of a timer.

As each dish was finished, all eyes turned to watch a small table set off to one side by the doorway leading to the rest of the hotel.

Some poor Diplomatic Group taster sampled each dish while everyone watched him ghoulishly to see if he died. Though Kate had brushed off Terry and Rikka's protests as she tasted each dish herself, she couldn't help but join the staring contest.

If the agent survived more than a minute with no symptoms of poisoning, the dish was served.

Once each course was out of the kitchen, the ball came back into play, and they all attacked the next one as a team.

It felt like forever until the final rhubarb-strawberry tart with an *à la mode* of apricot sorbet and a fresh-ground dark-chocolate flake made it out of the doorway.

By the end of the service, she hadn't managed to kill the taster.

10

KATE FELT WHIPPED, WHUPPED, AND WIPED OUT BY THE TIME service was complete. The sun had long since set outside the tall windows along one wall of the kitchen. The tall trees along this side of the hotel were now softly lit by the lights shining out the windows.

Chefs sagged against counters or collapsed into chairs.

Their monitoring agents, who instead of being edged out were recruited to help, didn't look any better. Only T-2—no, she wasn't going to slip into Rikka's nickname—only Terry had remained completely uninvolved, watching everyone and everything. It was just as well. If memory served, the man couldn't boil water without burning the pot.

Kate poured herself a glass of Scotch whisky and passed the bottle around. Soon all the cooks had a glass, though none of the agents or guards did with Terry watching over them. A couple of the Brits clearly thought such self-restraint was a crying shame because the bottle going around was hotel's own Inverlochy Castle eighteen-year-old Grand Reserve.

The staff raised their whiskys on her cue.

"To Chef Vivienne Jacquard. She created the finest *brigade de cuisine* that it has ever been my honor to cook with."

"Yur in Scotland, lass, not cooking with the Frenchies," Dirk the *sous chef* spoke from where he'd collapsed nearby on an upended crate, "we're a bleedin' 'Kitchen Brigade.' Despite that, t'would be an honor to cook with yer likes on any day."

Kate toasted them as they all called out, "*Sláinte!*"

With her glass half knocked back she turned enough to see that Rikka had surreptitiously shouldered the television camera. She'd tucked it safely out of the way on a shelf after Terry returned it. Kate had been aware of the great glass eye that was always staring at her throughout the meal, but she'd been too busy to shove it aside. Rikka should have capped the lens to protect it.

Then Kate spotted the red recording light above the lens... the light had been on throughout the meal service.

The whisky caught half-down her throat, then burned there, making her try to breathe—a huge mistake that drew the fiery liquid into her windpipe. She blew out her mouthful of whisky in a fine spray all over Dirk who burst out laughing as he wiped his face.

"Crivens! Can ye na hold yur liquor? That's good scotch ye be wastin' there, woman."

Kate ignored him and turned on Rikka.

The rest of the kitchen joined in the laughing about her spraying Dirk, or perhaps about her inability to drink whisky.

To steady herself, she knocked back the second half of the glass and swallowed it down to sit warm in her stomach before speaking. Then she slammed down the glass so hard she was surprised it didn't shatter.

"If you caught that on film, Albert, you're fired."

"Recorded, signed, and sealed," Rikka didn't show the least remorse. "I filmed the whole thing, did you know this camera also has a remote control which gave me limited pan and zoom.

So useful as the meal moved down the line. I was thinking it would make a good special in the *Kate's Kitchen Raid* series. Or maybe its own series, *Kate's Kitchen Rescue*."

Kate looked down at herself. Somewhere along the way she'd shed her Hermes jacket, acquiring a white chef's jacket and the blue-and-gray stripe apron the others wore, though she had no recollection of doing so. Her hair was hanked back in a ponytail with a length of cooking twine meant for tying roasts. She also wore...she pulled it down to look at it...a blue chef's cap like Dirk's. Must have been too tired to argue. She could always kill it in edit, though she wouldn't be surprised if Rikka would have a way around that already worked out.

A ripple swept from the far end of the kitchen. The chefs shifting as if suddenly on military inspection. The Specialist Protection Branch AFOs moved adroitly aside to make a path. They acted as if they wished they bore rifles to hold at parade rest, or perhaps ceremonial swords, not handguns in their holsters.

A wholly unpresuming woman, on the low side of thirty, immaculately dressed in a dark dress of fine Merino wool glided down the line. She had a cheerful face that Kate would expect to see in a party photo, and a flutter of dark hair that brushed her shoulders with perfect styling.

"Ms. Stark, I am Irene Watson, the manager of the hotel. I don't know how to thank you for what you've done for us this evening and under such circumstances." Her bright and slightly lopsided smile might fit on a college grad, but her self-assuredness, firm grip, and steady blue eyes indicated that she was a force to be reckoned with.

"My pleasure, Ms. Watson."

"Irene...Watson?" Rikka's whisper carried in the momentarily silent kitchen. "But that's not right. Holmes should be..."

"My assistant, Erika Albert," Kate made introductions hoping to fend off the worst of it.

Irene didn't blink, instead turning with perfect manners. "To make matters worse, Ms. Albert, my maiden name actually was Holmes."

Rikka's squawk of protest silenced the rest of the kitchen.

The hotel manager smiled pleasantly as Rikka sputtered.

"But Irene Adler never would have married the good doctor!" Rikka sounded deeply offended. "Conan Doyle said she was Holmes' one true love. His only equal and the only woman to ever defeat him."

Kate never quite understood Rikka's view of the world. It was a jigsaw puzzle of both reality and fiction, and at times the fictional portions were far and away the more important.

"Doyle stated: 'To Sherlock Holmes she is always *the* woman.'," Irene spoke with a perfect calmness and a slight smile. "And that Holmes was incapable of love. But I am personally biased to accept your interpretation. My full maiden name, Ms. Albert, was Irene Adele Holmes, testifying to precisely your point of objection. My dear father was and is a literature professor at the Lochaber Secondary School here in Fort William."

"And you married a Watson? How could you do such a thing?" Rikka crossed her arms over her chest and tried to glower, but Irene was more Kate's height than Rikka's so it didn't work well.

"Nonetheless," Irene Watson née Holmes proved unflappable, "that is precisely what I did. He is a doctor too, though a veterinarian not a medical doctor."

"It's not right," Rikka mumbled to herself, but they both wisely ignored her.

Irene turned back to face Kate, "Should you ever wish a position as *chef de cuisine,* Ms. Stark, you will let me know. That meal was fully worthy of poor Vivienne Jacquard's high standards. I hope that I may impose on you to stay with us at least through the G-7 meetings over the next two days."

Kate opened her mouth and then closed it again. She loved to cook, but this was a Michelin-starred restaurant. Worse, the diners were nine of the world's most important leaders: the G-7 and the two representatives from the European Union. Not to mention spouses, interpreters, and advisors.

"I…" she stopped again, unsure what to say.

Rikka was grinning at her. Because of the way she held the camera, for the moment only Kate could see her silently shout, "T-2."

As if staying near Terry constituted a valid reason to accept such a crazy offer.

She again opened her mouth to beg off when her cell phone rang.

11

"KATYDID, THANK GOD!" PAUL COULD BARELY HEAR HER OVER the pounding rotors of the helicopter they'd rented at Glasgow Airport. He and Sam were squashed into a tiny Robinson R22 helicopter. He'd kept shoving Sam over trying to get more room until he realized that the man's broad shoulders were already against the door on the far side.

"Paul, where are you?"

"Good to hear your voice. Rikka's message made it sound like you'd be dead by now. Had me terribly worried, I can tell—"

"Paul." She cut him off in that tone she had. "Where, are, you?"

"How am I supposed to know? It's the middle of the night here in Scotland. I think we're close to you, but there's an RAF attack helicopter hovering about a hundred yards away and they have a lot of guns aimed at us. Can you do something about that?"

He heard her mumbling to someone in the background. A minute later she came back on.

"Follow them to the helipad, they're turning on a landing

light right now. If you have any weapons with you, they will shoot you."

Paul hesitated and looked at Sam, "Does that sound right to you?"

Sam was glaring at him. No help there. Man hadn't said a damn word on the whole flight; left it to Paul to fill the uncomfortable silences all the way across the Atlantic.

"What?" he asked Kate over the radio. "Does the UK have laws against that?" His fib at Customs was merely to avoid any hassle.

Sam rolled his eyes, Kate cursed at him. "I told you that you are never allowed to handle a gun. What part of *never* don't you understand? I'll warn them. They will confiscate it on your landing. Make sure it has no rounds in it, try not to shoot yourself while doing that, hand it to them empty and butt first."

She hung up.

"Well how was I supposed to know that?"

Sam didn't answer him.

Well! Paul was done with entertaining the man. He kept his own silence and simply watched as Sam followed the armed helicopter down toward the elegant hotel sitting on a bluff and lit by tasteful floodlights.

12

Kate tried not to feel offended when Sam walked by as if she wasn't there and stalked up to Rikka.

Terry tried to stop him and was brushed aside. An Abrams tank couldn't stop Sam Fierro when he was in this mood.

Irene Watson hadn't bothered to remain for this minor upset; she had the G-7 waiting upstairs.

Kate put her hand on Terry's arm to keep him in place. Kate could feel the easy ripple of his powerful forearms. He had the solid strength of a professional agent in peak form. *Lucky wife.*

"Marine Force Recon," she told him. "Sam was in for twenty years, Terry. You *want* to let him go where he wants to go."

"My ass is on the line letting him come here at all without a full background check."

"So run your check. He's clean," she turned to see what was going on.

Kate could hear that Rikka was assuring him that she was fine, though Sam's powerful frame blocked any sight of her. She ran down the facts as well as any trained operative could. Twice, Sam turned his glare upon Kate. And twice looked away.

Yes, they had a history. She wished to hell he'd get over it, but apparently that wasn't going to happen in any lifetime that would be showing up soon.

It hadn't been her goddamn fault that the Vice President was gunned down on her watch. Other than her being the last backstop on his Secret Service Protection Detail. She'd failed, whether or not they'd exonerated her. Apparently quitting the Service that she'd loved wasn't enough for Sam Fierro.

One of these days she'd pin him down until he explained himself.

Or get Rikka to.

When Rikka finished, Sam stood stock still for ten seconds, nodded his head once, and then shifted around Rikka so he no longer blocked her from view. But he also made it absolutely clear to everyone present that he had Rikka's back.

"Where's Paul?"

"I'm here," he called from the outside door, "but they won't let me in."

At Terry's hand signal, Paul was escorted in with a Protection Branch armed officer holding him from either side. One of them produced a Glock 19 and handed it to Terry.

Kate wanted to scream at him.

"What?" Paul tried to shake off the two agents holding him with absolutely no success. "My buddy told me that's what the NYPD carry. That seemed safe enough."

A man with no training carrying a gun with no safety except the trigger pull. He was a disaster waiting to happen. She should let him keep the damn gun and he'd off himself. Of course, knowing her luck with her twin brother, she'd be the one to catch the round.

"Terry, promise me something for old time's sake?"

"What?" he narrowed his eyes at her suspiciously.

"Do not, under any circumstances, ever return that weapon to my brother."

He smiled at her. "That I can promise." Damn but he'd

always had a good smile. Paul might think he was ever so blond and handsome, but Terry's tall, dark, and powerful truly was.

An agent came striding up to Terry with two sheets of paper. He scanned the first one, then read aloud.

"Vivienne Jacquard was killed with something called BTX, batrachotoxin. Whatever the hell that is."

"Poison dart frog venom," Rikka piped up. "It's a neurotoxin, takes out the nervous system. To do-in a woman of Vivienne's size that fast, you'd need a couple tenths of a milligram. It's ba-trac-ho-tox-in, by the way, not bat-rako."

Terry's attention zeroed in on her.

"What? I read stuff, T-2. Don't you?"

He scowled at her then turned back to his report.

"It was in a wine bottle that we saw her open on Ms. Albert's video. It was in her desk drawer where she stopped for a quick glass. According to the tape transcript, she was quite nervous about finally meeting you, Kate. So, she wanted a glass of 'nerve steadier'."

"Damn," Kate felt more tired than ever. She, in turn, had been daunted by Vivienne Jacquard's reputation. If they both hadn't been such idiots about it all, perhaps Vivienne would have skipped the quick glass. Of course, then who knew where that bottle might have traveled from Vivienne's private stash before being served. She, Kate, and Rikka might well have shared it after dinner. Or it might have gone up to the G-7's table.

But it hadn't. It remained in Vivienne's office until it killed her.

"Double damn!" That also meant that every one of the sauces had been fine and could have been used. Too late now, dinner service was long gone.

"But how did that happen with a sealed bottle?" Paul might be a con-man, but he had a real blind spot for the nastier types of work. Kate always found that to be one of the most refreshing aspects to her brother. He lived in a far less hazardous world than she did.

"Syringe hole in the cork?" Kate leaned forward to check her guess, but Terry turned to the second page. His scowl confirmed her guess anyway.

He looked at Kate for a moment, then kept reading. He glanced at each of her team members in turn.

Then he flashed a hand signal.

Shit!

Kate knew that signal from her days in the Service.

Neutralize target—four fingers to tell his agents how many targets—and the clenched fist said to restrain with all force necessary.

She could only hope for the Secret Service's sake that Sam was feeling cooperative. But after five hours in a plane and thirty minutes in a helicopter with her brother? It didn't seem all that likely.

Especially not if they grabbed Rikka first.

13

"You like poisons, Stark?"

"You like harassing innocent people, Tyrell? Because you seem to be getting off on the power trip."

Terry had forgotten that Kate Stark could be as snide as he could when she was in a bad mood. And holding her entire team for questioning after they'd served a first-class five-course meal to the world's leaders definitely put her in a foul one.

The Inverlochy Castle Hotel offered no privacy. Every space that wasn't in use by the G-7, Terry had packed with G-7 protection.

The chef's tiny office was in the final phases of a full forensic inspection, which hadn't uncovered a single new thing. Terry's people had questioned and released the rest of the kitchen staff. They were supposed to be back at four a.m. to start breakfast prep and it was already after midnight. Every one of them had gone home with a British PG agent in tow to make sure it was an appointment they kept. He didn't want any witnesses or potential suspects to wander off in the night.

Terry held back Kate and her team. He'd had to settle with confining them to different corners of the kitchen so that they didn't talk...which had no effect on Rikka Albert or Paul Stark. They simply talked louder.

Posting agents to shut them up hadn't slowed Rikka and Paul down for a moment. Terry had listened for a while, unable to decide if they hated or loved each other. Ms. Albert was pounding Kate's brother about bringing a gun in the first place, into the UK in the second place, and being late in the third place.

Terry wished he knew *late for what* but neither asking nor demanding produced any comprehensible answer. Instead, he'd received a lecture on tact as exercised by Michael Biehn compared to Arnold Schwarzenegger in the original *Terminator* movie.

"You don't steal a man's Harley and clothes and expect to get the babe."

Sam Fierro's studied silence hadn't masked his complete lack of use for Paul and that he considered Rikka to be top priority, not that Terry could see she needed any protecting. However, Marine Recon for two decades. Terry had to respect that. Those guys were unbelievably good by any standard, including the Service's.

Kate looked tired and pissed.

She was her usual completely put together stunning beauty —woman had grown prettier over the four years since he'd last seen her, which shouldn't be possible. Her protectees were always safe because the bad guys were too busy being distracted by Kate Stark, right up to the moment she took down their asses.

All except once and that had been bad in so many ways.

Her clothes were a serious notch up from an agent's charcoal gray suit; her hair had grown longer and shone with health that had been somehow leached out by the brutal demands of the Secret Service job. She looked stunning...and seriously pissed.

Kate Stark pissed off was definitely not a good thing.

For lack of any better interrogation space, Terry led Kate to the hotel's black Rolls Royce Phantom. He'd received a severe lecture from the chauffeur before he would allow them to enter the Rolls. That Terry could ignore, but the stern look from hotel manager Irene Watson threatened dire consequences if he so much as tracked a stray leaf into the interior? She might seem to be a cute twenty-something, but she managed her hotel like a drill sergeant of the Royal Marines.

He'd frequently sat front seat detail in the Presidential limousine. *The Beast* was a fifty-thousand-dollar Cadillac turned into a three-hundred-thousand-dollar fortress on wheels.

The Phantom was a half-million-dollar work of art with every cent of that pumped into luxury. Ralph the chauffeur hovered, opening and closing Kate's back seat door. He'd glared at Terry for not waiting to have his own back door opened.

The rear door swung backward, opening where it met the front door. It was heavy with sound insulation, though nothing like the Beast's with heavy with armor and three-inch-thick windows. The chauffeur hustled around to show him where an umbrella hid, built into the door jamb of the front door should the starry night turn unexpectedly inclement during his questioning. The umbrella's handle protruded from the door frame enough to grab comfortably. A Rolls Royce *RR* was engraved into the handle so that away from the vehicle itself, no one would question your ability to afford one.

Terry nearly had to pull his sidearm to shoo the man away from the car.

"Nice digs," was Kate's only comment as he turned on the tasteful interior lighting against the late-night darkness that had fallen over loch and moor.

A glance at his watch and he clicked on a micro-recorder, "Twelve-thirty-one a.m., Inverlochy Castle Hotel, Fort William,

Scotland. Subject: Kate Stark, chef and owner of Cooks Network."

"Don't forget to add suspected murderer of the chef she was supposed to be interviewing. Now I have a program schedule slot, but no show to put in its place. What the hell am I doing here, Terry? What was on that second sheet of paper?"

"Now, Ms. Stark," he was well aware he sounded like a pompous ass, but the recorder was running. He couldn't figure out where to set it, everything in the car was curved and luxurious, not a flat spot to be found.

Exasperated, Kate grabbed the recorder from his hand and tapped her fingers against the back of the front passenger seat. They were both in the back, but Kate sat behind the driver's side, a slight weakening of his position. He didn't climb into UK right hand-drive cars all that often.

The seatback before him opened and lowered gracefully and silently completely unlike any airplane tray table that he'd ever wrestled with. It revealed a foldaway video screen for watching movies, though it was dark at the moment.

A drive-in movie in the back of a Rolls Royce with Kate Stark.

Now where in the hell had that thought come from? She'd always made it clear, to any dolt dumb enough to ask, that she didn't date inside the Service. Except she wasn't in the Service anymo—

Kate slammed the recorder on the table hard enough that whoever listened to this for voice-stress analysis was going to have their eardrums blown.

With Kate, he had no doubt it was completely intentional.

"Stuff the 'Ms. Stark' up your backside, Terry. You try playing that game on me and I'll get 'Ms. Albert' in here to make your life a true misery."

He was scheduled to be running a nice quiet patrol of the grounds right about now. He'd planned a double-check of each security station while the night owls among the G-7 leaders settled into the hotel's majestic two-story Grand Hall after a late evening session to sample one of the better whisky bars in Scotland. Instead, he was sitting here questioning a former Secret Service agent, the best and definitely the prettiest he'd ever worked with, about her role in murder.

He rubbed at his eyes. The day had started at four a.m. Washington time, now it was five a.m. there again or some such madness.

Wait, no. It was the other way. It was dinner time back in DC, it only felt like five a.m.

He wondered what his wife was having for dinner.

And who she was having it with.

Crap!

Seven months apart, the divorce final two weeks ago, and it felt like shit every single night. She had someone and, as he'd promised not to investigate, all he knew was that the someone wasn't him.

"I know, Terry. It sucks," Kate rested a hand on his arm. "What was on that sheet of paper that makes you think I killed the woman I traveled ten hours to meet?"

What *was* on that sheet of paper? For half a moment, he'd thought she meant his divorce papers, but those were all signed, processed, and now—after the six-month mandatory waiting period for District of Columbia—done.

He pulled out the *eyes-only* Secret Service report and handed it over to her.

Not that any of it mattered any more. He watched Kate read it over. When she concentrated, her brow remained unfurled, but her eyes darkened and her shoulder-length hair always swung forward to partly mask her face.

His own wife—Damn it!—ex-wife was a slight, lithe woman with shining eyes, a bright smile, and a joyous view of the world. Rather she'd *had* a joyous view. But seeing him at risk every day—ready to block the crucial bullet with his body and his life—had been asking too much.

Kate once lived that life, it wouldn't push her away. The woman embodied rock steady. She'd taken down the Vice President's shooter clean while covered in the man's blood.

Four years since he'd seen her. She'd always been full-figured in all the right ways. Nor had she neglected her physical training for a single moment since leaving the Service.

"You still run 10Ks?" *Smooth.* He'd now told her that he'd been checking out her body. *Idiot.*

"Mostly on the treadmills now. Manhattan sucks for long distance runs," her answer was distracted as she continued to study the report, thankfully missing the implications of his question.

He forced his focus back to her face and resisted the urge to brush back the hair that now shadowed her well-defined cheek lines. He hadn't so much as touched a woman in five months. Longer if the truth be known, other than that awkward goodbye hug.

"I know all this," she protested. "Who writes these things anyway?"

14

KATE TOSSED THE PIECE OF PAPER BACK TO TERRY.

He missed it and it fluttered to the floor of the Rolls Royce. He bent down and smacked his head on the tray table, knocking the recorder to the carpeted floor.

She managed not to laugh in Terry's face, but it was a close thing. So, he'd been checking out her body? She had that effect on a lot of men and, while it wasn't something she sought, it was a fact of her life. But he'd commented on it. That was weird for Terry; his hundred percent propriety was as much a part of him as the nose on his face.

With utmost care, he retrieved the recorder from the floor and rested it back on the tray table. The fall had knocked the recorder into the Off mode. If he wasn't going to notice it, she wasn't going to tell him.

"This report—" he started, but she cut him off.

"Talks about a psycho ex-Marine who murdered two people on the set of my television show using a medical drug that has no relation to the poison that killed Vivienne. We caught him. We took him down. It's done."

"But—"

"If you want to know what's missing from the report, you'll have to talk to FBI agents Marcus Reynolds and Leona Edwards, New York Office. It is part of an ongoing investigation that doesn't have shit to do with you or the G-7, Terry, and I'm not at liberty to talk about it. So, get a grip. Start working the real problem. Who killed Vivienne? Because I know for sure it wasn't Rikka or me. And Sam and my idiot twin brother weren't called until after Vivienne Jacquard died."

"I find it strange that the exact same group that were ultimately involved in whatever this was," he shook the recovered report at her, "all show up here so neatly. You and this Ms. Albert arrived less than twenty minutes before Ms. Jacquard's murder."

"Trust me. I wish it had been twenty minutes after."

"And when I run a report, Ms. Albert's past is sketchy. It feels wrong, though I can't quite..." he trailed off and frowned.

There were four people aside from herself who knew why Rikka's background was invisible: FBI agents Marcus Reynolds and Leona Edwards, a dangerously brilliant North Korean ship's captain named Rang Jin-ho and his wife. Five. There was no keeping a secret from Sam, which was probably the safest place to hide one. Kate certainly wasn't going to—

"Witness Protection Program."

Terry had never been stupid.

"But I should have been able to see the code in her report that—" He pulled a sheaf of papers from another pocket in his jacket that he'd been handed during the other interrogations and flipped to the page with *Erika Albert* in bold across the top.

Kate peered over his shoulder and was glad to see that there was no more information there than she and Rikka had planted.

"It's not here," Terry stabbed a finger at the box reserved for special code symbols like the Witness Protection Program. It was empty.

"The bad guys punched through the veil on her once already. I made sure it couldn't happen again." It had required tampering with federal records and doing half the work herself so that Rikka didn't show up, especially in the US Marshall's files. But it saved Rikka's life, at least twice.

"Let me get this straight," Terry started flipping through the other profiles.

Kate slid down into soft leather and lay her head back. It was so comfortable that she could go to sleep right here.

Instead, her brain started churning on tomorrow's menu—three meals she had no intention of cooking, but her brain wouldn't shut up. If she riffed off the quail egg-seafood omelet she'd served on the bruschetta at the start of dinner, then she could start the guests on a culinary journey where each meal built on the one before. That meant adding another protein during breakfast, and not bacon—too predictable. She'd—

"Stark!"

"Huh? What?"

"You going to sleep on me?"

With those dreamy brown eyes of his, she could think of things to do that had nothing to do with sleep. But that would be make-up sex for Harold moving on.

"Kate?"

"No. I'm trying to decide what I'd cook tomorrow if you haven't locked me up and I haven't shown the good sense to flee the country, by express freight if necessary. I'm telling you, I've done it once and I'm willing to do it again." Though it had not been a comfortable experience.

"I'll ask one more time. You and Ms. Albert, who—"

"You know she gets a real kick out of every time she can make you call her that."

"—who just happens to know about Amazonian frog neurotoxins," he plowed ahead, "simply happened to arrive right before the cook—"

"Chef," she corrected him.

"Chef…" he ground out the word.

"You're so much fun to tease."

"—right before the *chef* at a G-7 meeting was murdered?"

"Yep."

"And then a highly decorated Marine Force Recon soldier and your billionaire brother show up within hours because you called them."

"Rikka did that, and it was a text. But you've got the right idea."

"Sounds fishy to me," he crossed his arms over his chest.

"I washed me hands and face afore I come I did," she put on her best Eliza Doolittle accent. She and Rikka had recently watched *My Fair Lady* together and then spent the entire evening impersonating Audrey Hepburn at each other.

"What?"

"You obviously weren't raised on old musicals." Neither was she, but that didn't mean she was going to let Terry off the hook so easily.

"I go back to *Aladdin* and *The Lion King* and that's about it. Now, c'mon, Kate. Would you buy your story?"

Crap! She slouched lower in the back seat of the Rolls.

No, she wouldn't.

15

CECILIA BARSTOWE FLIPPED THROUGH MESSAGES ON HER PHONE as she lay on the crappy hotel bed miles from Inverlochy. The Secret Services of eight countries had booked out everything for miles around and it was the closest she could find.

She sneered, Harry from *The Wall Street Journal* was over thirty miles out, halfway to Perth—which she'd thought was in Australia but apparently Scotland had one too.

Her room itself wasn't crappy at all. It was...weird. A quilt on the bed, flowered wallpaper, cheerful rugs with hunting scenes—every frill and trim in place until she felt as if she was trapped in one of her six-year-old niece's fantasies. This wasn't a B&B; it was the Hollywood version of one. But admitting that it was comfortable and cozy was not something you ever let anyone else in the Press Corps know or you'd lose massive brownie points on the suffering-on-the-road scale.

Extreme suffering? At a G-7 jaunt? Not so much.

Landing in Libya the day after Qaddafi went down, that hadn't been so comfortable, especially as an American black woman. However, it had been far more interesting.

While being a photographer at a G-7 meeting was a damn

sight safer, it was pretty much the dullest assignment she'd landed in a decade of working as a freelance stringer. Talking heads and nothing *but* talking heads.

The arrivals were at least tolerable: nice handshakes and not so friendly ones.

Africa's latest genocide? They could all agree that sucked.

The former Soviet bloc countries in yet another civil war with yet another intervention by both Mother Russia and NATO, each looking for new ground to duke it out on a grand scale? Except now Mother Russia was no longer fomenting civil war. Instead, she'd placed a new focus on the *war* part of that equation.

Always added a nice tension to the whole arrivals' scene, with pretty much everyone at the meeting hating Russia this year—par for the course according to the regular G-7 media hounds.

France never was terribly buddy-buddy with Italy or England, and now there was the EU versus England mess on top of that to spice things up.

But Germany and Japan sitting on either side of the US on the whateverth anniversary of WWII battles on the Pacific island of Tinian, and Hitler's retreat from the Narva River—two places she'd never heard of before and never would again—wasn't that exciting after the third or fourth memory card worth of shots.

And poor Canada always sitting off to the side and wondering how she'd wound up at this table in the first place.

The preliminaries looked...dull. That meant that the next two days were going to provide nothing but a tedious Hell. Dante undoubtedly needed to add another circle of Hell to his hierarchy: 10th level, political tedium beyond imagining. The reporters in the press gaggle were looking pretty excited about the whole thing; the photographers all looked as if they desperately needed a drink. She certainly did, except she never drank on assignment. There'd been that time in Jakarta, and it hadn't gone that well. She'd woken up in strange beds before, but that particular time…ew!

Cecilia lay on her walnut sleigh bed and continued to scan her phone for anything amusing.

E-mails dull.

No decent assignments coming in.

Why didn't anyone want a freelancer to pop over to Beirut or at least jump in on the Tour de France? Nope. For Cecilia it was, *Joey broke an arm and he's in a cast, would you cover the G-7?* And she'd been so lamely desperate that she only charged her usual late notice fee. Though she'd gotten expenses *and* per diem, it was hardly worth the boredom.

Facebook. Her friends currently assigned to hot zones around the globe didn't have time for it. Her settled-and-reproducing friends from high school had too much time for it. They needed to get a life.

Twitter. Mostly noise from people she never should have followed in the first place.

MI-Vid. She'd received an MI-Vid. She'd installed the app, then never found a friend who used it. But now the white MI logo bore a red *1* beside it.

She tapped in.

An image popped up.

It was a close-up of the meal she'd photographed at the G-7 dinner four hours ago. She'd sold that shot on the side to a cooking blogger.

Her main client was only interested in the people, a detail she'd worked into her contract. So, she'd set up several other side contracts for the trip: travel, hotels, food, and…yeah, it was a hundred percent yawn. The short notice coming from her side instead of theirs meant the fees were pretty lame, but it gave her something to do and roughly doubled her income for the trip.

Across the face of her picture of the turbot in Mexican chocolate sauce—it had struck her as weird but everyone sure gobbled it up, lowly photographers not eating on site—someone had written across it, "What were they supposed to eat!"

Then the picture disappeared.

The MI-Vid ran the requisite seven seconds, then erased itself. That was the whole point of the system. You watched the message and then it went away.

You could reply, but there wasn't anything to forward—the image played, then died.

She hit reply, looked around and spotted her camera bag. She shot an image of the case's cover—the only object in the whole room not covered in flowers and stag-hunting needlepoints—and then used her finger to draw a question mark on the black background. The app, after waiting a moment to decide she'd finished writing, changed it to the blocky *Mission Impossible* font, red outlined in silver with the horizontal gap a third of the way down the letters, and sent the message.

Question mark for why the exclamation point at the end of *What were they supposed to eat!* and also for *What the fuck?*

Then she pulled out her previously unopened press packet that they'd issued to her on arrival. She scanned the papers, stopping near the back of the pile.

Now wasn't that interesting.

Though Cecilia managed no deep sleep and checked her phone often, there was no reply.

16

"GEORGE MADSEN?"

He came back from that dreamy place that Stephie could always take him. He knew she hated the nickname, but he'd always thought of her that way. She'd become tolerant of his usage and now it was a pet name exclusively between them. He liked the feel of that.

"Geor-rge," she ground her hips against him in a leisurely circle; enough to ensure that sleep was going to completely elude him a while longer tonight. That, and she always kept the lights on when they made love. He'd come to like that. First, because it revealed her elegant bedroom, all feminine and cozy and soft, like he'd breached some inner sanctum of womanhood. And second, because he could see what it did to her when he breached that threshold in herself.

"Yeah, babe?" He cracked open one eye and looked up at her.

She licked her upper lip clear of a thin sheen of sweat. She had a magnificent face that glowed in the aftermath of what they'd done to each other. Her glorious mane of red hair draped forward over her shoulders, despite the fact that she leaned back.

Her 34F breasts—he'd checked her bra drawer when she wasn't around—soared proudly through the shining copper red curtain of hair that was darkened here and there to a deep auburn by the sweat he'd worked up for her.

He ran his hands up from that workout-trim waist that she maintained so vigorously to hold those magnificent mammaries and began teasing them back to life. He wished he could do the whole thing over again right now. Never in his life had he been with a lover like her.

Lover? He'd bypassed that one a while ago. Have to figure out what that meant, another time when he wasn't still at least partly inside her.

"I was thinking, George," she hissed out a breath and arched in pleasure at what he was doing to her.

Her cream white skin fascinated him; so perfect he could spend hours stroking it and watching her respond.

"Perhaps I can stop you from thinking," he massaged and squeezed more vigorously.

She reached around behind herself, down between his legs, and cupped him right on that impossible threshold between pleasure and pain. Perhaps a touch toward the pain side.

"Two can play that game, honey."

For a moment they were at an impasse, but he was spent and eased off first.

"What were you thinking?"

"I was thinking about Thursday."

"Uh," he was thinking about the line of her neck and wondering if he could find the energy to sit up and nibble on that fair skin. No hickies though, man she'd been pissed the one time he did that. But to sit up, he'd have to let go of her breasts, so instead he lay there and enjoyed massaging them until she squirmed. "Thursday as in the day after tomorrow?"

"Yes!" The way she heaved that out as she cupped the backs of his hands hard against her breasts, he knew he was doing things exactly right for her.

"What about it?" And Stephie's breasts were so perfect.

"Our luncheon with Morgan." George's best friend was in the city for a rare few days.

She leaned her weight into his hands until he was holding her aloft by those hallmarks of femininity.

"Don't you think it would be fun if we told him a bit of special news?"

"News?" he managed to gasp out as she began working him once more between her legs. God bless whatever those exercises were called that women like Stephie did.

She leaned down the rest of the way until her tongue was somewhere in the vicinity of his tonsils.

He shifted his hands to her immensely toned butt.

"Ask me," she whispered against his mouth, "a question to which 'Yes' is the only answer."

"To which 'Yes' is the only...?"

She did something with her hips that sent a shockwave of pleasure roaring up into his system.

He got it. They'd been friends for a couple of years with the occasional weekend tryst, steady lovers for six months, and now were nearly living together.

Morgan occasionally ribbed him about when he'd be making an honest woman of Stephanie.

He thought about it, as well as he could, through the tidal waves she sent rocketing up from his crotch. Her hips, her mouth, her tongue seemed to be everywhere at once.

If he was going to make a bid for the White House in four years, or maybe eight, he couldn't pull it off as a single man. Having a woman of Stephie's considerable assets—monetary, social, and newspaper—at his side could be a huge advantage. To have a stunning, buxom redhead on his arm, who had long since proven how amazing she looked both in the press and on television, could only improve his chances further. He also kept fit and had no gray yet, so their seventeen years age difference wouldn't be much of an issue in the news.

Then Stephie drove down on him so abruptly with her hips that the two of them cried out in unison. They were always in such perfect sync in the bedroom.

And having a woman he could make respond this way, waiting in his bed each night...that idea led to his return to a full erection. It had been his fastest recovery since he'd gotten into Laura Donovan's prom dress twice in one night thirty years before.

"Yes," it made sense once he'd said it. "Yes, we'll tell Morgan at lunch on Thursday."

Stephie mumbled something incoherent from the depths of her passion about "Step Two" and then began to show her deepest gratitude as only a woman like her could.

A part of him wondered what the hell he'd agreed to.

But that part didn't have a lot of blood running to it at the moment and the thought soon drifted away.

17

As George slept, Stephanie went to the bathroom to clean herself up. Done in chrome and steel, she liked this room more than the bedroom which she'd prettied up to create a specific impression. The bedroom was a place for men to feel confident and powerful, entering the *woman's innermost domain.*

The bathroom carried a message that no male guests ever noticed: there is pure steel and power at the core of the woman. Her office that doubled as her gym was more so, but the only male who ever entered there was her personal trainer. That room of rosewood, oriental carpets, and a high-end gym was her true inner sanctum.

It never ceased to amaze her how little men understood about power. As long as they had somewhere to put their dick, their certainty of absolute control remained unassailable. She blessed every day that she'd been born female and had mastery of where the true dominance belonged.

Thursday's lunch would be the culmination of six months of hard work and two years of planning. The key was the timing. Thirty-six hours remained to drive home the final nails in the coffin and cement it beneath her path to the future.

She'd left her phone in here so that she wouldn't be tempted to check it while cornering George.

An MI-Vid reply was waiting for her.

A red question mark on a black background from that reporter she'd hired. She closed the app without responding.

Step Three complete.

That came closer to giving her an orgasm than Majority Whip US Senator George Madsen ever had.

18

Kate's people were waiting for her when Terry finally let her go. They sat in the kitchen around a small side table that looked as if it was primarily used for staff to share their meals. A Secret Service and a DPG agent stood stationed at either end of the kitchen.

She checked the storerooms, but they were kept cool enough to remind her of a meat locker...or a morgue. She finally stumbled on the butler's pantry and nodded for her friends to join her. Once they crowded into the room and the door was closed, there wasn't a whole lot of space.

Sam sat on the floor with his back against the door and his arms propped up on his knees. The Marine Force Recon tattoos on his massive forearms showed clearly: one bore the winged skull wearing a SCUBA rebreather and perched over crossed oars; the other the Recon motto *Celer, Silens, Mortalis* in large, ornate Marine Corps-blue lettering. Swift, Silent, Deadly.

Rikka hopped up onto the marble counter and sat cross-legged next to a silver tea service like the hookah-smoking caterpillar from *Alice in Wonderland.*

Paul started poking around, inspecting the china and silver

behind the glass-fronted cabinets, then pulling out drawers in the fine walnut lower cabinets to reveal vast arrays of shining silverware.

"Wow, look at these." He held out a small display case that he'd popped open. Inside lay an ornately engraved silver spoon. The Canadian Prime Minister's name was inscribed along the handle and a maple leaf carved into the bowl. The back of the handle also said *G-7* and the date; the front was a masterpiece of smithcraft.

"Paul. Put that away. Can we focus here?"

"Sure, Katydid. Sorry." He tucked it back away with a series of identical blue gift boxes, slid the drawer shut, and leaned back against it.

"So, what do we know, Kate?" Rikka was calm and quiet, as calm as she'd been at the DPG's command center. Kate had her complete attention and appreciated it because she was far too tired to be thinking straight.

"We don't know anything we didn't know before except how to pronounce batrachotoxin."

"Crap! I'm sorry, Kate. But I was afraid the Secret Service would uncover more than that about me and I was trying to distract them."

"You're safe."

Rikka nodded her thanks. Then she hopped up onto a countertop and perched there cross-legged like a merry elf.

Paul looked at the two of them strangely for a moment, then shrugged. He knew there was a secret and that he wasn't privy to it. Oddly for him, he'd resisted nosing around on it. Kate had declared Rikka's past off limits. He'd respected that, for once.

"They have no evidence and can't hold any of us," Kate wanted to be far away. "Personally, I think we should get out of here."

"What about the cooking?" Rikka asked.

"I'll disappoint them if I'm the one doing the cooking. They're used to world class."

"Stop being an idiot, Katydid. I've eaten plenty of top-end meals and I'll put you up against those master chefs any day."

She kissed Paul on the cheek, "Sometimes you say the sweetest things, including when you're totally full of shit."

"You'll disappoint Irene," Rikka pointed out.

"I was trying not to think about that." She hated leaving the hotel in the lurch, but she suspected that if she remained, then the others would insist on doing the same. "Terry made it pretty clear that we're a major disruption to his security plan and that he didn't appreciate it one bit. I think it will be better for everyone if we were gone."

Rikka offered an uneasy shrug.

Sam didn't look happy either but was on the verge nodding his agreement when Paul cut him off.

"Nope. We gotta stay, Katydid."

Kate checked with Sam and Rikka, but neither knew why Paul suddenly sounded so assured.

"Look, I know it's stupid in about eight ways."

"Like all of us winding up dead or in prison. Or at least Kate," Rikka commented acidly.

"Yeah," Paul nodded, "that's two of the ways toward stupid that I was thinking of."

"So..." Kate waved Rikka to silence and she subsided. Then she turned to face her brother, "...why are we staying?"

He offered that funny smile of his that always seemed to charm the ladies.

She tried not to think of how many times growing up that exact same smile had charmed her.

"Because. The game isn't over."

"Game? A chef is dead."

"It's a game, Kate."

Rikka looked down at Sam, "Do you want to kick his pansy ass or should I?"

"Look," Paul leaned back against the cabinetry and rested his elbows on the marble counter looking like he was relaxing in a high-end bar...or lady's boudoir. "Someone's killed a chef at the G-7. What's the point?"

"I don't know. What is the point?" Kate had no idea what he was talking about.

"Exactly. We don't have a clue. But Kate, there's the G-7 meeting in the Great Hall on the other side of this wall."

He was pointing toward the lake out front, but she decided not to straighten him out.

"Do you think the Secret Service is going to know how to protect them?"

"That's their job. And Terry's damn good at it." She felt protective of him despite Terry suspecting her of murder.

"Yeah, let them deal with it," Rikka agreed.

"No! Damn it, Sam. Back me up here."

Sam looked pained at the request, but Paul didn't appear to notice as he continued.

"There's no point to killing the one chef and then stopping. You think I'm so damn innocent Kate because I can't shoot a target a million yards away or cook like a magician or do whatever the hell you do with computers," he flapped a hand at Rikka. "But I know how the game is played. Vivienne Jacquard was the opening gambit not the goal. You want to spoil their endgame, then you're going to have to stay in and play the hand you've been dealt."

Kate wished there was a reason Paul was wrong...but wasn't having any luck finding it.

"God but it sucks when Paul is right," Rikka rested her elbows on her knees and propped her chin on her folded hands. "You're totally ruining my image of you."

Paul grinned at her pout.

"Okay," Kate could accept this. "Okay. But I want the three of you out of here by first light."

"Not gonna happen, Katydid."

"No way, no how," Rikka agreed.

Sam's emphatic nod closed the deal.

Suddenly exhausted, Kate leaned back on the counter beside Paul and looked at them.

"For your information, if one of you ends up dead, I'm going to be beyond pissed."

"Oooo!" Rikka pretended to duck and cover. "We're so scared!"

That was the Rikka she knew.

"What if it's Paul who ends up dead? I'd be fine with that. How about you, Sam?"

His pained expression testified to how painful that trans-Atlantic flight had been.

Oblivious, Paul gave her a hug across the shoulders.

Sam flexed his hands as if he was making sure he was ready for anything that came at them.

WEDNESDAY

19

―――――

"DID YOU SLEEP WITH HIM?" RIKKA HOPED SHE DIDN'T HAVE TO say who *him* was. Kate couldn't be that dense.

"What part of 'married' don't you understand?" Kate stood at the big stainless steel double sink with a bucket of eggs. Well, at least Kate knew which *him* she was referring to.

The lights this morning were overbright, mostly because Rikka had managed less than two hours of sleep after the meeting in the butler's pantry. It was still dark outside the kitchen windows for crying out loud. She could stay up all night, but she wasn't a big fan of sunrises; hadn't seen a lot of them over the years.

Kate looked as if she hadn't slept at all as she scrubbed off the eggs that had, well, stuff on the shells that Rikka didn't want to know about. She knew eggs came from chickens and that they were dirty, but she preferred American eggs that came from pretty cardboard cartons and didn't have brown stuff stuck to their shells like when these were delivered from the farm in a bucket.

"The part..." Rikka continued slicing lox, brined Scottish

salmon, into perfect diamonds for whatever crazy breakfast Kate had designed, "...where he isn't married."

Kate fumbled one of the eggs that dropped into the steel sink with a crack and a wet splat.

Hmm. An interesting chink in Kate's I'm-not-really-interested facade.

"No, he'd never divorce her. He's a real family kind of guy." Kate's protest sounded half-hearted.

Rikka pulled out her phone and tapped for the document she'd found last night. This morning. Whatever this was.

"Maybe she dumped his ass, though there's not a whole lot wrong with him that I can see. Is it the ugly butt tattoo from his secret life as a Chippendale dancer?"

Kate's laugh barely cracked Dutiful on the snort-o-meter. What was up with that? It had been a decent enough line, especially at this hour.

"Here's the divorce decree, signed and filed with the Washington DC court. Went final two weeks ago." She aimed her phone at Kate who didn't bother looking; yet kept scrubbing at her eggs like they were more important.

Rikka considered being pissed. A cool couple of discoveries, yet a null response. First, a guy that Kate actually liked. She was the best and could afford to be picky but, man, talk about tough to please. And here Rikka had found that Kate's *like* was available—and getting *nada* back.

She checked in with Sam at the nearby butcher's station, but he wasn't paying any attention. Which meant he knew what was going on around him but chose not to have any input.

Then she saw the look on Kate's face.

Oh, duh, Rikka.

Kate didn't look at the document Rikka had found in the court's filings because she believed what Rikka said. She didn't need the proof.

Rikka wasn't used to unquestioning trust, so it surprised her every time Kate gave it to her. It generated a weird feeling inside her, somewhere between a smile and the confusion of the moment before an alien race blew up the planet but first told everyone all about it so that they could gloat.

"Excuse me."

Rikka turned to see a tall, sleek woman with walnut-dark skin and oak-light eyes sidling up to Kate. Despite her nice outfit, her unruly hair and a slightly awkward manner spoke of *dressed up* not being her normal state. She looked way out of place.

But Secret Agent T-2 had let her into the kitchen, so she must be cool. Her Press Corps clearance badge dangled from the G-7 strap along with her cameras. A long lens on a Nikon D6 and a short zoom on a Z 7II—she wore about twenty grand of gear and that looked to fit her far better than her business clothes. Serious toys that Rikka wouldn't mind playing with.

Kate looked up and the woman stumbled back a step.

She came near to planting her butt in a bucket of ripe tomatoes that would have splattered pretty impressively.

Rikka resisted the urge to give her that last bit of help. After all, they needed those tomatoes. She'd helped Kate pick them this morning. In a garden. From green viney, bush things.

"You're Kate Stark, aren't you?"

20

SAM FIERRO PAUSED WITH HIS CLEAVER RAISED OVER THE LAMB carcass spread out across the wooden chopping block—and waited for the other shoe to drop.

Kate had recruited him to do the day's butchery. He enjoyed the work, it was a calming, meditative task that he could do with minimal thought. Each animal was different, so attention was required. But each animal was also the same, allowing his mind to spend most of the time doing as it pleased. The family butchery in Brooklyn had taught him to appreciate the balance.

A simple lamb-and-pork breakfast sausage for breakfast. Crab-stuffed lamb chops for lunch and bacon-wrapped crab as a dinner appetizer eventually leading to a pork roast main course. Kate was making good use of the whole animal, something he appreciated.

They'd never cooked together before. The few times they'd worked an op side-by-side had been more about information gathering, defensive strategies, and fallback safe points. His final years in the Marines had been as a specialist in VIP security, especially in the *dust bowl* of southwest Asia. Kate had traveled there for a while as a field agent for the

Secret Service protection details. She'd been damn good at it too.

Their few shared meals were the local version of fast food: falafels in pita, goat curry over rice, whatever.

Sam and Rikka had cooked together several times over the last month with him providing the meat and her making the vegetables so elegantly prepped and sliced that he felt guilty eating them. Watching Rikka wield a knife made him feel thick-fingered and clumsy.

"And is that Sam?"

He lowered his cleaver. He'd wondered if Cecilia would recognize him; he'd spotted her while the Secret Service agent at the kitchen's entry verified her credentials.

Sam had pulled Cecilia Barstowe out of a small village in Rajasthan in the midst of the local opium lords blowing the shit out of the place. Labeling it as mere in-fighting among different factions, the western press had been dumb enough to send a pretty American reporter into the middle of it.

She greeted him with a smile and a kiss on the cheek that lingered and included enough body contact all the way down to state that the offer remained open if he ever wanted to go back there. She'd been fun, once over the standard caught-in-the-middle-of-a-battle jitters. They'd been trapped in a farmer's hay shed for three days. They hadn't been bored.

Sam spotted Rikka's expression.

Woman didn't miss a damn thing.

He offered Rikka a smile that she didn't return, then he faced away from Cecilia and put his attention back on his butchering.

Out of the corner of his eye, he spotted Cecilia's slight pout as she processed the disappointment. But she was a smart girl and hadn't missed his glance at Rikka.

The two of them eyed each other up and down. He could hear the unspoken conversation.

He'd want that bit of a thing when he could have a real woman? You awkward stick figure. Why would he want you?

Funny thing was, they were both exceptionally skilled women in their own way and suspected they would like each other...under different circumstances. His best course? Keep his damn mouth shut.

He raised the cleaver and swung it down to separate the lamb's head. His blade hit the block with a *thunk* loud enough to echo around the kitchen that hadn't yet geared up to its normal mealtime mayhem. Six other chefs worked their stations, but only quiet prep so far.

Kate watched him. A single arched eyebrow sent a double message.

First, she thought it was funny that two women were battling over him.

Second, that Kate would prove quite how lethal a field agent she'd been if Sam ever disappointed Rikka in the slightest way.

Sam had no intention of doing that and let his level gaze speak for him.

Kate nodded and returned to washing the eggs.

21

CECILIA WATCHED ALL THE SILENT COMMUNICATION INTENTLY. She'd learned to do that as a photographer. The reporter was supposed to do all the talking, but it was by being the silent observer that she could see the dynamics building toward the actual story. A picture *was* worth a thousand words, if it was the right picture.

The best photos had to be anticipated, not *captured* as most people thought. If the photographer wasn't ready when the moment came along, it was already too late.

So, Sam had found himself a petite Japanese girlfriend. Odd couple, considering Sam's Marine Corps powerful frame. At least she was a pretty thing.

Sam possessed good taste; he'd picked herself at one point, after all. And while he'd been fun, it had never really clicked with them no matter how good he looked out of his clothes. Three days had been about the limit for both of them; Sam wasn't a laugh-it-up, chatting-together type of guy.

Wasn't this a fascinating collection of personnel.

Kate Stark rather than Chef Vivienne Jacquard—Cecilia had checked the Hotel's website last night.

Sam Fierro butchering lamb at her side.

The tiny chef—*really, Sam?*—doing sushi things with lox so quickly that you'd have to shoot video at high-speed and slow it down to see any of the technique.

Whatever it was didn't look like Roasted Pigeon Breast Monte Cristo sandwich with a Baked Rosemary Grapefruit listed in the official press packet. And she certainly hadn't photographed Turbot Chowder, Roasted Seabream with Oban Scallops, or a single Cinnamon Brûlée last night.

Safest point to engage?

She dismissed the other chefs tending a baking oven, firing up grills, and clarifying butter. They all looked as if they belonged here.

Starting with Sam—studiously doing things to a lamb carcass she'd rather not be watching—would provoke the woman with the long slender knife, not that the man ever put two words together, or even one all that often.

Kate Stark now cracking pairs of eggs into a long line of ramekins. In addition to being generally acknowledged as an exceptional chef, the woman owned the most successful cooking network in existence. Her management skills transformed her and her brother from merely wealthy into billionaires. That meant she was smart and would easily avoid any question she didn't feel like answering.

Cecilia was about to place her bet on the wildcard and start with the new girlfriend who still eyed her cautiously, when a miracle walked into the kitchen.

22

"Hey, sis," Paul Stark strode into the Inverlochy Castle Hotel's kitchen, seriously annoyed at the British agent who'd frisked him at the entry and then double-checked his ID. "Where's the coffee?"

Kate used a frying pan she'd just pulled down from an iron hook to point at a large brass teapot. It was mostly hidden by an ornately knit tea cozy done in cables like a fisherman's sweater.

"You gotta be kidding me? Tea? Where the hell are we, England?" He found a mug with a thistle on the side and poured it anyway.

"Scotland, you utter doofus," Rikka shot back with a more than her usual asperity. Someone had put a bug up her behind this morning. Something gone wrong with Sam?

He hadn't realized they were an item, not until he'd been caught on the wrong side of a Secret Service agent last night as Sam rushed to her side.

Surprised the hell out of him.

He took a swallow of the tea. "Ow! Shit!" Hot as Hell and honestly, he didn't brew coffee this strong. It dribbled down his chin.

A lovely woman with dark skin and bright, inquisitive eyes handed him a kitchen towel. She required a second look. Her hair was fine-textured and looked as if she'd been out riding a motorcycle, not attending a stuffy G-7 confab. Long and lean, looking both sexy and uncomfortable in blouse, blazer, and neatly creased black slacks that were a testament to long legs. Practical shoes rejected, the toes of black cowboy boots peeked out on the rubber kitchen floor mats. He decided that they were the only part that was truly her, other than the cameras dangling from her delicate neck adorned by only a thin gold chain that dropped into her open top.

In fact, she looked uncomfortable enough in those clothes that it was easy to imagine her stripped out of them. Very easy indeed. It might be fun to discover what was at the other end of that gold chain.

"Hi. I'm—"

"Paul Stark. I'm Cecilia Barstowe, here photographing the G-7." She held up one of her cameras to prove her identity.

When they shook hands, he noted that she possessed a firm grip despite the fineness of her fingers that went with that slender frame.

"I'm not on for an hour. Would you care for a walk?" Her voice was mid-tone and carried a simple frankness. No games with this one, straight ahead all the way.

Well, he'd often been propositioned that bluntly and found no reason to complain about how often it worked out in his favor.

"A pleasure, Ms. Barstowe," he offered his arm.

Kate rolled her eyes at him. When Rikka did the same, he stuck his tongue out at her.

Sam's gaze remained level and assessing. For a moment it made Paul feel as if he was screwing up worse than last night when he'd arrived in Scotland only to have his new handgun taken away. At least he'd known not to call it a revolver; that should have counted for something.

23

"WHAT THE HELL, KATE?" TERRY RAGED AS HE STALKED UP TO the station where Kate was leading the crew in plating the G-7's breakfasts. The sun and the dignitaries were both up.

The kitchen roared in full, meal-service mayhem. If Terry weren't shouting, she wouldn't have heard him. Servers hovered. Chefs rushed over with bites for her to taste because she didn't have time to go to them. The dishwasher blasted away as the appetizer plates—swept clean of local Greek yogurt, fresh berries, and thistle honey—poured back into the kitchen.

She, Dirk, and Rikka were frantically plating the Gouda cheese omelets beside fresh-made miniature bagels spread with goat cheese, topped with a diamond lacework of Scottish lox, a single caper placed in each open hole in the pattern, and minced chives. Sam was following a step behind plating the best breakfast sausage patty she'd ever tasted. The hint of maple syrup cooked in was eloquent on the palate.

"I don't have time for this, Terry. Go away."

"Yeah," Rikka chimed in as she dressed the next plate with a trio of the small fresh-boiled and baked bagels each dressed in a different pattern of lox. "Go away. You can have sex with her later."

Terry sputtered, but he didn't say it would never happen. Earlier, when Rikka mentioned his divorce, Kate hadn't thought about that. She'd felt bad for Terry; he'd honestly loved his wife back when he and Kate were working together.

Now? Definitely too busy to think about such an option. She'd give it due consideration soon though.

"I mean this!" Terry held out his tablet computer.

Kate ignored him. While trying to land ten perfect omelets simultaneously, the last thing she had time for was a pleasant chat. Less than a minute behind these would come the ones for the First Spouses, eight of whom came along for the trip.

"Read it!" Terry was practically shouting.

"You read it!" she snarled back and wiped the corner of a plate where an omelet left a small smear of cooking butter as she'd positioned it. She gave him a hip check to get him out of the way as she circled the plating station.

"'Poisoned! Chef dies at G-7! World leaders next?' God damn it, Kate. I thought we were going to keep a cap on that. There's a goddamn photograph of you cooking."

That surprised her enough to glance up from the last plate. There she was, wielding a skillet as if it were a weapon.

Earlier this morning.

Showing Paul where to find the pot of tea.

"Looking pretty good in it, Kate," Rikka commented as she dropped violet petals over each omelet for a touch of sweetness and color. The purple and farm-egg yellow looked wonderful together.

Kate looked back down to make sure each plating was perfect. The hovering servers swooped in and the plates were gone. Sam began spreading out the pre-warmed spouses' plates as Kate and Dirk rushed back to the cooktop for the eight additional omelets that the rest of the staff had been prepping.

"Find Paul," she told Terry without looking up. "Betting he's with a photographer named Cecilia Barstowe. Start looking wherever there's a comfortable bed."

She pictured Terry shooting her brother dead. While it was tempting to let him, it perhaps wasn't the best option.

"Better yet, Terry. Give me three minutes then we can hunt him down together." It wouldn't be the first time she'd had to save his hide—or wanted to rip it off.

24

FBI AGENT MARCUS REYNOLDS LOOKED AT HIS PARTNER LEONA Edwards. Her grim expression matched his own.

The three-a.m. call physically hurt, left him feeling nauseous at the hard jolt from deep sleep. Worse, none of their standard coffee places were open yet. At least they'd been together; it saved them time. He had a place out in Brooklyn, but Leona's cozy rent-controlled loft was on the Lower East Side of Manhattan was much closer to both FBI headquarters and this morning's call-out. The emptiness of the still-dark city streets allowed them to hustle to midtown.

Leona spent the whole drive up from downtown on the car's laptop inhaling information and making notes on her pad. He liked a lot of things about his partner: how she felt, how she tasted, how her dark skin and his light...

Damn! They'd been sleeping together for close to two months and she kept sidetracking his brain every single time he thought of her.

He, *take a breath and focus Marcus,* liked the way that someone so good with computers was so retro that she did most of her fieldwork from a small pocket notepad and a pen.

An NYPD officer, nearly asleep at the Cooks Network's main studio door, let them in. Yesterday's crime scene, for that's what it was, was a train wreck by this morning's inspection—nothing remained undisturbed.

They were in the main filming studio of Cooks Network. The last time they'd been here was for the poisoning murder of a chef and a movie star. The prime suspects: Kate Stark—the network's owner, and Harold Merritt—a guest judge. They'd been cleared, but it sent shivers up his spine being in the studio.

The overhead grid of pipes, lights, and camera tracks remained the same. Work lights shining down from above projected a shadowed grid pattern onto the studio floor.

The set this time included to his left: two rows of audience seating, a three-position judge's table in front of the first row—knocked askew with two chairs on the floor, and two fixed camera positions.

To his right: three work kitchens, three large worktables. Two tables were down, but one remained upright. It displayed a seriously cute *WALL-E* robot amidst his sugary world of collected clutter. He looked, sad-eyed, down upon the wreckage of the other two sculptures, desperate to be released so that he could begin the clean-up. He'd repack it all into neat stacks of sugar cubes.

The entire area of the studio floor was covered in the shards of the two shattered contest entries.

Blood stained the floor where a Maxwell Klugman had been killed by his own sugar sculpture.

"Who knew sugar sculpture was a thing," Leona surveyed the damage.

"What was the sculpture?" Marcus decided not to mention that he'd normally have taped the show but hadn't been back to his own apartment in a couple days to set it on his machine.

"The ice castle from *Frozen*. Using sugar, not ice."

"But still he ended up on ice."

Leona rolled her eyes at him despite the early hour.

Marcus crunched a bit of sugar back to fine crystals under the toe of his shoe. A thousand shattered crystalline bits lay scattered about, worse than smashed window glass because there was so much of it. At every move it crunched so loudly underfoot that he could either move or speak—but his words wouldn't be heard if he tried to do both.

Leona started briefing him, "Reports state that Klugman's sculpture went over first. Somewhere in the ensuing panic, one of the other competitor's sculptures went down too."

No way to tell what it was, for it had shattered spectacularly.

Based on the concentrations of the bits and pieces, it looked as if most of the colored sugar came from the second sculpture. The lethal sculpture was all white, except where it was brown with dried blood.

Marcus spotted a piece of the second sculpture sufficient to provide a positive ID of the theme. A small, bright orange fish with one shrunken fin smiled up at him from where it swam intact through the wreckage.

"Heck of a survivor there, Nemo," he told the hand-sized sugar form and stepped carefully around it.

Tracks in the sugar were confused, but he traced them around the perimeter.

He called over to Leona who was inspecting the most heavily bloodied area. "I've got a couple of tracks running from the studio seating toward the victim. Can't tell where they went after that. The rest must have gone out the audience exit doors. Hold it...I might have them returning. Yes, sugar tracks returning from the main floor leading out through the lobby doors."

Leona pulled out her ever-present notepad, "According to interviews, these tracks would include the victim's girlfriend. Ouch!"

Definite ouch. He imagined a poor woman sitting there watching her lover get pithed by a two-hundred-pound sugar palace. Then he imagined it happening to Leona and felt positively ill. They'd been lovers since, well, the last time there'd been a murder in this exact same studio. He tried not to think what this one might bring.

"The second set of tracks," Leona kept reading her notes, "was a John Doe who kept the girlfriend from approaching the body. This time the operators all killed their cameras, so there's no tape. Eyewitness reports say that one nondescript escorted the girlfriend out into the hall where she was handed over to a Cooks Network staffer."

Thankfully, the first responders had taken photos before the cops arrived and began stomping around. Between them, the medical team, and finally the coroner; the site had not fared well. The medics' early snapshots were going to be more useful than the forensic team's careful crime-scene investigation photographs.

Kate Stark had personally invited the victim to be on the show at the last minute. NYPD already deemed Kate a *person of interest* and wanted to bring her in for questioning.

That she was in Scotland made it an international matter that was escalated to the FBI. After the episode with the North Koreans, Marcus had set a flag in the system so that anything that came to the FBI involving Kate Stark came to his attention. That's what had brought them up from downtown at this early hour to inspect the crime scene. Perhaps he'd update that flag to notify him of *anything* about her on any law enforcement system. It would have notified them twelve hours sooner.

"Check out this table," Leona squatted beside it.

Marcus crunched his way over, the air growing sweeter as each step shattered more sugar into fresh puffs. Sugar rush without eating the donut.

"NYPD said it might be murder because someone cut the legs..." He stopped when he saw where Leona was pointing.

The table legs had indeed been cut. Scorch marks showed where the steel had been heated. But there was a flash pattern across the bottom of the table for several inches around the leg.

Not merely cut, cut by an explosive.

A line of caulk led from each table leg toward a metal box that could be part of the table's structure, except it would serve no purpose where it was positioned.

He checked the other tables.

No mystery box.

Leona used the tip of her pen to peel back the edge of the caulk. A single wire.

"The steel table itself must have been the other half of the circuit, so they'd only need the hot lead. The wire is thin enough that when the charge triggering the explosives in the legs fired off, the wire would have overheated and vaporized. But the caulk kept the hidden sections of wire isolated from any oxygen so they couldn't burn. Whoever did this was good, but not great."

"So, what's inside the box?"

Marcus rested his hand on Leona's before she could prod it with her pen.

"I'll call in the bomb squad and we'll let them find out."

25

IF CECILIA BARSTOWE HAD BEEN POSITIONED DIFFERENTLY, SHE'D have thought the whole thing carefully orchestrated.

She'd arrived late for the breakfast, only seconds ahead of the heads of state and their wives. Photographers and interpreters were supposed to be in place at least ten minutes before each event. So, she'd won the honor of the *worst position possible* in the Red Dining Room. The other newsies all offered her a friendly sneer of superiority.

Well worth it. She'd dug up the dirt from a pliant Paul Stark —she hadn't known that billionaire guys were still intrinsically guys—then composed her piece and run it down the wire. Pure bonus over her contract as it focused strictly on the food.

She'd agreed to meet up with him later. After all, he was a nice billionaire, with a Hollywood-powerful smile and the looks to match. A perfect gentleman, who also made his interest perfectly clear—not a combo she was used to. It took her longer to extract herself than normal once she had her story. She found that she didn't particularly want to be extracted, but her photographing-delegates-even-when-chewing-their-cud contract called.

Cecilia perched in the darkest corner of the room, tucked halfway behind the massive sideboard that a King of Norway had gifted to the hotel. It rose in two tiers of dark wood, walnut maybe, one thigh high and one shoulder high—which ruined every good photographic angle. Massive with carved lions or monsters or something in place of the vertical supports at the corners. One was so smug she wanted to slap it, instead she snapped a photo. Maybe that would steal its evil spirit.

From here, half of the delegates' backs were to her. The red floral-papered walls and rich carpeting required a more distant perspective to make sense. Because of the designs, the smallest corner of the wallpaper in the image would be too distracting. Her choice of shots kept looking worse.

Worst of all, she faced the windows. They faced westward, so that every single shot was backlit by the morning sun shining off the lake and trees of the pastoral setting: instant silhouette. Her best shot, pun absolutely intended, was to use a long telephoto, brace the lens on the edge of the monstrous sideboard, and confine herself to close-ups that dodged both the bright windows and the wallpaper as much as possible.

She made a point of photographing the meal, not a single dish matched the information packet. Of the snarl of reporters and photographers who'd managed to finagle a press pass, she alone knew why.

Soon, many, many more would know. And she could lord getting the scoop over the others for at least a day or two.

She hadn't checked her phone during the meal to see if the garish headline on her article had been picked up. But the look on the Secret Service agent's face when he came into the room told her that the word went out fast and wide.

He scanned the room and then spotted her. With a slight tip of his head he indicated that she should exit through the door behind her and meet him outside the room.

Instead, she snapped his picture and caught Kate Stark's

arrival close behind him. She fired off three more. Nice looking couple. Kate's perfect jet-black hair, high cheekbones, and startling blue eyes—eyes that looked equally good on her twin brother—and the agent's rugged good looks were an awesome combo.

At the tiny sound of Cecilia's camera clicking at an incongruous moment, the *maître d'hôtel* turned and noticed the intrusion.

Cecilia spotted Irene's instant of surprise through the long lens, but she'd schooled it by the time Cecilia clicked the shutter. Instead, she captured the woman's perfect composure overlaid with pleased surprise; perhaps she could sell it back to the Inverlochy Castle Hotel as a marketing piece.

Irene Watson turned to the room as she held out her hand for Kate to step up beside her.

"Ladies and gentlemen," the manager disrupted several conversations without seeming to do so. "I am so sorry to interrupt your meal, but I wanted to introduce to you our guest chef. Our own chef departed unexpectedly on a personal emergency."

Being dead. The ultimate in personal emergencies.

"In her stead, my dear friend Kate Stark, you may know her television network, happened to be visiting us. She has graciously agreed to step in and cook for us. Dinner and breakfast were her creations. I hope that you look forward to more of her fine cooking as much as I do."

Interpreters translated from their taller chairs placed behind their leaders. The height of their raised seating allowed them to observe over the heads of those seated at the table, yet whisper next to their leader's ear when they leaned forward.

On a swell of applause, Secret Service Agent Terry Tyrell casually crossed the room, took Cecilia's arm in a vise grip and escorted her out the back door without breaking stride.

His grip was firm enough that if she hadn't moved quickly to follow, she'd have done a faceplant on the carpet and been dragged out.

Her attempt to make it look graceful proved about as useful as her usual attempts in that area.

26

Kate could feel the high as she left the Red Dining Room and returned to the Great Hall. The applause from the world leaders and their spouses had *not* been perfunctory. And Irene Watson's pleased smile spoke volumes.

Kate's love of cooking stretched back to before she could remember. She'd wandered away from it for the five years of work in the Secret Service—she never figured out what that aberration had been about. Then shortly after her return to the networks, her parents had died. Either her or Paul...she'd taken over the helm.

She'd hired managers for the other stations, good ones so she only heard from them at the quarterly meetings.

But she'd kept Cooks as all hers.

Most people thought of her as the executive who kept hosting shows to promote her own network. Few understood that it was the food and the chefs she cared about, and the network provided a vehicle to do more of that. Kate owned a play world in which she created entertainment for millions by wallowing in the world of food.

So tonight, to garner such accolades from people used to

eating world-class cuisine touched her more than she'd expected. President Kennelly's radiant smile had matched her husband's, but that might have been for an American stepping in when needed. The President was a notch or two overenthusiastic about pretty much everything for Kate's taste.

Kate—and the phalanx of Secret Service and British Protection Group agents that Terry had shackled her with—waited in the Great Hall while Terry escorted the photographer around through the service spaces.

Earlier, on their way to the Red Dining Room, she and Terry were moving so fast, Kate hadn't had a chance to appreciate the space.

Despite being set up for the meeting, the Inverlochy Great Hall still presented as an elegantly cozy space. The warmth of the dusky red patterned rug, the gold curtains, and the tastefully papered walls all spoke of luxury. The chandeliers hung from a painted-sky ceiling mural two stories above. Dark woodwork and period furniture, other than the modern meeting table, only reinforced the atmosphere of the room. The view out the window of Ben Nevis, the tallest peak in the UK raising its rocky head above the trees, stunned without humbling.

She'd never stayed here but could be talked into it quite easily. Of course, it was the sort of place you wanted to share with someone and her only candidate at the moment was Terry. A possibility that existed only in Rikka's wild imagination. Any glimmer of interest she'd had was pretty thoroughly quashed when Terry yelled at her during the plating of the breakfast service.

Kate's phone rang sharply enough that she jumped. The three agents posted around her jumped. Hands moved abruptly but stopped before diving under lapels toward shoulder holsters.

She pulled out her phone.

Why would FBI agent Marcus Reynolds be calling her?

Quickly in her mind, Kate ranked the risk of a call from the FBI against the more immediate hazard of the Secret Service escort. An escort that she didn't appreciate at all. *Thank you so much, T-2.*

He brushed into the room with Cecilia Barstowe in tow, already talking at Kate, "Is this the woman—"

Fine. Two could play that game.

"I have to take this," she answered her phone before Terry could switch gears to protest.

"Speakerphone," he snarled.

When the photographer made an attempt to free her arm, Terry didn't let her go. She finally gave up and glared at him.

Good! Made her like the photographer a bit despite the story she'd published.

"Hi, Marcus," Kate hit the speakerphone switch. "You're on speaker with the Secret Service so keep it clean. How's Leona?" Kate felt partly responsible for them getting together.

"She's right here and she's fine, Ms. Stark." His tone was neutral and relegated Kate back to her formal name. Why didn't that sound good?

She moved farther away from the door to the Red Dining Room so that she wouldn't risk disturbing the G-7's breakfast. Like a sticky cheese sauce, her Secret Service escort flowed with her. The photographer was also dragged along, though she no longer resisted.

"Has anyone called you regarding events here at the station?"

"Events?" her throat was suddenly gone dry. "You're at Cooks Network?"

"I'll take that as a 'no' on your being contacted."

"I've been busy here in Scotland." And she'd been too busy cooking last night when several messages had rolled in. Then she'd forgotten to check them between Terry interviewing everyone in sight and planning the next day's menu. She'd slept...uh, not a wink that she could recall.

"I'm standing in the main studio with Leona and we're waiting on a bomb squad tech."

Kate shoved a Secret Service agent aside to reach a chair and sit on it; she'd bet that the news was about to get worse. She tried to choke out *bomb squad* but didn't manage so much as a croak.

Not her beautiful studio!

"A Maxwell Klugman was killed yesterday when—"

"Max?" she managed. Only a few months ago he'd been the second chef in the competition where Marianne Rimaldi was murdered. She'd felt so bad that she'd offered the slot to him when there had been a last-minute dropout in the sugar sculpture competition.

"Yes, he... Why does that name sound familiar?"

She told him and Marcus answered with a long silence.

Definitely didn't look good. Max survives one show where Kate was a judge, and the other guest chef is murdered. So, Kate invites him back personally and this time he does go down, hard.

Not good at all.

"Well, he was killed when small explosive charges cut two of the legs holding up the sculpture's support table. We've called in the bomb squad to take apart the trigger mechanism; we don't know yet if it was remotely controlled or what. The collapse of the legs dumped a six-foot tall, two-hundred-pound sugar sculpture onto the cook. He was impaled by his own creation."

"Chef..." she corrected him absently with the only part of her brain listening at the moment. The rest of it was busy looking at the new pieces that had landed on Paul's game board. They couldn't be connected, but what if they were anyway?

Rimaldi and Klugman. The only connection she knew of was her network, but they'd arrested those responsible for Rimaldi and determined that Kate had been the actual target.

Hadn't they?

Was the new Council of Five member Senior Captain Rang Jin-ho breaking his word? Well, if the North Koreans were back, she had a few surprises of her own for them. It didn't have their feel though.

"Death was near enough to instantaneous," Marcus' voice continued out of the phone and resonated thinly in the Great Hall. "NYPD wants you for questioning because you invited Chef Klugman to join the show on such short notice. When they discovered you were...out of the country," his pause made it clear that NYPD thought she'd fled the country, "we were called in."

"You suspect me of murder?"

There was a long pause.

"No, Kate, we don't," Leona spoke up. "If we did, we wouldn't have called you, we'd have had you arrested and extradited."

"Small comfort." At least Leona used her first name.

Two dead chefs.

"What time?"

When they told her, she sighed. Klugman and Chef Vivienne Jacquard had died within minutes of each other. And, again, the only connection was herself.

Rimaldi on the cooking show a few months ago, Klugman surviving that show only to die on this one, and Jacquard...all three linked solely through Kate Stark. If she were in the FBI's shoes, she'd have arrested herself already.

Kate heard the quiet snick of a camera shutter, and didn't react—a strategy to stop this Cecilia Barstowe from snapping a more dramatic expression for her next photo. Kate felt satisfaction when there was no trademark follow-up of three quick shots that the woman invariably used.

Terry grabbed for the woman's camera, but she managed to pull it aside in the nick of time. With the other hand she reached for her press credential and waved it at him.

"I'm the only common thread," Kate acknowledged over the phone. "However, I'm having similar problems here in Scotland. I'm already in loose custody here for the murder of a chef I came to interview. I'm guessing that the US Secret Service wouldn't be amused if I were to try and leave the country at this particular time to answer charges in New York." A glance up at Terry confirmed that suspicion.

"Well, I have more bad news," Leona's voice came over the phone.

Kate closed her eyes. "What?"

"Your brother was seen in the main Cooks studio the day before the show."

"He...what!" Paul rarely came to the studio unless he was bored or in deep enough trouble to send him looking for Kate.

"We have him arriving in Colorado three hours later. The next morning he passed through La Guardia mere hours after Klugman's death, and he has now left the country."

"He's with me." Kate couldn't imagine what Paul was doing at the studio.

"May I speak to him?"

"He's not with me at the mome... Hang on."

Two agents entered the room quickly and were whispering with Terry.

Terry turned to face the photographer whom he hadn't released.

"Ms. Barstowe, do you know the whereabouts of Paul Stark?"

"I left him out front by the Rolls Royce chatting with the chauffeur about engine performance and road handling characteristics. We're meeting up later." She didn't have the decency to blush. Instead, for the first time, she looked worried.

They all turned to the windows of the Great Hall that looked out over the driveway.

No car.

"The Rolls Royce was out front earlier," one of the agents said. "It was scheduled to take a couple of the First Spouses on a sightseeing tour of Fort William and the surrounding countryside after breakfast, roughly twenty minutes from now."

Kate pictured Paul joyriding the Highlands in the Inverlochy's Rolls Royce.

Murder was too good for what she was going to do to him.

27

Cecilia's press credentials came to mean less and less over the last thirty minutes.

The last time that happened to her was when Sam had pulled her butt out of Rajasthan. An increasing hail of bullets in both directions were unimpressed by her status as a stringer for Associated Press. The RPG that had flown in through her hotel window and destroyed the small building as she watched in horror from the back of Sam's speeding Bajaj motorcycle had only emphasized the point.

Then it had been, *Keep down and get out.*

Here at Inverlochy she'd been prepared to dig in her boot heels and fight the good fight for Freedom of the Press in a civilized country.

Then Agent Tyrell had clamped down with national security and risks to the President and the First Man. Bet he enjoyed that title—First Gentleman hadn't survived ten seconds past the election. First Dude had been floated and thankfully sunk within days.

Cecilia prepared to fire back with the Constitution when Kate took her aside.

"You can fight the battle, Cecilia. You'll lose. Or you can go with the flow and maybe get a career-making story out the back end."

Cecilia wanted to argue, but this was Kate Stark handing out the advice. She was a through-the-roof-savvy marketer. The way Cooks Network shot into the stratosphere since her parents' deaths had been an amazing thing to watch.

"Can I get an exclusive?"

"For all I care," she offered an elegant shrug.

Cecilia wished she could make gestures like that, but they always looked stupid on her. Even after she'd practiced them in the mirror. Especially then.

"What about my cameras?" They were presently in the clutches of the Secret Service.

"That one's up to you."

"Fair enough," she strode back up to Agent Tyrell. "Here's the deal. I get my cameras back. I publish nothing about this story without your clearance, but I get to photograph anything I want. *And* I get an exclusive once it's cleared."

He started with a snarl, "And on what basis can I trust you?"

"Because I'm trustworthy. You want scout's honor? I was in until the other girls voted to sack me for being the first one to screw the quarterback."

Agent Tyrell, about to snap something vicious, glanced over Cecilia's shoulder.

It would be a bad loss of *chutzpah* if she were to turn and see Kate Stark's look. But whatever it was had the agent cursing again.

"Fine," he shoved her cameras back into her hands. "From this point on, one word or image of this story traces back to you before I clear it, and you're under arrest for endangering the life of the President. Do we understand each other?"

She gave him her best three-fingered Girl Scout salute, barely resisting the urge to make it a one-finger salute.

His half smile told her that he saw it the way she meant it anyway, and he turned to talk to an agent behind him. Damn but he was almost as handsome as Kate was beautiful.

Her phone buzzed in her pocket.

She pulled it out.

Another MI-Vid.

28

Cecilia Barstowe's gasp had Kate glancing over her shoulder as the woman played a video on her phone.

Kate moved in fast, which caught Terry's attention, and brought him back close enough to her side in the Great Hall that she could feel the heat of him.

It was—

The video ended.

"Play that again!" Kate demanded.

"I can't."

Terry moved in closer until their shoulders were brushing, "Play what again?"

Kate tried to process what she'd seen while ignoring the man, "Did I see a video of Paul tied up in the trunk of a Rolls Royce?"

"Play it again!" Now Terry was in on it.

"I can't!" Cecilia protested. "It's an MI-Vid."

"A what?"

Kate had heard of it. "It's a seven-second—like 007 in *Goldfinger*—plays-one-time-only, video-based social media. Then it does a secure erase from your phone as well as from the company's servers. She can reply, but she can't watch it again."

"What do you mean—"

"Shut up, Terry. Don't interrupt. I need paper and a pen, now! Cecilia," Kate led her over to a seat at the delegates' table close beneath the Great Hall's towering windows and shoved her down into the French delegate's chair, "I need you to write down everything you just saw. Don't tell me. Write it. Sketch it. Every detail you can recall no matter how stupid or trivial it seems."

She opened her mouth, but Kate rolled right over her.

"Time for questions later. You're our only clear witness; I only saw the last two seconds. We need everything you've got."

Terry was being too slow.

Kate grabbed a notebook covered in columns of Japanese characters and tore them off none too neatly until she had a clean page. She found a Montegrappa Miya Argento fountain pen at Italy's desk and shoved it into Cecilia's hand.

The woman was so wide-eyed, there wasn't a chance of her remembering anything.

Kate took a calming breath, squatted down so they were at eye level, and rested her hands over the photographer's before speaking slowly.

"Do what you can, then we'll talk. Don't second guess yourself. Get it all down in any order as you remember it and then we'll look at it together. The best way to start is to recall how you were standing, what was the light doing, where was your weight on your feet as you answered your phone. Repeat those physical actions if necessary to help jog the memory. Can you do that for me?"

Cecilia nodded once, like a puppet. Then again, more steadily.

Kate turned her to face the table, then patted her on the shoulders when she began writing. Cecilia had a heavy stroke that was sure to upset the Italian Prime Minister over the abuse to his seven-hundred-dollar pen, but Kate didn't care.

Terry pulled her aside.

"What the hell did you see, Stark? Paul tied up in a Rolls Royce? Is this one of his jokes?"

"No," Cecilia called out though she didn't stop her writing. "I bet it's from the same person who clued me in on the menu change and the chef's murder last night. It was a picture I'd sold to a foodie site about last night's dinner. Across it they wrote the words: 'What were they supposed to eat!' ending with an exclamation point. I sent back a blank image with a question mark but there was no reply."

Irene Watson breezed in from the breakfast room and took in the odd clustering of Kate, Cecilia, and the agents at a glance.

"Is there a problem?" She hadn't risen to her position of *maître d'hôtel* by being slow on the uptake.

Kate moved to meet her.

"Is there a good pizza shop in Fort William?"

"Yes, a more than good one. Are you planning to go out after you cook lunch?"

Kate wished. "No, you are going to have Dirk make a gourmet salad and you're going to bring in a truckload of pizzas for lunch."

"Am I now?" She managed to mask her horror quickly behind what sounded like a terribly sedate British query as to the expected weather next week. The sort of tone you might get from a British bobby if you walked up to him on the streets of London while carrying a missile launcher and informed him you were on the way to blow up Big Ben.

"They'll love it, Irene. It will be casual; break down barriers. Don't plate it at all. Send in the boxes. You'll earn a laugh and a sideline article for wit and creativity. I can promise you that. Right, Cecilia?"

"Uh, sure," she sounded distracted. Then the photographer focused, "Absolutely. On a major American foodie blog."

"Thanks, keep drawing." Kate could see that she'd shifted from writing to sketching.

"When was the last time, Irene," Kate asked her seriously, "that anyone in that room ate a superlative takeout pizza? If they have 'local' toppings, emphasize those, but also bring in a few standards."

"There's a corn crust-and-lamb sausage that is a particular favorite of the staff."

"Perfect! Four of those, at least."

Irene looked skeptical, "Is there a problem in the kitchen?"

"Kidnapping this time I'm afraid," she did her best to match the *maître d'hôtel's* droll manner. "My brother may have been taken."

Like the soldier of the service industry that she was, Irene squared her L. K. Bennett-clad shoulders and then nodded her agreement. She briefly rested a hand on Kate's arm.

"Is there anything I can do?"

"Not at the moment. But thank you."

As Irene headed off to see to matters, Kate called after her.

"You'll have to send someone other than your chauffeur as I have reason to believe that your Rolls Royce will also be unavailable."

That earned her an arch look that she did her best to ignore.

Then Kate returned to look at the sketches over Cecilia's shoulder and wished that the woman was less of an artist. They looked far too real. She hoped that this was one of Paul's jokes and that someone else wasn't going to kill him for her.

29

Kate exited the Inverlochy Castle Hotel through the heavy-pillared front entrance with Terry and Cecilia in tow.

The two of them were having an argument. Cecilia insisted that she had rights to an exclusive story. Terry snapped back that the photographer should be going the hell back to her job because she wasn't welcome during an ongoing investigation, and *exclusive* did *not* mean an all-access pass.

Kate spotted Sam and Rikka playing chess with the giant set on the front lawn. She knew Recon soldiers were brave, but holy crap!

She stopped for a moment to appreciate being out in the sunshine. It was her first moment of that wisp of freedom since the helicopter landed her here just twenty hours earlier. She'd only seen the kitchen and the inside of a Rolls Royce in the middle of the night. The fresh air tasted better than last night's turbot.

As she crossed the lawn toward them, Rikka lugged one of Sam's white pawns off the board by the throat. She plunked the piece, as big around as she was, down on the grass and patted it on the head. The board itself had already seen a lot of play considering only that single piece had been taken.

"Fear not. You shall have companions soon, my pint-sized friend."

"Did either of you see Paul?"

Sam stood with his arms crossed, glaring down at the results of Rikka's attack, his sleeves rolled up to reveal his tattoos.

Kate would take that as a no on his part.

"Maybe," Rikka perched on the flat top of one of her black rooks. "I saw the Rolls pull out of here, I can't believe you sat in the back seat with T-2 for over an hour last night and didn't do any necking. It's a Rolls Royce for crying out loud. How often does a girl get an opportunity like that?"

"Rikka! About Paul?"

Rikka waved a hand toward the drive. "The Rolls left as we came out on break from your sweat shop of a kitchen," her quick smile turned it from an insult to a tease. "Chauffeur at the wheel, might have been Paul riding shotgun. No, wait, we're in England."

"Scotland," Kate's ancestors might have been Lowlanders, but they were absolutely Scottish. And Inverlochy was in the Highlands which made it more so.

"Whatever. Other way around. If it was Paul that I saw, he must have smooth talked the driver and been at the wheel. Chauffeur was a pretty fussy sort, so I'm guessing it would take all of Paul's con-man skills to pull that off. Who knows where they— Hey!"

Sam had taken Rikka's knight with a bishop. Not a move Kate would have made. He picked up the knight easily with one of his big hands and set it on the grass behind his lines.

Rikka jumped down off the rook.

In a flurry practically too fast to follow, Rikka toted his

bishop, two pawns, and a knight over to her collection. Sam countered with adding four pawns and her other knight to his.

Terry arrived at the last of it—without Cecilia Barstowe.

"You shed Camera Girl, T-2," Rikka addressed Terry without ever turning to face him.

Kate looked around and spotted the reflective surface of a Protection Group car's windows on the far side of the circular drive. It had parked there after the disappearance of the Rolls. Terry missed it though and continued to look mystified at how Rikka spotted his arrival across the quiet grass.

"Good move," Rikka continued facing the chessboard but went on speaking to the Secret Service agent. "Linda Hamilton —brunette. Kate Stark—brunette, well, black hair but close enough. There's hope for you yet."

"Nobody gets Linda Hamilton in *Terminator Two,* short stuff. Did either of them see the kidnapping?" He addressed the last to Kate, rightfully concluding that a frontal attack on Rikka was a waste of time.

"I know that, doofus," Rikka wasn't actually paying attention to him. Or perhaps she saw it as a moral duty to harass all authority figures in every way possible. "But the young and dashing Michael Biehn does get Linda in the first *Terminator.* Gets down with her too, pregnant and everything."

"I don't think they did," Kate answered the kidnapping part of Terry's question. She waited, knowing that sometimes it wasn't worth trying to re-track Rikka until she was done with whatever she was riffing on. But nothing else appeared to be forthcoming, so she continued, "It's hard to tell, but I can't imagine it happening on the property with all this security."

"And then Michael Biehn ends up dead, short stuff," Terry continued his conversation with Rikka. "Not my ideal choice."

Kate would have to talk to Terry about not fanning the flame. But she gave him points for trying to keep his ground with Rikka.

"A woman like Kate standing here and you're worried about a little death. Jeez! Though, you try any unsafe sex with Kate, and I'll have Sam cut your balls off. Slow."

Sam confirmed his absolute agreement with the threat by not bothering to look up.

Rikka continued to face toward Sam and the chessboard. "Who was kidnapped anyway?" Rikka had indeed followed the conversation and chosen the parts of it she thought were more important.

Sam stood once again cross-armed and staring down at the chessboard. But that was okay; Kate knew that Sam missed absolutely nothing, ever.

"We think that Paul was. We saw a video of him tied up in the trunk of the Rolls. Something called an MI-Vid."

Rikka and Sam exchanged a look that Kate couldn't interpret then Rikka spoke as Sam returned his attention to the board.

"While we both think that might be pretty funny, considering who they grabbed—I mean who would want to keep him? Though I suppose that it's something we should deal with. Do we have time to finish the chess game first?"

With a look at Kate, Sam moved his queen and captured the rook that Rikka had so recently perched atop.

"What? No! No! No!" Rikka rushed around the chess board and knelt to give her castle a hug after Sam set it down with the other pieces he'd taken. "I'm so sorry. I never thought he'd be so cruel. I was going to build you a buttress and a keep wall and everything. I've failed you."

Rikka rose slowly, walking at a funeral pace with her head down, back to her position near Kate. Her deep sigh was heartfelt.

"Well, I guess we should go find what Paul's done to himself this time."

"What about the rest of your game?" It wasn't like Rikka to be so suddenly cooperative.

"Sam won. He'll have me in four moves, and I can't see any way out of it."

Kate looked back at the board. First, she couldn't see it. Second, how many moves had Rikka processed how quickly to know she'd lost? Third, Kate still couldn't see it.

"Okay," she decided that was at least a moderately safe response. "Congratulations, Sam."

Any reply he might have been on the verge of not making, Rikka cut off as she looked up at Terry, "Do you play chess?"

"Not much."

"Well then you and Kate should get along absolutely fine. Neither does she, not well. She tries, it's sweet, but..." Rikka shrugged Kate's incompetence.

Kate already knew that and didn't need the reminder.

"She totally rocks Scrabble though, just saying. Way out of my league." Rikka turned to Kate. "Okay, let's go find Paul. You sure? This could be your big chance to be done with him."

Kate admitted that the thought was attractive, but figured she'd better go find her brother anyway.

30

WHILE RIKKA AND SAM RESET THE CHESS BOARD, KATE HAD AN idea. She pulled out her phone and dialed Paul's cell.

Maybe she'd get Paul, maybe the kidnapper.

A nearby hydrangea, a purple one to the left of the stone entryway, rang shrilly. In moments, she and Terry unearthed Paul's phone from beneath the bush. Its case was the same color as his Ferrari, sunshine yellow with a blue racing stripe. He loved that phone but was always losing it somewhere. Someone might have dumped it, or he might have set it on the lip of the front archway's stonework while chatting with the chauffeur, or having a quick grope with the photographer, and hadn't noticed when it tumbled into the shrubbery.

"So much for that brilliant thought," Kate inspected the screen. "Wait, he's got an MI-Vid message, too."

"Don't we all?" Rikka looked at the screen.

Terry jerked in surprise at finding that Rikka and Sam had silently arrived beside him, so close that his twitch caused his elbow to bump against Rikka's shoulder.

Kate could sympathize. It violated all of her beliefs about her own Secret Service training in situational awareness, but she'd become resigned to Rikka's light-footedness and Sam's Recon-honed stealth.

"You sending him crap?" Terry looked down at Rikka. Pretty good rate of recovery, as she'd expect from a top field agent.

"Hey, teasing Paul is a God-given right. Ask his sister. I have a *carte blanche* on that, don't I, Kate?"

"Sure, open season. Do your worst, Rikka," Kate reached to tap the message icon.

"Wait," Rikka pulled out her own phone. "This is *super* tacky, by the way. Considered to be seriously bad form to take a video of a phone playing an MI-Vid. The whole point of these messages is that they play and die, like they did for Jim Phelps and Ethan Hunt."

Kate wanted to cheer. For once she'd caught one of Rikka's movie references without needing it to be explained. Paul had watched every single movie in the series multiple times and Kate joined him on occasion. She could rock *Mission Impossible* trivia.

"But we'll record it just in case it's anything interesting. Okay, go. Regardless, if Peter wouldn't approve."

"Peter?" Kate racked her brain but couldn't come up with any Peter character in the *MI* series. "Peter who?"

Rikka looked up at her with a wicked grin, "Peter Graves. Star of the television show. You didn't think I was referring to the lame movie remakes, did you?"

Damn. Kate thought she'd finally had one.

"You said Ethan Hunt," Terry put in. "That character was only in the movies, short stuff. Nice try."

Rikka stuck her tongue out at the Secret Service agent.

Kate didn't want to think about how many previous Rikka-traps she'd been led into.

"My brother?" Time to get this back on track.

"Yeah, okay, I'm ready." Rikka held her phone about six

inches above Paul's, set it to record video, and then they all shifted to be able to look around it.

They crowded close. Terry's shoulder was warm against hers on one side, Rikka's on the other, with Sam watching from close behind. His big hands practically enveloped Rikka's waist. It was casual, intimate, and had Rikka glancing down at them in surprise...then she seemed to decide to leave well enough alone.

Kate waited a moment for Rikka to recover, took a deep breath against what this message might reveal, and tapped the icon.

The MI-Vid was a single image of...

"I think I need to see that one again, Rikka. That wasn't..." She couldn't quite say it; some things were too weird for words.

Terry sounded equally doubtful, "That was your brother?"

"Every naked inch worth."

"And surrounding him, are those..."

"I think so." She watched as Rikka re-ran the video she'd shot of the MI-Vid on Paul's phone.

"Yep!" Rikka confirmed. "That's what you saw."

"Someone please tell me I'm not going mad." Kate looked at her three companions.

Not a single one of them volunteered to reassure her.

For once, Sam wasn't the only one who remained stone silent.

31

PAUL WOKE TO A HIGH SQUEAL THAT SLICED THROUGH HIS BRAIN like a dentist's drill on a hyperdrive going warp twelve. It wasn't merely an external sound; it cut and jabbed and hurt like mad.

"What the hell?" He clamped his hands over his ears and looked around. He was in a steel box filled with straw that itched like hell because he was...*stark* naked. Christ his head hurt—too much to laugh at his own joke.

Four people stood looking down at him over the raised tailgate of the trailer, because that's what this must be. Kate, that Secret Service guy standing way too close to his sister, Rikka, and Sam. He was only partly masked by the six sheep sharing the trailer with him. Well, he wasn't going to heap itchy straw all over his privates in order to make them more comfortable, though he did draw his legs together. One never knew what a sheep thought worth nibbling at.

Again, the hard squeal and the thudding boom shook the trailer.

Besides, over the years, more than one irate husband had caught him naked, so that didn't worry him much. Instead, he kept focused on protecting his ears.

"What is that?"

"Pipe and drum band. As in bagpipe." Kate kept her tone dry, but she looked quite happy. Usually she came across pretty grim when rescuing him from a plan that went unexpectedly sideways.

Except this time he couldn't remember... "How did I get here? Where is here?"

"You're in the middle of the town square in Fort William, Scotland, about three miles from the Inverlochy Castle Hotel."

"And you're naked."

"Thanks, Rikka. I kind of noticed that."

Sam made no comment.

"What's with the sheep?"

He hoped that the others could see them too. No hallucinogens except once or twice in college. If this was a flashback, he was glad he'd never had the original experience. Way too bizarre.

The closest sheep stared at him balefully from less than a foot away. Its long nose was covered in tight white curls, its body close shorn, and it wore a white saddle blanket with a large number 5 across its back. Atop the blanket sat an orange-furred teddy-bear jockey—wearing a blue-and-white striped knit cap and jersey. It tilted forward and a bit sideways to glare at him glassy-eyed.

"Fort William has an annual sheep race through the town square. It's how we found you. Someone sent a video of you and the sheep. Irene knew of only one place in Scotland that we'd find teddy-bear jockeys riding sheep."

"Who?"

"The hotel manager, the pretty one..."

He didn't buy Rikka's innocent look for a second. That should warn him of something, though he couldn't think what. Irene *was* pretty. And when wrapped up in all those fine British manners and sophistication, she posed an interesting challenge to—

"She thought," Rikka made a gagging sound as she pretended to stick a finger down her throat, "that you looked cute asleep among the sheep. Don't worry, I told her what an asshole you are, like *Austin Powers* but with none of the redeeming qualities."

Figures.

Another loud squeal and thud rattled the trailer. The pipe and drum band must be returning. The sheep in the trailer continued to nibble at the straw. He wondered if they conditioned the sheep to bagpipes like they conditioned police horses to not be startled by gunfire—Paul figured that the horses got the good end of that deal. An image of a bagpiper wandering up and down the sheep pasture was a good one though. Especially because then they wouldn't be so close to the other side of the thin sheet metal trailer that his head might explode at any moment.

"What's the last thing you remember?" The Secret Service agent was all business, despite how close he stood to Kate.

"Can I have some clothes?"

Rikka tossed him a sheep's jersey with a brown teddy bear dressed in green and yellow knit goods tied to it.

"Something more substantial?"

Kate handed him a t-shirt and a kilt over the transom.

"Not quite the family colors." The kilt was the blue-white-black plaid of a Clan Clark tartan. Starks were part of the Donnachaidh who wore a red-and-black plaid. How much misery would a Lowlander get for wearing a Highlander plaid? Less than strolling naked through the town. He wrapped it around his waist. With nothing to wear under it, he felt mostly naked. The wool wasn't all that much less itchy than the straw had been.

The t-shirt must be Rikka's doing. It was bright green with

garish yellow lettering that boasted of the Fort William sheep race. *I raced the sheep, but the sheep won. Now I'm standing in...* and a frownie face.

Perfect.

They let him out of the trailer right when a big Scotsman came up. "Here now, what the hell are ye lot doing among me sheep?"

When Kate's tall and powerful Secret Service agent turned to the man and began questioning him in turn, Paul felt unexpectedly thankful for his presence.

Sam showed a surprising solicitousness when he wrapped an arm around Paul's waist, led him through the crowd, and along a back street to an empty table. He appreciated it, because his body showed no interest in cooperating. Like he was drunk, except his brain felt fine, mostly. Like he'd been...

He staggered to a nearby garbage can and heaved out his guts. Drugged. Someone had drugged him. He held onto the can until he was sure he was done with it. And then stayed there until the shakes subsided.

Kate, Sam, *and* Rikka, which was something of a shock, were unusually kind as they led him to a small table far from the roaring crowd that beat upon his headache despite the distance.

He'd woken up in any number of strange beds and situations over the years, but none quite like this one. He'd long since learned that a roll in the hay required a thick blanket. At the present, every inch of his skin felt as if he'd taken a quick roll on a bed of nails.

One thing detail that he knew he could count on from past experience: the blank spot between leaving the G-7 meeting and waking in the sheep trailer was not going to turn out to be good.

32

"THE LAST THING I REMEMBER IS WE WERE ABOUT HALFWAY FROM the hotel to Fort William. A Rolls is as nice to drive as you'd think. Not all the fun of my Ferrari, but I might..."

Kate glared at Paul until he dropped the topic. But she'd bet that one day soon Paul would be adding a Rolls to his toy collection.

"There was a herd of sheep crossing the road. More sheep; theme of the goddamn day."

Rikka had scared up a paper cup of strong tea and set it on the small café table in front of Paul. For the moment, this quiet corner remained theirs; nothing nearby except closed shops and sunshine.

Later, after the parade and sheep races ended, this backstreet café would reopen and start serving... One glance at the chalkboard in the café's window had Kate turning away. It didn't seem fair. On sheep race day they were serving lamb curry, lamb burger, lamb...

She focused her attention back to her brother. He looked ragged, not a normal state for him by any stretch of the imagination. He rarely worried her—pissed her off plenty but rarely caused her to worry. This was different. She took his hand as much to reassure herself as to reassure him.

"The chauffeur had us open the doors and leave them open like a barrier. Then we stood to either side of the car doors so that none of the sheep came up toward us instead of crossing the road sideways from one pasture to the other."

Paul rubbed at his forehead as she and the others crowded close around him, as he struggled to draw out the memory.

"We got back in the car. I think there were a couple vehicles behind us, I don't remember. Maybe one. I started the car. There was a sweet odor. I was going to remark on it…"

"Then what?" Kate knew that Paul typically earned whatever happened to him, but it didn't sound as if this time was in any way typical.

"That's it. Next thing I knew I was naked in the straw looking at you. You're a sight for sore eyes, sis. What the hell is going on?"

Kate looked at Terry, who nodded in reply. Sweet odor. Violently ill after waking up. Chloroform or a variant.

Harmless enough in the long term.

She suspected that the short-term question of *Why?* would prove much more dangerous by the time they resolved the answer.

33

DYLAN SAW A LOT OF STRANGE THINGS IN THE SIX YEARS HE'D been tending bar at The Plough. With a long history as a hard-drinker's bar before he bought it, he saw no reason to change a thing. Most of the folks here were solos or came in with their mates, drank with their mates, and left with their mates. The regulars at the bar hadn't built any community to speak of. The Plough was not a place anyone came to meet people. Business girls came here to not be bothered while they drank.

Having done his time in the Royal Marines, Dylan's one hard and fast rule was no fighting indoors. Folks knew if they started a fight, they'd be having a free trip out the door—the reason it swung both ways. And if they didn't land until they hit the trash bins on the far side of the alley, that was their own problem. He kept the music soft enough to not block out the football game on the telly and the crowd never became too loud to hear the announcer.

When Megan Dumfries and Kiya came in. Megan slapped a hundred quid on the bar and shouted, "Rounds for all!" Well, that beat anything in a long while.

The last time Megan and Kiya had five quid to rub together

was months gone. When flush—which was pretty much never —they weren't the sort to give a beggar bloke a brass farthing.

He waited, had seen enough drunks to know the story would follow, eventually. It took six pints and two shots—at twenty-three Megan was well on her way to having a dedicated alky's tolerance, though young enough for it not to show yet on her body—before the tale finally spilled out. She could maintain her place on the stool, but it was a close thing. If she landed on the floor and stayed there, others would be using her for a footrest before long.

"Two thousand quid," her voice slurred heavily. It took both elbows on the bar to keep her propped upright. "Up t' the north. We tossed this canister o' shit in the back seat of a Rolls. Bloke gets in, slams the door to, and goes sleepy-bye as pretty as a hundred-dollar whore. Kick out a vid of him bound up in the boot of the Rolls and another after we strip him and toss him naked in a sheep trailer to sleep pretty as a— Wait. Already said that. But he was pretty, if you're into guys."

Dylan knew what Megan was into: Kiya, in interesting and seriously kinky ways—bondage marked only a starting point for the two girls. He waited, but that seemed to be the end of it. He gave the story a nudge.

"One who paid you say why?"

"Guess the bloke was a coach for the Rangers footballers though he didn't look the type. Celtics prank or something like. Never got it clear," she shrugged it off and slammed back the whisky that Dylan knew would be the one to finish her off when it hit her system. "Scammed another five hundred American out of the bloke's wallet."

"You keep the wallet, Megs?"

"Do I look dumb? Kiya, tell Dylan—" she turned to her girlfriend who'd already put her head on the bar and was out for the count, but that didn't phase Megan. Her focus wobbled back to him as she continued, "Kiya knows I'm na dumb. We tossed it in the boot of the Rolls along with his cute tush. His clothes? Them got the toss into a wheelie bin. We be clean as faerie dust, Dyl."

Dylan noticed others listening in—some regulars, a couple not. He leaned in and whispered soft, "Why don't you give me your stash, Megs? I'll keep it safe for ye 'til tomorrow."

She looked at him cross-eyed.

They had a history; when she and Kiya were broke and desperate, they'd trade certain favors for a clean-slate bar tab. Not too spendy on his side and always worth it. He only had to pay actual costs on the alcohol whereas they—

Megs shook her head, "Nah, Dylan, I'm good."

Well, she'd be rolled later tonight and wake up broke as ever. Since she was flush at the moment, he debated bringing up her and Kiya's bar tab, it was climbing a might high.

Naw. He'd wait to collect his pound of flesh until after she'd been rolled.

The girls did a fine job of delivering full payment.

Gave him a stiffie just thinking about it.

34

STEPHANIE SHED THE RED LACE TEDDY THAT GEORGE LIKED HER to sleep in. As they'd become engaged last night, she kept it on right through serving him breakfast in bed, as a special treat.

But he was preparing to go to his office now, so she changed into her morning workout Lycra. She wore no sports bra, which both George and her trainer always appreciated. It was going to be a busy day over in Scotland, but she planned to enjoy every minute of it right here in New York.

She smoothed the wrinkles out of the top and tucked the stretchy material beneath her breasts for extra sheer lift, while admiring the article about the G-7 poisoning that showed up on her tablet. She loved that she could poke something here and watch it emerge over there.

The news must be rippling through the G-7 like a whirlwind. Heads of state would hesitate with every bite. Eyeing each other with suspicion until the meetings verged on collapse. Though they mustn't do that, so she'd fed no more clues to the flat-chested photographer she'd hired.

She'd stir the pot, but it mustn't boil over until late tomorrow.

George's phone rang as he came out of the bathroom, already dressed to head out the door.

She closed the news-reader app.

He sat on the bed to answer his call.

Stephanie made it simple for George, she acted as if it was the most natural thing on the planet to sit next to him. She'd been training him that it was more than natural; that it was a given that she knew *everything*. To emphasize her point, she slipped a hand far enough up his thigh that her pinky *inadvertently* brushed him. She tactfully ignored the near immediate bulge in his pants and with her other hand tapped a manicured fingernail against the speakerphone button.

Morgan was calling to warn him that there might be trouble in Scotland at the G-7. He'd be coming to lunch tomorrow, if he could, but with twice the number of Secret Service he normally traveled with.

Vice President David Morgan. Irrevocably married to his high school sweetheart, he'd proved far too straight for Stephanie to, uh, distract. That had her playing the long game. She was getting damn tired of the long game, but if everything went well, the game would get much shorter very soon.

As Vice President, of course they'd be ramping up Morgan's protection based on the perceived threat to President Cheryl Kennelly.

Stephanie needed Morgan to remain safe. He was her inside man, though he'd never know it. If that meant he came wrapped in Secret Service agents, she'd support every additional one.

Instead of revealing her presence, Stephanie nodded for George to assure his friend that it was no problem.

This kept getting better.

She'd received copies of the MI-Vids of Paul that her hacker sent. The two girls had certainly earned their money on that one, not that they'd live to spend it. She'd made sure to pay them too much, taping their payment out of sight inside the Rolls Royce's trunk when she'd stayed at the hotel a few days ago. Payment on delivery, girls.

Of course, word had somehow leaked out that they had a high-paying job going down today. She didn't slum around often but that particular jaunt through the wrong side of Glasgow, paired with her visit to Inverlochy, proved to be most useful.

And now the Secret Service team would be all jittery over the kidnapping of Paul Stark. And better, the Brits would stop trusting the Yanks because Kate Stark would make sure that her brother continued running around loose.

A few more nudges and then the cards dealt would start to fall her way.

The one question that she hadn't answered yet to her own satisfaction was when to let Kate Stark know there was a game in the offing.

Stephanie resisted the temptation to call Kate now, herself.

No. Let Kate figure it out, but by the time she did she'd be in a deep dark hole with no hope of escape. The woman had let Stephanie's brother die mere steps from the White House. The VP-elect for one lousy day before he died. She could have had him in the Oval Office inside of a year, until that bitch let an old girlfriend shoot him.

Well, that wasn't going to happen this time. Stephanie and George were going to go all the way.

Of course, Stephanie's second target would stay in the dark until it was altogether too late.

35

KATE, AND EVERYONE ELSE AROUND THE TABLE OUTSIDE THE closed Fort William café, jumped when Paul's phone rang once shrilly.

By the rising crowd noise and worried sheep bleats from two streets over in the main street, Kate could tell that the sheep race was imminent.

She pulled out her phone, then his.

"You've got an e-mail from Cecilia Barstowe."

"That's private," Paul reached for the phone, but Kate slapped his hand aside and tapped to receive the e-mail.

"Photo attached," Kate tapped to open it.

Paul struggled once more to grab his phone, but she blocked him easily. Too easily. He wasn't clear of the drug yet and that worried her.

It was a photo taken from the main entrance of the Inverlochy Castle Hotel. A pizza delivery van parked in the driveway. Pulling up behind? The immaculate black Rolls Royce Phantom.

"Radio your people, Terry. I want to be the first to talk to the chauffeur."

"Second. I'm first," Terry then raised his wrist-mounted microphone to his lips and keyed his radio. "Chauffeur arriving at Inverlochy. Detain and isolate. We'll be there in ten for questioning."

There was a roar that echoed along the building walls until it filled even their quiet corner of town. The sheep were released and the race was on.

"Your Ford is on the far side of that, T-2," Rikka made her tone all sweetness and light.

"Better make that twenty minutes," Terry growled into the mike.

Kate patted his arm in sympathy and received a pained smile in exchange. He obviously hated giving up a single round to Rikka.

36

DUE TO A BIT OF POOR PLANNING, NOT BRINGING AN SUV, PAUL sat in front and Kate was sandwiched in the back of Terry's car. There was no way Paul could fit in the back with Rikka and Sam three across—Kate did little better.

Rikka sat in the center and was lost in studying Paul's phone. Sam was as talkative as usual.

That left Kate speaking to the back of Terry's head.

"So, Terry, what's your working theory on how I killed a chef in New York and Scotland at the same time and kidnapped my brother while I was with you?"

"Who's dead in New York?" Paul half turned to face her.

"A chef named Max Klugman was killed by a sugar sculpture in the main studio yesterday afternoon."

"That's weird."

Kate wished she sat on the opposite side of the car so that she could smack her brother on the back of the head.

"A chef dies on air in my studio and all you can say is, 'That's weird'?"

"I mean I was in the studio the day before while they were setting up the competition."

"And..."

"What do you mean 'and...'?"

"Paul," why did every conversation with her brother go this way? "What were you doing there? You never come to the network."

"Looking for you. I received a text to meet you there; said we'd go out to lunch. Once I entered the studio, you sent another text. Pretty lame apology for standing me up, sis. You owe me."

Kate counted to ten. It didn't help. "During lunch day before yesterday I was in Boston with Rikka filming a spot at Evelyn and Angel's, eating the best chocolate truffles on the planet."

Paul twisted in his seat to glare at her, "Then why were you texting me?"

"I wasn't."

"She wasn't," Rikka held up Kate's phone.

Kate didn't remember handing it to her. Yet Rikka was holding two phones, Paul's and hers.

"These texts aren't from Kate's phone. They're from a clone. Someone cloned your phone, Kate. What have I told you about leaving it lying around."

"I didn't. I don't—"

Rikka waved Kate's own phone at her, "Wasn't sleight-of-hand, honey. You left it on the table while you checked out photo-babe's message on Paul's phone. And when you handed off Paul's phone, you weren't looking at whose palm you were putting it into."

"Wait a minute!" Paul waved his arms to stop them. "So, if you didn't want me in the studio, who did?"

Sam shook his head sadly and kept his thoughts where he always kept them, to himself.

"Because, brother mine, someone followed you in. Rode in on your security clearance; installed the charges, the trigger and explosives that killed Max. I'll bet...oh no. Dammit!"

"What?"

"The chef who was suddenly injured at the last minute and dropped out of the competition. How much you want to bet their broken leg was no accident?"

That brought on a silence in the car as they finally cleared the last of the Fort William congestion.

"Wow, Katydid. Someone sure has it in for you. Framing you for both Max and Vivienne."

"But it isn't holding up," Terry said that as he stood on the accelerator, rocketing them north toward Inverlochy.

Kate reached forward to squeeze his shoulders in thanks. Nice, strong shoulders; she could feel the muscle rippling close below the surface, shifting with the simple act of steering through the curves on the narrow road.

She pulled her hands back and flexed them to remove a bit of that feeling.

Rikka, for once, didn't give her the eye. Instead, she concentrated on the phones. Kate would have to remember that for the future; technology—the great Rikka distracter.

"The Send and Reply header on the MI-Vid doesn't match."

"Which means what?" Terry turned in at the stone pillars of the hotel's front gate. He stopped at the gatekeeper's cottage—normally an extra guest room, but right now a major security clearing station. A team of agents began going over the car with mirrors on wheels for the under-chassis, sniffer dogs, and all the rest of it.

"Means they're good enough that it's a masked address with no way to trace it. Hey Mr. Agent Man."

"What, short stuff?"

"I need your computer." There was a laptop mounted between the two front seats of the car where it could be turned to either side for easy access.

"It's bolted in. Wait until we get to the Castle and then you *can't* use it once we're parked there."

"I promise I won't ask for a single password."

"Done," Terry grinned at Kate in the rearview mirror.

Kate did her best to keep a straight face.

Terry had no idea that passwords were not Rikka-tolerant.

37

AFTER TERRY PARKED THE BLACK FORD CLOSE BEHIND THE ROLLS Royce in front of Inverlochy and climbed out, Kate watched Rikka slip into the front passenger seat. Sam moved up behind the wheel of the otherwise empty car to sit beside her.

Terry dangled the keys outside the open window, then smirked at Rikka as he pocketed them and turned away.

He missed it, but Kate saw that Rikka had flown past the login screen before Terry had finished the *grand gesture.*

Sam glanced over at Kate through the driver's window and offered a *Damn but ain't she an amazing woman?* look.

He puzzled Kate. She knew he was pissed at her for her role as the head of security detail in the Vice President-elect's death. She'd always assumed that his anger at her stemmed from her letting the man go down on her watch. But the more she poked at it, the less she understood of why Sam reacted to her the way he did. For one thing, after years of keeping his distance, Sam had now twice rushed to her aid.

Later. She'd get it out of him later, but not much later. Marine Force Recon or not, she'd take him down if he didn't explain himself.

She nodded an acknowledgement to Sam about Rikka being amazing and kept the other thoughts to herself as she walked away.

Kate didn't turn to look as the sound of laughter slipped out of the nearby open windows of the Great Hall. Apparently, the gourmet pizza was working out better than she'd expected. She'd come up with the idea mostly to distract Irene while she raced off to find Paul.

She, Terry, and Paul moved past the windows and were halfway across the lawn to the north end of the hotel when Cecilia slammed into Paul's arms. He caught her solidly enough that Kate knew he'd shaken off the last of the drug.

She and Terry continued around the north end of the building alone. It was nice to walk beside him, if only for the moment. A steady and solid man lived behind the growly exterior he tended to present. It would be truly convenient if she liked him a lot less, because he was both kind and attractive. It kept distracting her thoughts.

In quiet harmony, they descended the slope where the ground cut away to reveal the outside entries of two offices tucked below the ground floor of the hotel.

They'd isolated the chauffeur in his office. In addition to the agent standing guard outside the door, Irene Watson and Dirk Cameron, the *sous chef,* also stood by. Irene looked quite irritated at being denied entrance, giving in to her irritation enough to be tapping the toe of her practical Jimmy Choo flats against the gravel pad outside the two doors. And if Dirk was here, that meant dinner prep was not underway...probably because Kate hadn't told him what they were cooking yet—as if she had a clue.

The two offices were tucked into the space directly below the silent kitchen, each with its own entrance. One belonged to the groundskeeper and his staff. The chauffeur and the sportsman shared the other.

With Terry and Kate's arrival, the agent barring the door finally allowed their admittance. The small office was instantly overcrowded.

The chauffeur, a round-faced man in his sixties, sat in a brocade wingback armchair. The brocade followed the repeating pattern of the castle's coat of arms: white-stitched patterns of a lone castle turret embraced by two thistles on olive green fabric.

Dirk immediately moved beside him, "How are ye, Ralph?"

"Well..." the chauffeur's voice quavered with nerves. Kate decided to give him a moment with his coworkers to calm down a bit.

The sportsman's area took up most of the space. It looked tough and manly, especially when compared to Ralph's part of the room. It might have a badminton set propped up in the corner, but next to it stood a skeet launcher and a glass display cabinet boasting a selection of exceptional shotguns: Beretta, Miroku, Browning, and... damn!

"Hey Terry," his looming over the poor chauffeur wasn't helping anything, "did you ever fire a Purdey?"

He came over to look through the glass-fronted case, "I've never seen one in real life. That's beautiful."

"It be Gerald's personal weapon. He's our sportsman." The chauffeur spoke hurriedly, looking for any safe topic before the silent and glowering Irene Watson. "Cost him a year's salary, used. *Foolishness* I says to him but he says as how he'd have paid two-years-worth to own it."

Kate noted that there was a fine selection of Martin recurve bows, not a compound bow in sight (probably considered too crass), and a pair of falcon cages (presently unoccupied), but with well-worn jesses and hoods hanging nearby. Also, an assorted selection of small sports equipment: croquet, Frisbees, and the like.

"Where is he? I don't think I've met him."

"Off to the hills, I expect. The Protection Group chappies weren't especially keen on anyone using lethal weapons with the G-7 underfoot, including spouses and such, so Gerald took his precious birds and went on holiday."

"I offered him four days' leave," Irene confirmed. "He left to fly his falcons shortly prior to the G-7's first arrival."

Personally, Kate preferred the chauffeur's portion of the room. By sharp contrast, it consisted of a comfortable chair, a fair-sized bookcase, and a reading lamp standing on a charming oriental rug. A small vase of cheery flowers rested on a side table with the latest Val McDermid mystery. A narrow wardrobe boasted three immaculate chauffeur uniforms from traditional billed cap to polished boots.

Paul had trailed behind after his brief *welcome back* encounter with the photographer. He looked more his usual self when he came to the doorway, though the agent at the threshold thankfully kept the photographer out.

Kate had been waiting to observe the moment when the chauffeur first saw him.

"Paul!" the chauffeur leapt to his feet, brushing Irene aside. "You're safe! Thank God! I woke up in the parking lot at the old castle ruins close outside Fort William, no idea of how I came to be there. You must go see it, Paul. T'isn't often you can see such a fine ruin of a thirteenth-century castle. I woke and had me no idea what happened to you. *He must be okay. He simply must,* I told meself again and again. I was sick as an old hound right there beside the car and then rushed back here to find you. Then this lot locked me up. Wouldn't tell me anything. What happened to you, lad?"

Paul, a bit overwhelmed at the effusive greeting patted the older man on the shoulder. "It depends, Ralph. If you don't mind waking up without a stitch on, among a flock of sheep ridden by teddy bears wearing knit goods, I'd have to say I was doing well."

"Och, ye got to see the races. Damme, oh, pardon my language, ladies. I'd been hopin' to take a couple of the G-7 lassies into town for that and maybe catch a glimpse meself. I put a tenner on number seven. Which one—" He stumbled to a halt as if only now becoming aware of Irene Watson's stern expression.

She still hadn't said a word. It amused Kate that she didn't need to.

"Now, Reeni, you know that—"

"How could you be so careless, Ralph? We had clients who expected you to be here and you were off joyriding with—"

"Now look here, Reeni," the chauffeur stood up to Irene Watson. It earned him Kate's respect. "I've known you since your ma was head of housekeeping and I used to change your nappies in this very room, so don't be getting snippy with me, lass. As if I don't know me job. If all happened as expected, I'd have delivered Mr. Stark to town in plenty of time to be back for the First Ladies. I had three of them as wanted to go and Mr. Stark also showed an interest, but I only had the three seats in the Rolls. So, I was delivering him early is all."

"Ralph," Kate stepped in before Irene could fire off her next broadside. She could also see Terry gearing up. He'd never mastered subtlety much. His forthrightness was part of his charm, if you weren't on the receiving end of it.

Irene gave way a bare half step to allow Kate to stand beside her.

"Paul only remembers the sheep crossing the road and a sweet smell on reentering the car. Did you notice anything else?"

"Aye, I recall that scent. Curious, I thought it was. *Neither lavender nor heather,* I recall thinking. 'Twas a bit of foxglove growing nearby, but that hardly smells a'tall."

"Anything else?" Kate should put in for a Nobel prize for

patience, between Rikka and Ralph she was getting far more practice than usual.

"There was this pair of girls, real city types that you don't see much out here in the north country. They'd come up beside the Rolls but stayed that tiny bit behind us. Can't say as I noticed what they were driving, though they were quite striking young ladies aside from their strange hair colors and such. *Just watching the sheep,* I thought to meself. They were certainly gawking like they'd never seen a flock on the road before. There's some as will climb right into a Rolls uninvited like they've never seen one of them either, but these stood by the open doors. I'd left the front doors swung wide, you see, to block more of the road from the sheep. I saw one as took a wee peek inside but did na more'n that."

"What next?"

"Naught but waking up wondering if my head was going to break from the inside. I have na had a decent cup of tea yet. Could I at least get that, Reeni?"

Dirk and Irene exchanged a look then glanced to the wall close beside Ralph's chair. A small sideboard had a sink, an electric kettle, and a supply of tea and mugs, all within easy reach but untouched. Without comment, Dirk squeezed the elderly chauffeur's arm.

"Let me be mother for ye, Ralph. Jest set down and let your wits come back to ye. No harm be done now. No harm be done," he aimed the last of that at Irene before moving off to fill the kettle.

"'Let me be mother'?" Terry whispered to Kate.

She had no clue.

Irene made sure Ralph sat again, then knelt in front of him on the rug and held his hands.

"It means," Paul kept his voice low, "to take the traditional woman's role of serving the family tea."

Kate looked down and could see the family. Irene looked so

young kneeling before the old chauffeur as she must have knelt a thousand times in her youth.

"Remember how you used to drive me to school?" Irene started in a wistful tone.

"You always did hate getting up a-time for the school bus to fetch ye, lass. I was in trouble with old Mr. McNulty more than once over you."

Dirk set out three cups on the small table beside Ralph's chair. He set a slice of lemon by Ralph's cup and a cube of sugar near Irene's without asking.

Kate stepped back to give the three of them—as close as family—more of their own space. Paul slipped her hand into his. He kept his voice soft.

"I'd thought to let the story of Vivienne's murder out to stir things up a bit, but it seems I stirred more of a hornet's nest than a snow flurry. Scared me, Katydid."

"Me too, Paul." So, his action made sense, as did someone's desire to scare them. It was the whole point and they'd done a fine job of it. So the question now? Who would be after scaring her family: Kate and Paul and her team?

If something she'd done put any of them at risk once again...

38

DINO CHECKED OUT THE VIDEOS AND REPORTS.

Dead chefs in New York and Scotland. MI-Vids of meals, a guy in a car trunk, and then in a sheep trailer. An escalating mess at the G-7. None of that worried him much.

There were layers of planning and money here that pointed to a major scheme that hadn't just been slapped together.

Then the Scottish punk girl's cell phone showed up on the black market. She might have lost her money easy enough, but to lose her phone like that? Bad sign. A quick news search revealed she'd gone out seriously bad.

His bitch redhead client cleaning up after herself? Could be. Not that she worried Dino. There were only three or four people on the planet who could come close to touching him. But it also didn't pay to be in harm's way.

His client had it in for the pretty chef.

Pretty? Hell! The client might be a rapacious redhead who loved to fuck, but the chef radiated pure class. Like a dark-haired Galadriel in *The Lord of the Rings*. Not the ditzy Arwen but the wise-woman and totally hot full-grown Cate Blanchett elf. A quick look at her file revealed Secret Service for five years. Beautiful and a hot shit? Cool! Didn't mean she wasn't going down if that's what the client wanted, didn't matter to him, but he'd sure enjoy watching.

Then Dino noticed something strange.

One of the Secret Service laptops he'd been using to monitor where the awesome black-haired chef moved dropped offline. Not as if it powered down, but there one moment and gone the next—like a black hole manifesting abruptly in the cyber-sphere.

He could see data moving in, but nothing came back out, nothing at all.

Well, he'd been planning to shift from the empty room over the pub in London where he'd been tapping their Wi-Fi. He'd delayed too long already. It wasn't smart to be lazy in this game; lazy dudes got their code slashed. Or—he tracked down the news on the Glasgow girls—their throat. Seriously time to get gone.

The small black hole didn't matter, not really. Some weird glitch he didn't care to take the time to trace. But as he shoved his gear into his knapsack, he didn't like it. Felt wrong.

Yeah, definitely time to move on to a highly secure bolt-hole.

39

S<small>AM LED</small> R<small>IKKA DOWN TO THE CHAUFFEUR'S OFFICE WHERE THEY</small> found two groups standing on opposite sides of the room.

Sam assessed the available weapons and wondered at the Secret Service. Yes, the guns and ammunition were locked up. But it was clear where a poorly hidden hide-a-key rested. A half-used box of shells had been left on the shelf with the neat stack of clean cloths and the cleaning kits. A full quiver of arrows hung beside the bows in plain view. He considered pointing out their security shortcomings but then decided that it was always good to know where a handy weapon lay in case of trouble. He left well enough alone.

"Wow, do I have bad news for you."

Sam considered poking Rikka sharply in the ribs. Her tendency to mouth off without thinking about how others were going to hear and react could seriously backfire on her one of these days.

Kate, Paul, and Terry laughed.

Sam reassessed. Maybe Rikka did have a clue.

"Hit me," was Kate's answer.

So, Rikka did, on the arm, rather hard. Proper technique,

too. He'd have to show her a trick or two... Kate rubbed at her arm. Maybe Rikka knew enough already.

"Ow!" Kate didn't look amused. "Next time I say that, hit someone else."

"Do I get to pick?"

"Sure. But not me. Or Irene. She might hit back."

Irene looked up from where she knelt before her chauffeur and the hovering Dirk. Sam listened to them with half an ear as Irene tactfully tested the man. Smart woman. The dose of knock-out gas would have hit the old guy much harder than Paul. It sounded as if the last of it was clearing out of his system.

"I'd never hit Irene," Rikka sounded offended. "She's too much of a lady."

Irene inclined her head in thanks and turned her attention back to the two men recounting the day they'd escorted Irene to her first formal *fourth-year* dance, whenever that was. High school sophomore? Everything he'd learned about the British school system came from Rikka forcing him to binge-watch the Harry Potter movies, one of her weirder choices. Eight movies straight. Long.

"If she's a lady, that makes me...?" Kate turned back to Rikka.

"Yep, chopped liver. That's our Kate. Or soon will be."

Kate laughed at her.

Sam watched her carefully. It wasn't that Kate disbelieved Rikka; it was that she didn't step forth in fear. That took years to beat into Marines' thick skulls, whereas that's how Kate always operated. Cautious, weary, frustrated, he'd seen all of those in her. But rarely anger and never fear. No wonder she was so goddamned formidable.

Sam decided they should continue this conversation somewhere else; nothing to be gained by scaring civilians. He led them out of the chauffeur's office and out into the early afternoon sunshine. Around the Inverlochy Castle Hotel to the west, they passed the two Protection Group officers standing watch at this corner.

He moved on until they were out on the front lawn well away from the hotel, close by the cow fencing where the Highland cattle kept the Inverlochy's lower acreage well grazed. They had long horns and shaggy red fur that hung down over their faces and entire bodies. It made them look like oversized, underage street punks. Lazy ones who couldn't be bothered to inspect the new arrivals.

Outside the fence, the Robinson R-22 helicopter that he'd arrived in with Paul remained parked at the helipad on the lower lawn. One of the rotor blades reached out over the fence; a sole member of the street-punk cattle gang grazed below it.

The ground beyond the fence dropped in long rolls down to the private lake. A small boathouse serviced the half-kilometer long lake. A possible hide, except for the agent standing close beside it.

A motorized skiff idled along the shore's edge. Then it circled the small, wooded island at the lake's center before repeating its route.

A quick scan. The security detail had grown fifty percent from their arrival last night. That was a good thing. Snipers on the two flat sections of the roof of the castle; one each. Easy to spot. They were the deterrents. That meant there were two more that he couldn't see and never would, not even after they'd shot him if they decided to do that. They'd be SAS snipers, the most powerful counter-terrorism force outside of Delta Force. It was as secure as they were going to get.

Time to face it.

Sam turned to close their circle and indicated Rikka could safely begin. He estimated the chances of a usable listening post that would capture all of their conversation despite the light westerly breeze as acceptably low.

"Okay," Kate turned to Rikka, "tell me."

"You didn't say 'hit me.' Do I get to hit one of them anyway?"

"I think Paul needs a break."

Sam was surprised to find himself agreeing. No man liked facing his own mortality. Though he'd bet that Paul would brush it off soon enough.

"And," Kate continued, "Terry will be bummed enough when he finds out you cracked his password in under fifteen seconds."

"Under eight."

"You what?" The Secret Service agent didn't begin to understand Rikka's hidden talents.

Sam knew she'd needed under five seconds, because he'd been watching when she did it. Nice of Rikka not to brag, too much.

Kate put a restraining hand on Terry's arm.

"If you want to hit Sam," Kate offered, "I'll leave that up to the two of you."

Real nice.

He looked down at Rikka.

She tilted her head back and inspected him through slitted eyes that did nothing to hide the green brilliance of them.

After a long pause she patted him on the arm, "Later, I promise."

How did she do that? The others laughed at the joke. But he heard that she was ready for the next step in their relationship. Not now, but not long.

He brushed a hand down her thick fall of jet-black hair that always felt smooth as water and as substantial as the ocean. He barely resisted kissing her on top of the head.

Rikka turned back to Kate.

"Remember when the Vice President died on your watch?"

40

Kate felt as if she'd been kicked in the gut. She wanted to curl up on the field grass of Inverlochy and die.

Four years ago, and it felt like yesterday.

Washington, DC.

Thirteenth and Connecticut Northwest.

Twelve-thirty-four p.m.

One of those perfect early November days in DC when the sun shone and the air warmed enough that you couldn't see your breath despite the snowstorm hammering on Boston and New York.

Eleven steps from the front door of the DGS Delicatessen.

Eleven lousy steps.

Her team reported *clear* inside the deli. Mr. Vice President-elect Earl Bronson had decided a DGS corned beef on rye and a root beer float would be the perfect cure for a victorious election-night hangover.

Nine steps to the deli. She counted in odd-numbered groupings today to keep her mind alert. Yesterday had been even numbers and tomorrow would be by threes.

Kate shifted from taking point to working rearguard, facing the street, scanning the most likely lines of attack.

They'd made her head of his Secret Service Protection detail when he'd started polling over ten percent. Kate had escorted Bronson during his Senatorial tour of the war zones. That's where she'd met Sam. Bronson had ended up making VP on the party ticket when Cheryl Kennelly edged him out for President during the third round of convention balloting.

Back in Washington DC, she used that memory to keep the edge on her thoughts. They'd kept him alive in Kabul, this should be a piece of cake, but she'd never treat it that way.

The outer ring of defense secured the block. The middle team halted all motion in or out of the surrounding shops, three to either side of the deli and the six directly across the street. They'd also swept the inside of the deli.

Seven steps to the door.

A bright bell announced the door swinging open.

That struck her as being earlier than expected.

Kate looked over both her shoulder and the Vice President-elect's to see a particularly stunning blonde step out the door.

That wasn't supposed to happen. Why had the inside team allowed someone to be on the move?

Then the cataloging portion of Kate's brain snapped to.

Patricia Clarice Abrahamson. Mistress—Earl Bronson, even though single, wasn't the sort of man who one could say had a girlfriend. That's why the inside team let her move. She was a *known*.

Correction. Former mistress, based on the perky collegiate brunette aide the VP had partied with and bedded last night after President-elect Cheryl Kennelly's acceptance speech.

That set off every alarm in Kate's head.

At five steps to the door, Kate stood too far behind to get between them.

She began her swing, but far too late.

VP-elect Earl Bronson opened his mouth to greet his former mistress with a smoothly placating promise to give her a call.

From her purse, Patricia Clarice Abrahamson raised the 9 mm Colt Defender that her daddy had purchased for her and taught her to use.

Kate's locked arms slammed into the VP's left side to knock him clear.

He'd stepped down with his right foot, making him well braced against Kate's blow from his left. As a former college linebacker, he automatically pushed back against the unexpected blow and remained in place.

It was his undoing.

Patricia Clarice Abrahamson unleashed three quick, precisely targeted rounds as she raised her arm. The last caught Earl in the open mouth, the second in his heart (if he had one), but the first landed below the belt.

Vice President-elect Earl Bronson's blood splashed outward from where the bullets passed through his body, showering Kate. Hollow-point cop-killers to leave such massive paths of destruction, mushrooming to many times their size before they exited.

Kate continued her spin now blinded by the hot blood from the back of Earl's head.

Three steps to the door.

Kate drove Patricia Clarice through the front window of the DGS Delicatessen.

The woman ended the day with four broken ribs and fifty-seven stitches.

And one dead Vice President-elect.

41

"I REMEMBER THE DAY," KATE MANAGED TO KEEP HER VOICE steady despite Rikka's gut punch. She looked out at the rolling meadow and the watching cattle, seeking any semblance of internal peace.

Totally failed.

"Can't believe you quit the Service because of that slime," Terry sounded grumpy. Patricia Clarice Abrahamson was only the most recent among the corral of women Earl Bronson had used and left behind. In front of how many of those, including Patricia, had he dangled the open role of Mrs. Vice Presidential candidate as an enticement into his bed?

"I know that no one on the inside liked or respected him," Kate admitted. "Including me."

You never allowed yourself to get personal about a protectee, but Earl Bronson scraped the bottom of the barrel. She'd known that when they were teens together on the Upper West Side and she'd dislocated three of his fingers before he learned to keep his hands off her.

"That doesn't mean you don't protect him," her greatest failure ever.

"Protect him, fine. Quit the Service? C'mon Kate. It's what you were meant to be doing."

She was on the verge of facing down Terry when she noticed Sam's sullen expression.

"You're shitting me, Sam."

He shrugged uncomfortably. Sam *agreed* with Terry?

Kate went toe-to-toe with him.

At her sharp jab against his breastbone, he rocked back on his heels but gave no ground.

"You've been giving me the raw edge for *four years* not because he died on my watch but because I *quit*? I allowed the first assassination in history of a Vice President and the first of a US head of state since Kennedy!"

"Well, duh!" Rikka said. "But none of us get why you quit."

"The Director was pissed as hell," Terry put in. "You're one of the best field agents we ever had. And you just quit. You're the one who should be standing beside President Cheryl Kennelly right now and everyone knows that. Been a hell of a load on Amy Franklin. She's been nervous as hell about you being here, I can tell you."

Rikka nodded, "T-2 is right for a change."

Terry didn't deign to snarl at the use of his unwelcome nickname.

"Hell, you tracked me and knocked me totally out of operation," Rikka continued. She flapped a hand at the cows chewing their cud as if they had relevance to an event six years before.

A couple of the cattle shifted, but that might have been to reach taller grass.

"You know how many tried before and since? Over a hundred attempts, though only ten or so I'd count as decent efforts. And only two found my third firewall, and no, I'm not saying how many I maintain. Their score? Zip. Kate Stark? One for one."

"Knocked you out of what?" Terry asked. "Who the hell are you?"

Rikka ignored him.

Kate looked to Paul.

He shrugged, "I knew you were hurting, Katydid. That's all that mattered to me. Secret Service or running Cooks Network, you seem to like both. I never did give a damn which one you did."

Thank God. One rational person in the world around her. She gave him a hug and received one back that seemed to re-center something inside her.

Over her brother's shoulder she saw Irene Watson waiting at the head of the steps that led up to the castle, Dirk Cameron at her side.

"Okay," Kate knew what was coming from that direction, dinner prep had to start soon. A second round of pizza wouldn't cut it. She waved at them to indicate she'd be with them shortly. Rather than departing, they sat on a handy bench to wait.

Crap!

She patted Paul on the shoulder and turned back to the group, doing her best to suppress a sniffle as he kept an arm around her shoulders.

"Hit me, Rikka."

Rikka unleashed a punch that Terry was barely able to block in time to save his arm. She turned her grin to Kate.

"I prowled through the FBI's servers on MI-Vid messages. No image capture, sloppy of them, and not full routing information. I mean if you're going to all the trouble of spying on the nation's data, you ought to do it thoroughly. I kicked them a quick 'how-to' for MI's data architecture anyway—that should be popping up anonymously sometime tonight. The message-routing packets on the MI-Vid servers usually lead to a lot of places. There should be IPs, routers, point of origin, and a track of multi-bounce off a long trail of servers. *Nada*. All I got was a signature."

"A what?" Poor Terry.

Kate was growing used to Rikka's technical barrages, not that she understood them. She did learn that Rikka translated them into layman's terms only after she was through her technical breakdown and analysis. That made silence in the early stages of her explanations the best strategy.

"C'mon, T-2," Rikka wasn't backing off on targeting him yet. "This is the digital age. Every hacker has a signature. A punk's is sloppy. But if they survive the FBI and assorted hackbacks long enough to get good, it hones down to a certain style, a unique set of custom tools. It's hard to shift a signature because it's based on a hacker's brain. What they put together works for how they think. You know the old saying: Once a Linux-head always a Linux-head. That's why no one can find me. I'm always rotating my paradigm. No one except Kate. How *did* you find me, anyway? You never explained."

"Another time, Rikka."

She harrumphed but was having too much fun inundating Terry with jargon to do more. She picked up where she left off.

"A signature evolves organically as—"

42

KATE DECIDED TO LET RIKKA HAVE HER STAGE SHOW FOR ANOTHER minute or so, to watch Terry squirm. He didn't. Instead, he stood there on the Inverlochy lawn and did his best to keep up.

Damn but she liked him.

"Lecture another time, Rikka." Kate cut her off sooner than she'd planned. Besides, Rikka had also been on the verge of tipping off into the deep end of her favorite topic. Once at that end of the pool, a naked Hugh Jackman prancing through the heather wouldn't shift Rikka's attention.

"Dino's playing against you," the sudden flat statement with no explanation almost caused Kate to stumble forward.

"Dino?"

"Yep."

Kate searched for references in her head, this had to be a movie thing.

"Dean Martin?" That couldn't be right. "He's dead, isn't he?"

"C'mon, Katydid," Paul squeezed her shoulder, "you used to be addicted to reruns of *The Flintstones.*"

"When we were three years old."

"And the name of Fred's pet dinosaur?"

"Dino," Kate must be going quietly mad.

Rikka smiled, "I met him a couple years back—"

"You met a cartoon dinosaur named Dino?"

Rikka patted Kate's arm. "A hacker with the moniker Dino. At the hacker convention in—"

Terry cursed emphatically before asking, "There are hacker conventions?"

"Sure, bunches. Next one is Black Hat in a couple weeks in Vegas; I can't wait. There are two of those happening simultaneously right before DefCon. DC is the big one for any idiot with an entry fee." Rikka made like she was knocking a cow patty off her shoes.

"Black Hat is the real one for serious newbies, security personal, government slobs, and so on. It's mainly the big stuff that scares the shit out of Jane Q. Public: hacking ATMs, tips on setting up IRS-sized Denial of Service attacks, easy hacks on security cameras, you know—the basics."

"The basics?" Terry gasped, short of breath.

"Sure, governments send their hot-doggers to learn. Security companies show off their counter measures, hopping about like bunnies just begging for someone to stroke their fur with a contract. All fun. But the cool Black Hat, the one for the most rad hackers, happens on a locked floor in one of the hotels. First, you have to find out about it, not easy. Then you have to be able to hack your way in through the Dark Web firewall. No invites. No one on the inside will admit it exists."

"You just told us." Kate knew little about the Dark Web other than it was a murky layer of code populated by arms dealers, hit men, and super hackers. As she preferred to sleep at night, she didn't ask for any more details.

"Yeah, right. I'm real worried about the four of you hanging out with Black Hat-class hackers. So not gonna happen. Anyway, I was the youngest ever at thirteen, took me three months to figure out how to get in. Each newbie is charged with reinforcing the firewalls so that their own style of attack won't work for anyone else. I laid down serious code in addition to that so no one got through for three more years. Except one guy. A short Jewish dude."

Kate wondered at how small a person he had to be for Rikka to call him short.

"He called himself 'Dino.' Scary good. Never went head-to-head with him."

"I'm being attacked by someone named after a cartoon dinosaur and who you rate as scary good?" Kate had no idea how to counter that. Or how to begin to think about—

"Don't worry, Kate. I'm better than he is. Besides, he's not attacking you. At least not directly. He's only doing work-for-hire to hide someone else's attacks."

A massive Highland cow eased up to the fence and reached her nose out to snuffle at Rikka's back.

Rikka jumped at the hot puff of grass-laden air that sent her long dark hair flying. She spun to face the cow and squealed in surprise, backpedaling quickly until she ran into Paul and the two of them tumbled to the ground.

Sam scrubbed the cow's cheek before turning to help Paul and Rikka back to their feet.

"Sam, you make sure that it knows not to do that again unless it wants you to chop it up for dinner." Rikka eyed the cow carefully and shifted her position to Sam's other side to stay well away from the monstrous bovine.

"Thanks, Rikka." Kate wanted to go find a nice quiet place where she understood what was happening, like... Well, she'd think of someplace. "You make me feel so much safer now."

"Good," Rikka kept a weather eye on the cow as it returned to tearing at the field grass. "Now the bad news."

"I was kidding about feeling safer." And if that wasn't the bad news, Kate felt a lot worse.

"Dino's signature is showing up in a lot of strange places.

Anywhere you've got a file, it looks like he's been there. Your Secret Service file, swept. The investigation into VP Earl Bronson's demise, he's been there and done that. I need something more than T-2's laptop if I'm gonna tromp on him. I need access to real gear."

"No," Terry held up both hands in self-defense. "No, you can't have access to our security van. There's," he waved a hand toward the hotel, "there's a G-7 meeting going on. Right...there. I can't have your private hacker war disrupting that. You are not getting inside our security."

Kate shook her head sadly.

"What?" Terry snapped at her.

"You don't know what you're messing with when you get to this level. But," Kate told him, "if it makes you feel any better, I don't either."

"Kate's right," Rikka pointed in the direction of the hotel's gardens where the security van sat parked in the trees. "I checked your system. Dino's already been in there. I started a couple of scans for logic bombs, but I don't see any echoes. Too easy for him; no challenge. Instead, he's got a sniffer that's looking to see if you have a hacker of your own that's good enough to be a problem. You don't, but I am. I left his sniffer alone so that he wouldn't be alerted to my presence. Besides, I learned a lesson from Sam."

Kate squinted at Sam in question, but he shrugged his own confusion.

"Come on people. Two decades in Marine Force Recon. Sam is frickin' invisible until he wants someone to see him. Same trick. Dino won't find any hints of me until it's way too late."

"Great. Thanks, Rikka." Kate did feel better for a moment.

The cow watched their group blandly. What the hell did they think about? Maybe she'd go and graze with them, thinking quiet cow thoughts.

Then she finally recalled one of Rikka's earlier comments. "But what about whoever is pulling Dino's strings?"

Rikka and Sam exchanged worried glances. Terry looked at her, but then his eyes slid aside uncertainly. Only Paul remained staunch by her side—stoic or naive, she didn't want to know.

Finally, Rikka shrugged uncertainly.

The cow ventured no opinion at all.

43

"WELL?" STEPHANIE TRIED NOT TO LET HER NERVES REACH HER voice or affect her composure until she was out of the workout room and had closed the door on her trainer.

She'd purchased a burner phone for speaking to this hacker Dino—a prepaid time cell phone off the Walmart rack. It had no camera, and she kept it in a black leather bag when she wasn't using it in case he could reach in and turn on the microphone after she hung up and powered it off.

She wasn't trying to be secretive, except from Dino. The fact that he was probably in her tablet computer and her personal cell phone was sufficiently unnerving to begin with. The burner phone gave her at least a feeling of anonymity no matter how false that sense of security might be.

Stephanie straightened her top in the bathroom mirror and began fluffing out her hair with spread fingers.

"Well," Dino drawled out the word like a hick from Texas, not a boy from the Bronx, "like I figured, they're pretty wide open over there."

"If they're so wide open, then why am I paying you so much money?"

"Because the Secret Service and the Brits are 'so wide open' to about three hackers on the planet. There might be a fourth, a Chinese guy who's getting close—they have seriously rad dudes these days. Mostly there's me, Buckbeak, and The Dragon Bitch."

"Don't like her much, do you?"

"I don't know if it is a her. The Dragon Bitch is their tag. It's gotta be a team, a big one like Anonymous. No one person is that good."

Stephanie liked the idea that she'd hired a hacker professional enough to know his competition by name.

"So, can you do what needs doing?"

"Jeez lady. Didn't I just finish saying that? Why are you so hot for this Stark chick, anyway? Because she was there when your brother got offed?"

Stephanie Bronson sighed. She should have known that bit of information wouldn't remain hidden any more than her identity. The best she could hope for was honor among thieves. No way was she offering herself to this shit, wherever he was.

Earl had been a philandering, womanizing bastard, but he'd also been her stepping stone to the White House. In four more years he'd have been doing the facade of for-TV, out-in-public appearances he so enjoyed and—like Nancy Reagan during the Alzheimer years—Stephanie would have been running the most powerful country on the planet.

No bitch child of Vernon and Betsy Stark took that away from Stephanie Bronson and got away with it.

"Not enough to kill her, huh?"

"Stick to your job if you want to get paid," Stephanie felt the world go cold in her gut. She wanted to do far worse to Kate Stark than mere death.

"I don't need the cash, lady. The world's banks are open anytime I need funds."

"Then why—"

"Because no one ever asked me to hack a G-7 meeting before."

"Then get it done." She shut down the phone, stalked back into the home gym, and stuffed the phone into the bottom of her Wek handbag.

Her trainer had given up struggling against his restraints.

She didn't just drop her Lycra shorts; she stripped down until she was wearing only her workout sneakers. Then she undid the handcuffs. She'd purchased a double-dildo and been planning to prove to him that turn-about was fair play. But that wasn't what she wanted.

"Just do it!" The trademark was emblazoned across his gym bag. "Hard!"

He did.

She'd bear the bruises for days, but those would be easy to hide from someone as naive as George. The scores of her fingernails on the trainer's back and chest would last much longer, but that was his problem.

And it was definitely worth it.

He purged the slimy feeling that talking to Dino spread through her system—most of it anyway.

44

"ENOUGH!"

They all startled at Kate's shout, except for a raven that had landed atop a cow's back and eyed her calmly. And Sam who nothing ever surprised.

"The line is in the sand. Here! Now! Paul, Rikka needs computing power. Call Roderick St. James, wave a big check at him and get her what she needs."

Paul nodded.

"Now, Paul."

"Right," he started patting his pockets.

Rikka pulled his phone out of her back pocket and handed it to him.

Kate held out her hand, Rikka passed over Kate's own phone.

"Sam, you're the only pilot among us. Take the R-22 helo that's parked over there and deliver Rikka to the Isle of Man. I'm trusting you to make sure she stays safe. I have no idea what's coming over the horizon once you're clear of the Secret Service and DPG's protective bubble around this place."

He nodded.

"Rikka, you find me a way in on this Dino-the-Dinosaur guy. We'll work other angles, but there's going to be a point where you're the only one who can stop that part of their game."

"Toast, Kate. Absolutely and so totally crispy." Rikka then stepped forward and gave her a hard hug. Truly hard.

Uncertain at first, Kate returned the hug as Rikka clung.

"You be careful, Kate," Rikka whispered into her shoulder.

"Only because you insist," Kate whispered back and received a last squeeze.

Rikka turned away quickly and hit Sam on the arm. Not hard, but enough to get him moving.

Kate watched them go. She hated sending off part of her team. But enough was enough and the time had come to start fighting back. If there was anyone Kate was going to trust without direct supervision, it was going to be Rikka.

She had to laugh at herself. The person she trusted above all others? Chaotic, brilliant, and one of the most dangerous hackers on the planet. A woman who had moved hundreds of millions in counterfeit bills, was still wanted by the FBI, the North Koreans, and several Chinese tongs, and whom Kate had arrested while she was in the Secret Service.

Kate ran a television network for crying out loud.

Well, at least Sam flew with her. That gave Kate some hope of a rational outcome.

The only large data center that Kate could arrange speedy access to lay on the Isle of Man. She and Paul had rolled some money into supporting a private space travel company, one of the twenty-two based there. In keeping with their own television network holdings, the company they chose focused on high-speed, high-quality data and image transmission across interplanetary distances.

The Isle of Man Aerospace Cluster consisted of a group of specialists and facilities that had been assembled to assist companies seeking a research and development center; pre-made infrastructure for your company. One service they offered was one of the most powerful for-hire computer systems in Europe.

Their head of IT services would be daunted by how much raw computing power Rikka would ask for, but Paul shot her a thumbs-up before the R-22's rotors were spinning. There were advantages to being both a local investor and the half owner of a multi-billion-dollar broadcast network.

Kate wanted to grab Paul and have all four of them go, but she knew Terry wouldn't allow it.

And Paul was right, until the murder of Vivienne Jacquard while inside the Secret Service / DPG protective bubble had been solved, she didn't dare leave. At least he'd stopped referring to her as *in custody.*

Kate sighed and watched Sam and Rikka soar aloft. Of the four of them, only Sam knew how to fly. She'd have to rectify that in her copious spare time so that she'd have an excuse to escape next time.

The sauces for dinner that she'd meant to build as a part of the lunch prep hadn't been started. And now Kate was short a butcher and a prep chef, as both were currently in a tiny helicopter flying toward a small island in the middle of the Irish Sea.

45

THE SEALAND ROYAL EC130 HELICOPTER MET DINO AT THE London Heliport and whisked him eastward. London, Chelmsford, Colchester, and any number of other interchangeable towns flowed below him in a mindless blur.

Dino would bet this was going to get down and dirty before the final credit rolled off the screen. There was something that Ms. Hoity Upper-east-side Stephanie Society-dame Bronson wasn't telling him. Probably several somethings.

Well, if the bitch wasn't careful, he'd take her down too.

On that, he'd wait and see.

Thankfully, he'd long since set up his present bolt-hole for such a job. Just because he'd been born in Tucson—land of sand and old dinosaur bones—didn't mean he was a desert dweeb. Sure, he'd hit the limits of University of Arizona hardware by the time he was sixteen, who wouldn't. All they cared about was *dem bones*. Assembling his own system hadn't been much better because the bleeding edge always lay a step ahead.

He'd cultivated a Bronx accent from *Ghostbusters* and loved that people thought he was big city. It kept them from suspecting that he always worked from out-of-the-way places. It had also made more than one corporate hit squad spend a great deal of time looking in a place he'd never actually been.

Intel, Google, and Amazon had all turned him down on job apps. One of these days, he'd take them down the same way he'd crashed the US military sites.

Titan Rain had breached Sandia Labs, Lockheed, Redstone Arsenal, and NASA all in one three-year sweep. He'd managed to lay all the blame on the Chinese military hackers—a sweet bonus. They'd been getting close on his heels and needed a smackdown. Dino had junked all the data he'd scraped because who really cared—not him.

The massive firewalls that the government put up against the Chinese after that slowed them down on a whole lot of sites. He hadn't set out to help beef up US military security, but it worked out okay. Until they'd passed the heavy protection code onto every major site around.

Finally, he'd gone overseas and found the access he needed. Plenty of people willing to pay for him to do what he did. The US was getting too damn fussy.

And psycho-sad.

He'd spent two years breaking into the inner conference at Black Hat and then found nothing but a bunch of squares who were into big nasty firewalls around their conference, for the sake of building big nasty firewalls. Where he'd expected to find a nirvana of hacker-heads, he'd found a bunch of guys sitting around drinking beer and talking social reform.

Hacking wasn't about good deeds.

Since then, he'd kept an eye on them and, sure enough, they'd created hacktivism and it was now a thing: Wikileaks, supporting the Arab Spring, and taking down the Church of Scientology's site every time they got stupider—those folks needed a new PR department.

Total fucking crap.

Though, he grudgingly admitted that the hacktivists who shut down Mossad's servers during the Israeli military strikes on Gaza laid down damn cool code.

The inner Black Hat conference was so lame that someone's jail-bait Japanese girlfriend hung out in there; fifteen years old when he asked. Seriously cute, but not even legal yet. Shit!

Those guys were pathetic; no way was Dino ever going back. He didn't plug the hole he'd used to get in, though someone closed it *hard* by the next day. He hadn't been stupid enough to drop a bomb or a worm on them. They might be pitiful, but what they lacked in edge they made up for in horsepower.

He'd at least met Buckbeak there. Dude was a rad hacker—more hyped on phones and comm networks than heavy data sites, but seriously good.

No one knew who the Dragon Bitch team was or, if they did, they were too scared to admit it. Whoever they were, they were more powerful than Anonymous, a pretty rocking group—even if they were wasting their time on social good deeds.

For this job, Dino only needed to mess with the US Secret Service and a television station. That needed care, but nothing serious.

Twenty minutes after taking off, the Royal helicopter soared out over the English Channel. Seven miles offshore lay the micro-nation of The Principality of Sealand. The helicopter circled once, something they did every single time he came here. The pilot must be under orders to piss all around the micro-nation like a dog marking his territory.

Dino leaned into the turn and looked down.

Sealand was an old World War II fort standing in twenty feet of water that had been dropped there in the middle of the war as an anti-aircraft platform. Fort Roughs base was a couple hundred-foot barge that they'd intentionally sunk to create the base.

From the barge rose two columnar legs twenty feet across and forty feet high. They stuck well above the thrashing waves to support a hundred-foot long, thirty-foot wide platform.

Half of the Sealand's platform was covered by a housing structure that used to be space for the gunners and now housed the Royal Family of The Principality of Sealand.

In the 1960s they'd declared it an independent nation and set up a pirate radio station. In the 1970s they'd ripped off the gunnery control tower and installed a helipad.

The Brits tried to take their fort back, but it was in international waters. The pirate radio operator British Army Major Paddy Roy Bates had declared himself Prince of Sealand, gave his wife the title of Princess for an anniversary gift, and fired on a British vessel who circled too close. Dragged into the UK court, he proved he was in international waters and outside UK jurisdiction. The court had agreed, and he'd claimed Sealand as a sovereign nation ever since.

All Dino cared about was that in 2000 when the Royal family's efforts turned to re-imagining Sealand as an offshore data haven. Their first efforts failed miserably, ending in a court battle between the family and the IT director for back pay of all lame things.

Now they were trying a reboot and had painted their URL down the side of the platform. He kept telling them to paint *v2.0* next to it, but that didn't seem to be happening. Frankly, the whole thing needed a good coat of paint, he'd lived in apartments that hadn't looked this bad.

None of that mattered. All he cared about was that they thought he was there to set up the data center for their new launch into the lucrative business of secure offshore data farms; as secure as any setup these days. What he liked about the place was that he had the excuse to buy, and a sponsor willing to pay for, seriously heavy-duty gear without attracting undue attention to himself.

Now, he needed a safe place to set up that hack for Stephanie Bronson—as soon as the helicopter finished with its dog-pissing routine and landed.

Black Hat started in a couple weeks. He'd drop in as The Guy; loaded with massive street cred. The dude who'd crashed the G-7 and American television's number one food network at a single stroke. Then they'd see exactly who was hot shit.

And it had been enough years now that the cute Japanese chick would be in her twenties. No longer a clumsy eighteen himself, he was now one of the top hackers on the planet. That would carry serious weight with any girl into hackers.

If she was still around, who knew what might happen.

46

"AND HOW PRECISELY MAY WE ASSIST YOU TODAY?" RODERICK ST. James was a welcome relief. He displayed only marginal British formality that Rikka found too tempting to attack when it was on full display. Though Irene had been great, giving back as good as she received.

Rikka wondered if the IT director of the Isle of Man Aerospace Cluster came to meet her and Sam's helicopter personally because of Kate, or because he felt protective of his data center.

"First," Rikka looked up at the flag flapping above the airport control tower, "can you explain that?"

His wry smile noted that she phrased it as a challenge. He didn't look up at the red flag with the three bent legs pointing at noon, four, and eight o'clock as if it were a clock face.

"Our triskelion of three armored legs with golden spurs all joined at the top of the leg does cause notice. Our country's motto is 'Whichever way you throw, it will stand.' We Manx are quite proud of that. The last six thousand years, the longest continuous government on the planet, by the way, have not always been comfortable ones."

"*The Gamesters of Triskelion.*"

"Yes," Roderick sighed. "We get that quite a bit from *Star Trek* fans. We're quite a bit more pleasant than they were."

"No slavery? No scantily clad blond gladiators?"

"I'm sorry to disappoint madam, but no."

"Well, I have a game I need to play and apparently you have the computing power I need." The air was fresh and crisp off the ocean. She breathed it in deeply and could feel herself shifting modes. Mostly the world moved too slowly for her. She'd learned to survive it, but this upcoming challenge revved up her nervous system in glorious ways.

"A game?" Roderick grimaced.

No serious IT Director wanted a gamer messing with his system.

Sam braced up at her side, but she leaned against him which always seemed to calm him down. Truth be told, it did the opposite to her. Being in the same room with Sam wound her up. He was such an amazing man...and he wanted to be with her. Not something she could easily process, but she was getting there. That's why she'd been going so slow, waiting for an internal shift from disbelief to acceptance that he meant it for real.

"Perhaps you'd rather think of it as a bit of sport on the British PM's behalf."

"Well, if that's the case," he calmed significantly, offered a scant smile. He led them over to his sedan, "Let's go have a spot of fun then. Shall we?"

To cross from the airport to the Aerospace Cluster's IT offices, they had to go from one town to another. The landscape was stark, only scrub grass on the barren hills. Not a tree in sight.

"Aren't we going kinda fast?" A glance showed that they were zipping along at a well over a hundred-and-fifty kilometers an hour—near enough a hundred miles an hour.

"No speed limits on the island. Let's us gad about rather nicely."

They soared along cliff-side roads with sweeping views of the turbulent Irish Sea. Rocky shores flew by as quickly as the miles and they soon slowed to descend into a small town that must rate as a major city around here. You could tuck the whole place into Brooklyn Heights and never find it again.

Rikka considered kidnapping Paul's Ferrari from New York and shipping it over to give it a try on these roads. Maybe she would; he'd never find it here.

When they arrived, all Rikka could do was goggle at the building they were parked beside.

"You've gotta be kidding."

"I assure you that we aren't," Roderick St. James sounded amused.

The block of buildings looked like New York brownstones. A long row of narrow, four-story townhouses. Except instead of being brown, their paint shone sky blue, the next black, the one in front of them a rather shocking sunset pink, the next apricot, and so on down the row.

Once through the old wooden front door of the pink building everything changed. They stopped at an inner door with a security pad on it.

Roderick swiped a card, which then turned on a camera. He greeted the guard by name and the door unlocked. Inside was ten degrees cooler than the warm July day outside, Sam immediately offered her his jacket. She accepted because it was Sam's, not because she was cold. She could wear it as a dress to her knees, which offered up a few interesting ideas for later.

Roderick led them to what must have once been a parlor. Big racks of servers wrapped around the room.

"IBM Blue Gene. Nice gear."

"Thank you, we're pleased with it." He led them past the former dining room, with a crystal chandelier and an elegant ceiling mural of a vast sailing ship coursing across the open oceans, when she stopped dead in her tracks.

"What's that?" Rikka went up to the main computing cabinet in a row of ten. "An Intel Paragon XP/S. Oh, that's so retro. Is it still running? Is it on the web? OSF/1 or SUNMOS?"

The Paragon had been the ultimate supercomputer of 1994. It was one of the few machines in history that broke Moore's Law about the steady state of increasing complexity of computing machines. The Paragon had been way above the curve in its day.

"That would be, yes, it works like a champ. Furthermore, yes, it is available upon the Internet. And no, it does not run SUNMOS. It was upgraded to the PUMA operating system in 1995, well before our acquisition of the machine."

"Oooo," Rikka embraced the tall black cabinet. "We're going to have such fun together. He'll never see *you* coming."

Roderick St. James looked at her strangely, but Sam nodded. He trusted her skills absolutely.

No one other than Kate ever did that for her. Ignoring the islander, she went up and rested her hands on his chest.

When he hesitated, she nodded that it was okay.

His kiss was gentle and sweet.

But, oh, it promised wonders under other circumstances.

She patted Sam's chest and turned back to Roderick.

"Does she have a name?"

"We, uh, call it 'The Paragon'."

"It? She's not an it! She's beautiful, dark, and evil." Rikka turned back to the machine, "I will call you Madam Deal."

Sam's bit-off laugh told her that he'd followed right along.

If Roderick hadn't read the World War II-era comic strip *Terry and the Pirates* that was their problem. Madame Deal was the *real* name of the beautiful and brilliant villainess The Dragon Lady in the comic strip. The Dragon Lady was, in turn, based upon the most successful real-life female Chinese pirate in history, Lai Choi San.

Dino, probably naming himself from *The Flintstones* movie and not the cartoon, had no sense of history.

There was no way that he was ready for Madam Deal, The Dragon Lady of the Intel Paragon—especially not with The Dragon Bitch at the helm.

47

FBI Agent Leona Edwards seethed as the bomb squad continued to work on pulling the cover off whatever was hidden on the bottom of the table in the Cooks Network studio.

They'd taken hours to arrive. Then for three hours, not counting a long lunch break, the studio remained off limits.

While she and Marcus were waiting, they'd interviewed the studio techs, cameramen, and the chef's girlfriend. Net gain of knowledge? Zero.

Big applause.

A small double bang.

One dead chef.

The two table-leg bombs had cut through the thin aluminum but no farther. The bomb boys were treating the box under the table as if it could level the whole damn building.

Blast pads were brought in. The floors immediately above and below were evacuated. A robot carrying a screw gun had finally slithered forward to open the box on the bottom of the table that had killed Max Klugman—she hoped it choked on the sugar dust as it ground back and forth in the studio.

Marcus handed her a roast beef sandwich on rye with extra horseradish and a Coke—red can, fully leaded. He'd learned her preferences faster than most men, he listened. And not only on the job. Like the fine agent he was, he paid attention to all the details to discover what she liked best.

"Chances this was Kate Stark's doing?" Marcus sat beside her. Together they watched the bomb team controlling the robot. Not a lot to do until these guys were done with something that would have taken her thirty seconds with her Swiss Army knife.

"I place it at about minus infinity," she bit into her sandwich.

The robot driver, after eighteen false starts, was finally having his machine remove the first of three screws.

"About what I figured. So why kill this guy? To keep us occupied?"

Leona considered their caseload. They were unraveling the hornet's nest Kate Stark had uncovered and given to them as a gift after facing down the North Koreans. It hadn't been the NK's doing, but rather a by-blow of the contractor they'd hired for kidnapping Kate Stark and another chef. But that was mostly down to paperwork and indictments now, not a whole lot new going on there. They had several ongoing cases like any other team, but none of them hot.

"Doesn't fit, does it?" He bit into his turkey, mayo, and lettuce on white bread.

She had to do something about his eating habits. He was less adventurous than a three-year-old. Once out of this, she'd take him out for an Indian curry. She'd make Marcus sit on the floor and eat with his hands. That alone should be worth the entertainment value.

"To attack the studio itself?" she countered.

"Makes about as much sense as attacking Kate. They've kept this whole thing hush-hush so far."

"Actually, honey," Mac Olson, Kate's chief studio director came whirling up to them. He was wearing a lemon-yellow shirt and black-and-white checked pants, an odd fashion statement, yet he made the ensemble look sharp with the addition of a Monet *Water Lilies* tie and yellow sneakers.

Standing only inches away—he had no sense of personal space—he clutched a hand on either of their arms.

"We only *thought* we'd kept it quiet," he sounded truly mortified, his words tumbling together. "An anonymous video showed up on the Internet several hours ago. It hit a million views before anyone told us about it. It's so horrid I can't stand to watch it again. The angles are poor, the quality, oh, the quality is so low grade that I don't know what I'll do if someone thinks this exemplifies our work here. Oh, Kate will be sick to her heart, poor dear."

"Mac," Leona used her best calming voice. At least the best calm she had as she heard the bomb techs in the background debate whether or not it was safe to remove the screw they had just unscrewed.

"Yes, dearie?"

"Would you mind telling us what has you so upset?"

"I can show you. Let's go to the Studio Two control room. It's all over the news, worse than the last time when poor Marianne... You know that she and I were so close, poor dear. Well, I never did like Maxwell Klugman much. Oh, I feel awful for saying that about the dead, but it's God's honest truth and we must speak truth about the dead. He was so stubbornly Teutonic. His sugar work, magnificent technically, lacked any heart. *Frozen* was too perfect for him and it finally killed him. Poor man."

Mac led them into the other control room after the bomb techs finally decided it was safe to remove the screw, yet another tool change on the robot.

There, on the large center screen, Maxwell Herman

Klugman—not a small man—was dwarfed by a breathtaking palace of white sugar.

It was a common Internet video site.

Then Mac started the replay.

48

"STARK, COME WITH ME."

"No!" She wasn't following Terry anywhere, *unless it was to bed,* her weary brain added. But that didn't seem likely; he wore his righteous manner for all to see.

Hadn't she delivered a dinner, for which the G-7 demanded her attendance for another round of congratulations? And they'd still laughed over the pizza luncheon. Hadn't she already done all the food prep for tomorrow so that she could manage without Rikka and Sam's assistance?

She'd shared a whisky with the British and French Prime Ministers to discuss cross-channel fusion cuisine. She'd found them both surprisingly approachable and open to letting her into their kitchens to film a state dinner...provided everyone stopped dying around her. Their wry smiles only marginally covered the earnestness of that one key criteria.

She didn't appreciate that unspoken addendum to every invitation and compliment, but you didn't tell the world's most powerful politicians to go stuff it. No matter how tempting.

Cecilia hovered about, taking the occasional picture as the

G-7 mingled and relaxed—as much as they ever would in each other's presence. Kate found that she had the attention of the cyclopean glass-eye of Cecilia's camera far too often for her taste.

Paul, fading out a while ago, now slept in a chair in the kitchen; the drugging had taken more out of him than he'd admit.

Kate, sitting by the fireplace, now understood that was a critical mistake, the same mistake Paul had made; she'd stopped moving.

No sleep on the trans-Atlantic redeye. She'd managed next to nothing last night between Terry releasing her from his Rolls Royce interrogation cell, meeting with *her team* as she was coming to think of them, and then she'd had to start prep for breakfast.

A single whisky and a pleasant chat by the warm fire left her hammered-down exhausted.

Terry leaned close so that only she could hear. She could smell him. Feel his warm breath tickling her ear and along her neck.

"You need to see something. It's bad."

Definitely not what she'd been hoping to have whispered in her ear by a hard-bodied man in what felt like the middle of the night. But, sadly, he knew her too well. He'd said about the only phrase that would get her moving. Had he said the kitchen was ablaze, she might have done a quick happy dance, perhaps stealing Rikka's arm-flapping chicken dance. But since he hadn't, she didn't.

And she couldn't say *no* to Special Agent Terry Tyrell, especially when he was being as serious as if he actually was the Schwarzenegger machine in *Terminator 2*.

With friendly excuses to the two PMs and their wives, she followed him out the door of the Great Hall.

In moments, he led her out into the cool night air. The stars sparkled high above as if everything was right in their world and they were laughing down at her.

She tucked her hand in the crook of Terry's arm. Not because it felt good, though she wouldn't deny that it did; unless Rikka was here, then she'd deny it. However, in truth, Terry's arm was the only reliable means for her continued ability to walk.

He led her out of the kitchen's back door, down the stone stairway, and through the small patch of woods separating the Inverlochy Castle Hotel from its kitchen gardens.

The black surveillance van, the size of a UPS delivery truck, parked close by the garden wall and blended into the night. They knocked on the back door. A blinding light flashed on in their faces, causing Kate to throw up an arm in protection. The door didn't swing open for nearly thirty seconds. They first must be inspecting the surrounding area through their security cameras. Even Terry being her escort didn't gain them rapid admittance.

The instant the door swung aside, she knew that no matter how much Rikka had scoffed, she was going to be majorly bummed that she hadn't gotten to see inside the Secret Service van. Good! It finally gave Kate something to tease Rikka with.

This wasn't one of those big tractor trailer-sized command-and-control monstrosities able to fight a major forest fire or a minor war. This was a small vehicle. There were seven stations: three to either side manned by agents, and a command desk at the head of the central aisle. The right-hand side was all surveillance—three lines of defense.

The one closest to the back door tracked the inner ring. It had feeds from every agent in the G-7 conference room or inside the hotel. Six command radios were stacked up, each on a different frequency. The screens showed every floor of the hotel with active tracking on agents, hotel staff, and protectees. Anything that moved without a tracker dot on it would be treated as a hostile.

The middle seat covered the grounds and all the agents in the area from the roadway to the hills on the far side of the castle's lake. Snipers on the rooftops and K-9 dogs on circling patrols—how did they know to ignore something as exciting as deer or rabbit scent, both being far more likely here than explosives or drugs.

The front seat on the right-hand side of the van showed the wide-range information. A phalanx of armored vehicles, helicopters, and ambulances parked and ready in a nearby farmer's field. Alert jet and helo squadrons at Scotland's Leuchars and Lossiemouth airbases.

At the far end of the narrow central aisle, stood a Senior Agent.

"Jessup!"

"Stark."

"They dug you out of intel for this? They must think this meeting is important or something."

"I was on vacation on Cape Cod until people started dying around you, Stark. Now I'm here, my wife is there, and I'm not having any damn fun. Whose fault is *that,* Stark?"

Clearly hers. Clint Jessup had always been a taciturn egghead, but his ability to spot a break in an intelligence pattern remained unparalleled. That his attention now focused on her was uncomfortable at best. She hoped that it didn't lead to the worst; Clint had taken down more bad guys than most field agents.

The van suddenly felt overcrowded despite its eight feet of width; the shallow desks down either side and herself trapped in the narrow central aisle between Terry and Clint. Definitely not cozy despite the closeness.

She looked down the other side of the van.

These three were the intelligence operators. Kate spotted in-bound reporting streams that she was able to identify just from their style as CIA, Mossad, MI-6...

"Hey Terry. I'm not cleared to see this level of information."

"Special dispensation, Stark. So don't abuse it," Clint snapped.

"If I'm so special, do you mind telling me why I'm here?"

"If I had a choice, you wouldn't be." Then he spoke without addressing anyone specifically, "Do it."

The center screen above the head of the middle intelligence operator lit up.

"Hi, Katie. Oh, you're looking tired, sweetheart. Are you getting enough rest?"

"Hi, Mac." A glance at Terry didn't reveal anything about why she was talking to her senior studio director on a secure Secret Service connection across the Atlantic. "I'm fine. Doing a lot of cooking."

"That's good, Katie. I know that you're always happiest in the kitchen. I think you need to do more of that. You know, I have a couple of show ideas that—"

"Mac." She didn't need to say more. He wasn't stubborn like Rikka; he was effusive and sometimes needed to be reminded to focus on the business at hand.

"Right. I'm here with the FBI." He reached forward and made an adjustment to zoom out the camera. When he pulled his hands back out of the way Marcus and Leona fit in the frame.

"Hi Kate," Leona offered a tight smile.

"We back to first names?"

Her smile opened up a bit at that, "Marcus is being stiff-necked. I'll give him a lesson in manners later on."

Kate had no doubt as to what kind of lesson and did not want to hear the salacious details. FBI agents were not supposed to have better sex lives than rich television executives.

"Bomb squad is trying to figure out which end of the screwdriver to hold, so I don't have anything more on the explosives or the triggers. But we thought you'd want to know about the new video that just released online."

"It's not our work, Katie. We killed all the cameras in the first tow-point-seven seconds. I swear we did." Mac might sound like a ditz, but he was her senior director for a reason; he was incredible at his job.

"Understood, Mac. Roll it."

Without further ado, he started the playback.

High on Sugar by Kate Stark! was the banner flash. It wasn't even her show.

Max Klugman and the cameraman huddled close to the sculpture's windows. It was a different angle, and the quality wasn't all that bad. It came from...the second row of the audience, she decided.

The view shifted up to look at the big studio monitors that showed the control room feed to the audience.

The hammer blow and the perfect shattering of the sugar floor to Elsa's *Frozen* ice palace.

"Wow!"

The audience erupted to their feet.

"I know," Mac agreed. "Who knew that the thick-fingered German was also a magician with sugar."

The video continued to bounce around as if...

"Helmet cam."

"Nobody in the audience was wearing a helmet. No cameras allowed in the studio."

"A hat with a hidden camera?" she suggested and knew she was right as soon as she said it. "A good one, it has image stabilization for a clearer image. Otherwise we'd be seeing the vibrations up their body from the applause."

"How do you know the cameraman was applauding?" Marcus asked.

"Would have stood out too much if they hadn't been."

The analyst seated in front of her inside the van nodded his head without turning, confirming Kate's interpretation.

Then, without warning, two of the table legs buckled and the palace began to tip toward the chef.

"Wait, run that back, Mac. Give me zoom and enhance on the rightmost corner of the table, to Max's left. Run it frame by frame."

A moment later, Mac had it set up. The corner of the table filled the screen. The tubular steel leg continued off the bottom of the screen.

There was a brief brightening along the leg that must have been the explosive charge firing out of sight below the table. Then a small vapor cloud shot to the side and was gone within twelve frames of the explosive cutting the leg.

"Less than half a second. The explosion was an expert match to the job. Okay, Mac. Give me full screen and standard speed."

Kate made herself watch it to the end.

The tumbling palace.

The mortal piercings of Max's body.

The view of the back of the blonde woman's head running toward the devastation.

The camera wearer caught her and held her back, not that Max had any chance.

Then the camera aimed down, filming the prostrate body as the last of the blood pumped away, apparently over the weeping woman's shoulder that made the only audio track. It didn't track aside, as if that was the sole reason he or she had been there.

The video cut off.

"Who the hell was that?" Kate demanded.

"Maxwell Klugman."

"No, Marcus, the man or woman who wore the hat. Find

them. Find their gear. Figure out who the hell committed murder in my studio!"

Kate shoved Terry out of her way and pounded the emergency release on the rear door of the van. She left Clint to deal with the inter-agency repercussions about the intrusion alarms that fired off.

49

Terry caught up with Kate as she entered the walled castle gardens. A stout wall of stonework bounded the garden. It stood a story high and looked as if it had done so for a thousand years.

He didn't speak, simply kept her company as she stormed up the narrow gravel pathways between overflowing planting beds. The damn garden was efficient without being...tight-assed. Gentle nightlights lit pathways without interfering with the starlight from above. They did love their gardens. Vivienne Jacquard had given him an earful about his agents not being allowed in here without an escort who *understood what was what.*

Well, she was dead, and Kate looked as if she needed a friend.

She finally careened to a halt near the middle of the garden. It was a crazy mix of growing things in beds, bounded by neat walkways and paths. Some straight, some circular. There was a small sitting area at the center, but the garden was about the plants and not the people. A low greenhouse ran along the north wall, below a three-story battlement of stone that commanded that end of the garden.

Mirella would know what all this stuff was. His ex-wife had loved her garden. Despite all her coaxing, he didn't have a clue.

He recognized that a few of the vegetables and flowers bloomed everywhere—their colors leached by the starlight. But he didn't know what those were any better than the vegetables.

Kate reached down and plucked a leaf off a low bush. She crushed it between her fingers and breathed it in like a drug.

She held it out to him; he took a cautious sniff. Italian pesto hit him in the nostrils like a sucker punch.

"Basil," she pointed, "sage, Italian parsley, oregano, marjoram, *fraises des bois*." She knelt and plucked a couple of the tiny red fruits and handed one to him.

The strawberry flavor was all out of proportion with the tiny berries. He'd eaten whole pints of the monster supermarket berries that didn't total one tenth that single berry's power.

"This is what I love, Terry. I love the food. You and Sam seem to think of me as a hotshot agent, despite losing the Vice President. I have a couple thousand people back in New York who think I'm 'The Boss.' What I loved was the time I cooked with Julia Child. I wanted to talk *haute cuisine* with Vivienne. I want..."

Then she turned to him. Those impossibly sad eyes looked up at him.

"And then someone does that," she waved a hand helplessly toward the security van. "Now I want to..." Kate bunched her hands into fists as if ready to kill someone, but her eyes remained sad.

So, Terry did about the dumbest thing he could think of.

As he leaned in, he knew it was a reaction to the divorce going final two weeks ago.

As his fingers cupped her jaw, he braced for the slap he fully deserved.

And when he kissed her, Kate Stark melted against him, her bunched fists coming up around his neck and her kiss deepening until he was pretty sure that he was the one who groaned first.

Kate Stark's body was incredible and every bit of it felt utterly amazing as he pulled her tight against him. She tasted of strawberries.

One hand up into her hair and the other one inches from slipping down her back. Soon he'd be inside her jeans to cup that amazing ass...but she eased back.

"God, I needed that. You're such a sweetheart, Terry."

Sweetheart? He'd wanted to throw her down and take her since the moment he'd first seen her commanding the kitchen staff mere minutes after Vivienne Jacquard's death. Rikka's constant jibes only made his imagination burn that much hotter.

Kate moved with a power, a grace, and a certainty that had never before existed all in the same woman, except for Kate Stark.

He forced himself to pull back. It felt like a tearing on nerve endings that wanted to grope, grab, possess. He wanted to hear Mirella crying out his name as he—

Damn it!

Kate, not Mirella.

Shit.

Mirella was gone.

50

"WHAT HAPPENED BETWEEN YOU?" IN THE MOONLIGHT, KATE could see the pain ripple across Terry's features.

"What?"

"It's written all over you," she brushed a hand along his jaw. "You loved her deeply."

"Shit!" he turned away and came close to trampling a bed of cherry tomato plants. Would have if she hadn't stopped him.

"I'm not saying I didn't enjoy kissing you, Terry. And for a moment, it was me not her that you were kissing. I can't tell you how much I appreciate that. But there's other baggage going on." She tried to leave the door open.

"God damn it!" He continued to glare down at the tomatoes as if they were the ones at fault.

Kate moved up to stand silently beside him, slid her hand into his.

He clamped down hard and held on as he ground out the words.

"She couldn't stand wondering each day," he took a deep breath, "if that was the day I was going to catch a bullet and come home in a box."

The Protection Detail, especially the President's Personal one was tough on families. Long hours, and the agent's first commitment wasn't to the marriage but rather to the safety of someone who half the time they would never vote for.

"Especially after Bronson went down on your watch."

"You're laying the breakdown of your marriage on *me?*" She attempted to yank her hand free, but he held on.

"No. God, Kate, you and I *know* it's part of the job. But that made it way too real for her to live with."

She stopped trying to free her hand. "Sorry, Terry. That must have suck." About as much sympathy as you could give a guy without him getting all weird about it.

"It did. It does."

They stood together for a long time, holding hands and staring down at the tiny tomato bush.

She rested her head on his shoulder and was well on the way to being asleep on her feet before he spoke again.

"I have to say though," he told the leafy plant, "I did like kissing you."

"Roger on that one, big guy." He was good at it.

What else was he good at? She'd wager a lot of things.

"Think I'll take a rain check on that one for now, though."

Then he did the sappiest thing. He raised their joined hands and placed a kiss on the back of hers.

Oh damn. She really did like Terry.

THURSDAY

51

Kate jerked awake when her cell phone alarm went off. It was set to silent so it lay on a nightstand mere inches from her nose and rattled loudly against the hard wood. She jabbed at it until the alarm stopped.

"Stupid-ass alarm clock!"

A tiny voice called from the phone, "I'm not an alarm clock."

She picked it up and held it to her ear, "Uh, hello?"

"Rise and shine, Kate. It's another beautiful day in the neighborhood."

"Rikka." Kate wondered where the hell she could get a cup of coffee. The room was dark except for a nightlight. There was a window cracked open to allow in cool night air with the curtains pulled back to either side. She could see by the dimming of the stars that breakfast prep needed to start soon.

Problem one, she didn't recognize the room.

Problem two, she could tell by the feel of the sheets that she was mostly naked—panties and bra only.

Problem three, someone's arm lay heavily over her waist and kept her pinned under the blankets.

"Where am I?"

"Oooo," Rikka's voice sounded pleased over the phone. "Why do I like the sound of that?"

Kate didn't.

It was a hotel room. Her clothes were neatly folded on a luggage stand close beside the bed. She shuffled out from beneath the arm.

A mostly clothed, thankfully, Terry Tyrell lay on top of the covers and blinked at her with sleepy eyes. So, they'd been on different sides of the sheet and blanket though in the same bed. At some point his body had curled up behind hers and hers hadn't thought that counted as anything worrisome enough to bother waking her about.

Pretty damn forward of him, though she could see the rest of the room now, and there'd been nowhere else for him to sleep. Place was miniscule.

"God damn, Stark. That is one amazing body you've got there."

"Uh," unsure how she'd ended up here and which of them undressed her. She managed a weak, "Thanks, Terry." It was a nice compliment after all.

"Yes!" Rikka squeaked over the phone. "Go T-2! Yes! Yes! Yes! High-five, Sam, you owe me twenty!"

"It's not—" Kate let it go; not worth the trouble and Rikka would never believe that nothing had happened. Had it?

The last thing she remembered was climbing into the passenger seat of Terry's car and leaning her head against the window. There was no point in trying to explain something that she didn't understand herself. "Can you hang on a minute?"

"C'mon, Kate. It's gonna take longer than a minute or I'm going to have to have a word with T-2."

"Go to Hell, Rikka," she clunked the phone down on the nightstand, hard enough to send a major shockwave over the microphone pickup. Then she pulled on her blouse and pants.

Terry didn't look away for a moment and Kate resisted the urge to see what would happen if she tumbled back into that bed with him.

She picked up the phone, "If you're not an alarm clock, what are you?"

"Your fairy godmother. Your own personal guardian angel. Your—"

"Rikka!"

"I caught one of Dino's bugs drilling into a couple of New York banks. Big ones. He's going after your and Paul's accounts. Someone wants to take you both down bad. I locked him out for a while, pretending I'm a high-security routine, but it won't slow him down for long. If I block him, he'll know someone's onto him."

"So, what's the answer?"

"Well," Rikka didn't sound happy, "he's going after your corporate accounts as well, and Cooks Network is cash heavy at the moment. So, he's going to need to see money moving soon or he'll get suspicious. Know anybody who wants to lose a quick half billion in your place?"

"Not off-hand."

"Bummer," was all Rikka had to say. "You don't feel like taking a shower with *The Terminator* man anymore, do you?"

"You did not give my day the best start possible."

Terry, awake now, headed for the bathroom. Leaving the door partway open.

"I'm going to have to hard block Dino sometime," Rikka explained. "But I'll hold off as long as I can."

Kate hung up the phone and stared at the sliver of bright light shining around the bathroom door.

She could follow him in and help him do a bit of forgetting about his ex-wife. Or hurry them along their way to go cook breakfast for the G-7 and be a half billion poorer by the time the Green Dining Room table was empty except for the crumbs.

52

THEY WERE HALFWAY BACK TO INVERLOCHY FROM THE FORT William hotel, when Terry finally woke up enough to think somewhat coherently. The majesty of the peak of Ben Nevis wasn't catching sunlight yet, but it glowed brightly as a beacon to the north.

He should have enticed Kate into the shower, but that didn't feel right. Damn! First time in half a year he'd wanted to be with a woman and he hadn't...

"Terry?" his radio sounded loud in his ear.

"*What?*" Shit! He sounded like...well, like he felt. Pissed at the whole damn planet. Well, the whole damn planet except maybe the woman sitting beside him in the car who he didn't dare risk kissing again, or he'd lose his mind. Mortal women weren't supposed to taste or feel as good as Kate Stark had last night in the castle gardens.

And then waking with his nose in her soft hair and his arm around her waist totally slayed him. Backlit by the golden glow outside the hotel window in nothing but black bra and panties against her fair skin...oh my God! Such sights must mean he was in Heaven. Or Hell for being allowed to see—but not touch.

He wasn't going to compare her to his ex-wife who'd been lean and trim in so many wonderful ways, but he wasn't going to go around complaining.

"Sorry, Amy," he spoke into the radio microphone mounted at his wrist. "What do you need?"

Amy Franklin was the head of President Cheryl Kennelly's Personal Protection Detail, so she hung close beside her boss. That's why Terry was getting the bum's rush runaround on this whole poisoning thing. As Number Two on Madame President's detail, he had more liberty to move around.

"Do you know the whereabouts of Kate Stark?"

"Yes," he didn't look over at her.

"Please escort her immediately to the Library."

"We're five minutes out," they were pulling up to the Inverlochy turnoff. He wasn't about to argue with that tone of voice. He parked his vehicle at the gatehouse; they were trying to keep most of the security vehicles out of sight and it was only a quarter-mile walk up to the hotel.

He was well up the driveway before he realized that Kate wasn't beside him. Terry turned to face her, stopped twenty paces back on the one-lane-wide pavement. A turn in the tall hedges close to either side already hid the gatehouse itself.

"What? Am I supposed to drag you there? You're not going to do one of your Stark-stubborn numbers are you?"

"Stark-stubborn?" Was she laughing at him? He could never quite tell.

"Yeah," he grimaced at the old nickname, surprised she'd never heard it before. Woman was as stubborn as a mule, as an entire pack of mules when she put her mind to it. She'd been notorious for that in the Service. It was part of the reason he'd recruited her from counterfeiting to protection; if her instincts said her way was safer for the protectee, no one on the planet was going to change her mind. Her instincts had proven their value many times.

She moseyed up to him, giving him a hell of a lot to admire. The woman curves left nothing to the imagination and her walk drew attention to every one of them without trying; she walked completely like a woman, always had. She reached him before he registered where he was looking and refocused his attention on her amused eyes.

"Me? Stubborn?"

"You say that in a sweet innocent voice that has not a thing to do with what you're doing to my libido. Okay, I'll take back stubborn."

"Good."

"And I'll replace it with pig-headed."

Her smile went beatific.

"So why the stall?" He resisted the urge to either kiss the smile off her lips or...bonk her on the top of her head with his proverbial club, drag her off into the bushes, and to hell with Amy Franklin.

"Nothing. Just wanted to see how far you were going to walk the road without the person you're supposed to be delivering to your boss before you noticed."

He glared down at her, not far down, Kate was only a few inches below his own six-one. She stood so close that he could smell her, could feel her heat against his skin, could once more have his arm around her waist with only the slightest reach.

"Well?"

"Well what?"

"Are you going to stand there all day, or are you going to deliver me to your boss? If the former, I have to go cook a meal. If the latter, you're going to be late if we don't hurry. Want to race?"

They *were* going to have to hurry and...

God damn it!

He dragged her into his arms and covered her bubbling laughter with his kiss.

They ended up having to run, and something else he'd forgotten about Kate Stark.

She was fast.

53

"To: President Kennelly. Swift Death!"

Nothing more.

Kate held the plastic bag gingerly, afraid that the message inside might reach out and bite her.

"It just printed?"

Amy Franklin nodded. The head of the President's Personal Protection Detail had been waiting in the Inverlochy's Library. She was a tall, slender woman with a narrow face and short-cropped dark hair. It gave her a no-nonsense demeanor including when she wasn't handing Kate a death threat.

"It showed up on the Hotel Manager's printer. The job in the print queue states that it originated from the computer in Vivienne Jacquard's office."

"And your obvious conclusion is that I'm guilty of two crimes: murder and stupidity."

"No," Amy sat wearily in a big leather armchair and waved Kate to another.

Terry stood with his back to the door that led into the service area which included the kitchen, the route by which they'd entered.

Another agent, who she didn't know, stood with his back to the door that led out into the Great Hall. Both doors were closed, despite the soft susurration of voices from the next room. The jet-lag-addled early risers were already in the Great Hall enjoying their morning coffee and pre-breakfast scones as they watched the sunrise light up the Scottish hills.

The Library itself was something of a dream. A cozy collection of books, comfortable leather chairs, and a fire—set but not lit—beneath a mantel of carved marble. She could easily curl up here and not go anywhere for, oh, a millennium or two.

"Then you are saying...?"

"That your brother needs to take more care about where he sends his messages from."

"What does Paul have to do with this?"

Terry took a step forward. Kate could see that he was in defensive mode.

"Don't, Tyrell," Amy's voice was sharp and commanding. "Don't think it or you'll find yourself back stateside protecting an Alabama congressman so fast it will make your head spin."

Terry grimaced, glanced at them both, then took the step back.

Amy Franklin's reputation when Kate had still been in the Service? Pure hard ass. She'd grown no softer with time.

Kate ignored whatever dynamic was going on between them. Terry had been in line to protect the next President— until she turned out to be female. The head of the President's PPD must be able to follow her protectee anywhere, including to a clothing change or the bathroom.

"Let me follow this logic," Kate kept her voice calm. It was the only thing that kept her from trying out her old hand-to-hand skills against a couple of Secret Service agents.

"My brother sets a trap in our own studio to kill a chef he's never met, which he achieves while simultaneously screwing a woman in Colorado by the use of technology and explosives. I'll tell you that this is a man who doesn't know how to work the stereo system in his Ferrari and answers his phone while driving because he broke the hands-free system past any technician's ability to figure out what he did."

Amy Franklin kept her face blank, so Kate continued.

"At the same moment, half a world away, he murders Vivienne Jacquard with a South American neurotoxin, that could have as easily have killed me a few hours later. We have our moments, but his desire to end my life have been minimal —actually non-existent since the last time I bricked him into his bedroom right before a big date in high school. I became quite skilled at brickwork building a barbeque pit with my dad out at our place on Fire Island. Give me a goddamn break, Amy. You know what my question is?"

Agent Franklin shrugged.

"What's my brother doing up so early? He always sleeps in."

"He arrived with the photographer."

Kate wondered if he'd had a, uh, *better* evening than she'd managed.

She rose to leave, but Agent Franklin held out a slim file folder.

With about as much joy as picking up a viper, she took the manila folder. She recognized the beginning of the numeric code across the tab: "Threat to the President's life." It was a code that no trained agent could ignore—retired or not.

It included two sheets. One was a listing of the print queue on Vivienne Jacquard's machine, the other was a surveillance photo of her brother at that machine. The timestamps matched —she checked her phone—seventeen minutes ago.

Kate tossed the file in the unlit fireplace. Paul's picture landed face up among the ashes.

It rang a bell somewhere. She slumped down in her chair and stretched her feet out toward the chill of the unlit wood.

There was a prank that Rikka pulled on her once. After Kate caught her and stuffed her into WITSEC. On her first day as the newest member of the White House's Secret Service office. Bare-chested Sylvester Stallone pictures running unstoppably out of the common pool printer at the White House with her station ID across the top of each one. Rikka's idea of a Welcome Day gift.

"Terry," she snapped her fingers, "call Clint Jessup out in the security van. Never mind. Clint!" she called out into the room figuring he'd have surveillance on them. "How hard would it be to rig something in my brother's e-mail queue so that the next time he logs on, a file prints? Can you see if someone hacked his account?"

Terry put his hand to his ear and listened for a moment, "Hang on, he's checking something."

They all waited. Amy Franklin sitting ever so poised in one armchair—poised like a jaguar stalking a peccary; Kate slouching in the other and trying not to think about the breakfast she wasn't prepping.

Terry and the other agent remained at the doors.

Kate watched as all three did that slight freeze of intent listening. If ever she wanted to attack a Secret Service agent, that would be her moment. That was assuming this mess eventually made her feel suicidal—it was three against one and she was the only one out of practice and unarmed.

Amy grimaced and Terry looked relieved.

Kate refused to ask for an explanation.

Finally, Amy looked at her and asked, "How can anyone be dumb enough to have a password of '1234' in this day and age?"

Kate sighed, "*That* is my brother."

54

PAUL SWUNG OPEN THE DOOR FROM THE KITCHEN AREA INTO THE Library—and slammed into it hard enough to hurt. The door only opened part way then stopped as if it hit a brick wall. While he leaned over to rub his knee, the door swung open the rest of the way and the overly broad-shouldered Agent Terrance Tyrell stood looking down at him.

Paul saw the way Tyrell kept looking at his sister and he wasn't amused. Kate always took care of her own affairs—and threatened to pound the snot out of Paul each time he interfered—but there was something different about this one. Tyrell seemed like a decent and serious guy; Katydid seemed to think that was her type.

What his twin needed was someone to lighten her up.

He spotted Kate in an armchair, literally slouching. Tyrell was a good influence on her after all. His sister never slouched; including when they binged on all three of the original Bourne movies right in a row.

"Morning, Katydid," he gave his knee a last rub and stepped into the room. "Have you got a sec?"

"Sure. Why not? I'm not doing anything," she waved a hand at the group of agents she'd been chatting with.

Paul didn't see any threatening looks from them, so they were probably catching up on old times.

"Good," he turned back and waved Cecilia forward. "Cecilia got another one of those messages. We thought you'd want to see it when it played."

The change in the room was galvanic. The female agent sitting in the armchair across the hearth from Kate jerked to her feet like a string puppet. Agent Tyrell cursed. And Kate hid her face.

"Is this a bad time? We can come back later." He spotted a blurry photo of himself lying in the fire grate. He looked down at what he was wearing. The shirt wore, a fresh-washed blue-stripe oxford that Ralph the chauffeur had found for him yesterday afternoon among the sportsman's wardrobe, was in the photo. His adventure with the sheep had cost him a change of clothes and someone had stripped five hundred dollars cash out of his wallet. He and Cecilia had ended up back in her room, a pleasant night indeed, but it left him still wearing the absent sportsman's clothes.

Paul was about to ask what was going on when Tyrell closed the door behind him with a loud *snick*. Then the man stood in front of it with his big arms crossed over that broad chest. Not quite as imposing as Sam, but he had several inches on Paul and the same kind of training that made Kate so scary at times.

"Hold on," Kate held up a hand as Cecilia raised her phone. "I want to get a copy of this so that I can send it to Rikka."

As Kate pulled out her own phone, it rang, nearly making her drop it.

She set it on speakerphone as she answered with a weak, "Hello?"

55

"This is a weird one," Rikka waited.

When Kate didn't reply, she started again.

"You there, Kate?"

Another pause. Sam squinted his eyes at the phone.

"Yeah, she's here," a voice sounded into the room at the Aerospace Cluster's data center.

"Go away, Paul. I need to talk to your sister."

"I'm here," Kate spoke. "Why are you calling this time, Rikka?" Her voice sounded shaky and tired.

The G-7 trip wasn't being as fun as it was supposed to be, at least not for Kate. Rikka seen enough of the Diplomatic Protection Group's software during in-processing to know how to crack it if she ever needed to, ridden along as camerawoman in a cozy helicopter, cooked with Kate as chef—abso-tively the best part—and was now acquainting herself with a truly exceptional block of old hardware. If this wasn't a grand holiday tour, she didn't know what was.

Rikka looked around the room on the third floor of the estate house on the Isle of Man.

Roderick St. James had set them up in the *young mistress'*

bedroom. The daughter of this household had grown up with ornate pink wallpaper, white-stained oak flooring, and frilly curtains. Rikka wondered what in the world the poor woman had ever grown up into with this insanity for a starter.

What had once been, based on the wear of the white floor stain, the footprint of the bed—she could just imagine the four-poster with an ick-pink chenille bedspread and mounds of embroidered pillows—was now a U-shaped workstation of astonishing caliber.

Three consoles fed straight into the heart of the Intel Paragon XP/S, Madam Deal; that saved her from having to do any screen switching once things heated up. She'd arranged three other stations on three different protocols, not a single one of them running Linux. It was one of the reasons she had no signature when it really counted, she kept rotating her combination of tools and platforms. One of these was running Microsoft Windows. It would make any hacker's brain bleed trying to see through one of the most opaque and convoluted operating systems in the business. A totally unexpected hacking weapon.

Sam sat close beside her. Close enough to observe, but not to interfere.

Rikka stroked her fingertips lightly over the word *Silens* of his tattoo. Sam didn't only have an outer silence, but an inner one as well that she was finally beginning to understand and appreciate. She did feel calmer and steadier for having him there. Something had shifted between them, something good. Usually, the build-up to a run left her much edgier, but this time she was steady and ready.

She'd thought maybe she and Sam would launch the next phase of their relationship last night, but she'd worked straight through 'til dawn getting the machine configurations the way she wanted them. Good thing she had—or Kate would be broke by now.

"We are set up so su-weet," she told Kate. "Don't know what this is costing you per minute, but it totally rocks. I'm not all the way in, but I don't want Dino finding us too soon."

"Are we safe to be talking about this over the phone?"

"Sure. I downloaded an app onto your phone a while ago. If it detects my number, it lays down a nice scrambler that even Dino can't get through—because it will sound like a disconnect to anyone except me."

There was one of those pauses that meant Kate was lost again.

One of these days she was going to have to get Kate drunk or find her ticklish spot until she revealed how such a non-technical person had ever caught Rikka back in her bad-ass money-laundering days.

The pause continued.

"We're fine. It's okay to speak."

"Okay," Kate's hesitation vanished.

She was good at that gear change, better than Rikka herself.

"So, what's a 'weird one'? That *is* how this conversation began." Kate also never, ever lost the thread of a conversation no matter how Rikka tried to sidetrack her with chess games and obscure movie references. The woman totally rocked. If Rikka ever grew up, she wanted to be Kate Stark.

"Dino's latest MI-Vid."

"We haven't watched it yet."

"I'll wait."

56

KATE STARED AT THE PHONE, BUT NO EXPLANATION WAS forthcoming. Rikka must be tapped into all of their...of course she was.

Paul, Cecilia, and the three Secret Service agents were looking at her oddly.

The more she understood about Rikka, the more Kate marveled that she'd ever nailed the woman down. In retrospect, two years of work and a fair bit of luck didn't seem sufficient. The tame hacker for one of North Korea's largest money-laundering schemes turned out to be a small Japanese-American woman working out of an MIT dorm room. One who'd never applied to the school yet somehow been enrolled on a full scholarship.

There'd been another hacker at MIT who'd done that, but not as cleanly. One of her techs told her about it because he thought it was amusing. That anomaly, stumbled on by chance, had been her first hint that she'd spent at least the first year looking in all the wrong places.

Finding Rikka had been an intuitive moment, that Kate

initially ignored, to send her agent through the rest of MIT's records looking for a similar anomaly.

It wasn't that I couldn't afford it, Rikka explained later. *It was more convenient to set it up that way. I didn't have to mess with rent, buying books, paying tuition, all that noise. I did have the North Koreans give a million-dollar donation to the computer lab; without either of them knowing about it.*

Rikka lived with integrity, even if it was her own peculiar form of it.

Kate turned to Cecilia, "Play it."

Seven seconds long. *Mission Impossible*-style font.

"Silent Death." Nothing more.

She turned her attention once more to her own phone. "Sam? We got a message through Paul's e-mail about twenty minutes ago that said, 'To President Kennelly: Swift Death.' Are you thinking what I'm thinking?"

Kate saw the Marine Force Recon motto every single time she looked at his forearm tattoos: Swift, Silent, Deadly.

He grunted in surprise. He also must not like the sound of it.

Kate dropped back into her chair. She was a chef. No, not even that; she was a television network executive.

"Someone is screwing with you."

"Thanks, Paul. That narrows it right down. Anyone else?"

"I hate when he does that," Rikka's voice was disgustingly cheerful. "Paul's right for a change."

"So, who is pulling Dino's strings?"

"That's the half-billion-dollar question, isn't it?" Rikka agreed. "He's got an air gap, so I can't tell."

"Air gap?"

"Like in plumbing...never mind. There's no connection between what he's doing to you and who he's talking to. Separate systems with no overlap so I can't use one to find the other."

Kate contemplated the question. She couldn't think of any companies that would risk breaking so many laws to take down Cooks Network.

To take down Paul? Paul was always upsetting husbands; mostly by seducing their wives or mistresses. But badly enough to elicit murder threats against the President? Not that she could think of. To the best of her knowledge, Paul had never met the President.

To take out Kate herself? She'd met enough vicious bitches and bastards in the corporate world to last her a lifetime, but...murders?

And the money seemed like an afterthought. The first attacks had all targeted Kate personally.

Terry had kept a respectful silence ever since she'd mentioned the *half billion* number this morning. She and Paul didn't keep that much liquid, but Cooks and their other holdings were lucrative. She needed to buy another company or two to chew up capital but hadn't had time.

There wasn't enough stock out in the public for that to matter, it was a family business. She'd started a profit-sharing plan for her employees. You could take your stock with you when you left, but the amount out in the world remained inconsequential. Most of her people simply didn't leave, the wonders of job satisfaction and decent pay.

Maybe, if she'd rolled down the car window and tossed her phone onto the heath on the way here, she'd be having a better day.

A gentle knock sounded from the door that opened onto the Great Hall. She pictured the Great Hall and realized that she hadn't seen this door from the outside. The layout of the rooms said they had to join, but when she visualized the other side of this wall, all she saw was a wallpapered wall covered with a tasteful oil portrait of the Queen Victoria. Secret door. Great.

Kate wanted to scream as the agent opened it. The already crowded room became more packed as someone else strode in. By the sounds that followed the latest arrival, the G-7 was on a break.

Agent Amy Franklin rose to her feet and glared down at Kate.

Kate twisted around to see who was entering from behind her, then she too bolted to her feet.

57

PRESIDENT CHERYL KENNELLY LOOKED LIKE OLYMPIA DUKAKIS: A tall, spare woman with patrician features, neatly coiffed silver hair, and a rod of steel up her spine. Her presence was commanding by merely entering the room. She'd been a highly decorated Navy ship commander prior to her election to the Senate and then the White House.

Without a word, she handed a cell phone to Amy Franklin.

The agent read the screen, swore without apologizing, and handed it to Kate. Terry moved to look over her shoulder.

"No one should have this number," Amy explained. "It isn't registered to the President and the number is known only to family."

Kate looked down at the screen.

"Deadly Death," she read aloud. "Rikka," she spoke into her own phone. "The President has just received an e-mail on her private phone that says, 'Deadly Death' and has a logo beneath it of a sword-wielding Pegasus with red-starred eyes."

In addition to Sam's forearm tattoos in the original Latin: *Celer, Silens, Mortalis*—Swift, Silent, Death—she'd also seen the Marine Recon's emblem tattooed on his other arm.

This wasn't it.

"A Pegasus? Like the flying horse from Greek mythology? That's all messed up," Rikka spoke up. "Marine Force Recon would be a skull with wings and shit."

"That's not what I'm looking at."

A rattle of keys sounded over Kate's phone, "You're right, that is weird. It's pretty though."

Suddenly Amy was right in Kate's face, "How did your person get access to this phone?"

Before Kate could speak, Rikka cut her off.

"Du-uh! Cross-referenced phone calls from close relatives of President Kennelly with cell-based transmissions originating in the Oval Office. It's all right here in the FBI's call-monitoring files. They should call a landline in like Oklahoma and then that would re-route to the President's cell if you wanted any reasonable privacy. It's also the only cell phone that consistently triangulates at the Oval office as well as the White House Residence other than yours, Agent Franklin."

Amy's scowl said she took Rikka's tease as a personal affront. At least the President looked somewhat amused. She sat in the third leather chair by the fireplace and waved for the others to be seated. Unsure what to do, Kate waited until Amy took her seat before taking her own.

"That logo—" Terry started.

"Sam says," Rikka interrupted him from three hundred miles away, and you could hear how much she enjoyed doing it, "that it's the Special Operations Aviation Regiment. That's the Army's 160th: helicopter guys who kick ass and certainly don't take names. 'Death Waits in the Dark' is one of their two mottos. The flying horse with sword, and the night-vision eyes, is theirs. Nothing about 'Swift, Silent, Deadly'."

"Who's Sam?" Amy glared at Terry for not having somehow already provided that information.

"Sam Fierro," Terry replied with a tone that stated *I sure as hell do know my job*, "is a former Marine Force Recon soldier. He was also Kate's butcher for breakfast and dinner yesterday."

"And he is where?"

"He's presently on the Isle of Man," Rikka provided. "With me."

"Mute that goddamn phone."

Kate pretended to do so and hoped that Rikka and Sam had the good sense to stay quiet.

Amy faced Kate once more. "You have a Marine Force Recon soldier in your party. And the President has been threatened by a death threat phrased in their motto. Care to explain why I shouldn't have him immediately arrested?"

"For one," Kate was getting tired of the constant suspicion of her friends and sibling, "he's on the Isle of Man, hard to arrest him as the US Secret Service lacks jurisdiction there. For two, he's Recon. They don't threaten. If it *was* him, she'd already be dead. Excuse me, Madame President, but it's true."

The President looked down at her immaculate powder-blue pantsuit and spoke the first words since her arrival, "I don't appear to be dead. At least not yet."

Kate did her best to mask the snort of laughter from the un-muted phone.

58

STEPHANIE ROSE EARLY. THERE WASN'T A SECOND TO WASTE today. She left George asleep in her bed, she didn't have the patience this morning to tease him to orgasm; the man took forever to arouse and then was gone in a single shot.

Instead, she started her day from her office with the door locked.

"Dino, is the money moving yet?"

"Not yet, lady. Jeez, keep your pants on, if you can," his voice was a sneer.

If she hadn't already had a plan to off his sorry ass, she would have made one now. Cocky shit.

"What's the delay?"

"They've got serious damn security on those accounts, way more than normal. I'm most of the way through them. When it spills, it's going to spill fast. So don't worry, you'll get your payout in the next couple hours."

"I damn well better." It was more than leaving Kate and Paul destitute. It was also more than taking over Cooks Network so she could flaunt it in their faces while they languished in prison for the rest of their God-forsaken lives for murdering the President.

Stephanie needed the cash if she was going to ensure her path to the White House. Her newspaper had its back against the wall, the Internet leaving her nowhere to turn. Cooks Network was cash heavy and was about to invest that cash in buying the next election for her. Campaign money and donations to the proper charities, starting with the party's national election campaign—a quiet fifty million there should be enough to buy the committee's loyalty. Another fifty should take care of any stray electoral votes.

"You'd better go back to the bedroom and spread 'em wide, lady. George is starting to wake up and he won't like being alone when he does."

Stephanie punched off the phone and rammed it down into her bag. So, the hacker had a spy cam in her bedroom somewhere.

Fine!

George was going to receive an extra special wake-up treat. Let that hacker shit see everything that he was never going to get.

59

KATE WORKED HER WAY THROUGH BREAKFAST SERVICE, THOUGH she wasn't quite sure how. Dirk had suggested Belgian waffles. She expanded that with fresh lingonberries, a side of bite-sized bacon-wrapped crab with a brush of lemon-basil pesto cream that hadn't made it into either lunch or dinner yesterday, and a fresh fruit compote in a heather-honey syrup on a bed of goat-milk yogurt. For lunch...she wouldn't think about that yet.

Some crazed hacker named Dino was looking for money. Her money. A lot of it, probably all of it.

He also risked threatening the President of the United States. That meant he felt secure behind his deep walls.

Swift, Silent, Deadly death.

Death Waits in the Dark.

The two were related, somehow. Surely a SCUBA-wearing skull astride a night-vision Pegasus.

Kate always thought better when she cooked.

She decided that she'd leave death threats against the President to the Secret Service, at least for now.

That left the money. Rikka said she could block the bank

attack, perhaps trace it back, but that would alert the hacker and still wouldn't remove the threat to the President.

Was the President's life worth losing a half billion dollars? Stupid-ass question, especially when asking a former Secret Service agent like herself.

So, focus on solving the money without revealing her actions to the hacker.

Someone attacking her, Paul, and Cooks Network. Since she couldn't see how the various pieces could possibly tie together, she'd focus on one piece at a time.

Money must flow. Once it flowed out of the Stark accounts, the chances of getting it back weren't the best.

Who would want to lose a half billion dollars, even a few hundred million?

There were five hundred billionaires in the United States alone, sixteen hundred worldwide, and she couldn't think of a one who would want to give away a half billion dollars to a hacker in order to deceive him. She certainly didn't.

Kate didn't have enough strawberries to make the spouses' fruit compotes the same as the G-7's, so she changed to blackberries and shifted to other fruits to maintain a good flavor/color profile including slivers of bright green kiwi.

Right, change her thinking. Adapt to what's available. Not who wanted to lose a half billion, but who *should*? Now there was an interesting question.

"Dirk, can you finish this off?" All that remained was serving up the finger-sized chocolate-stuffed croissant rolls with a lingonberry drizzle that would tie the meal together in a neat bow.

"Can do, lassie. But don't be wandering off too far now. I don't fancy the G-7 thinking we'd serve pizza twice in a row."

"No promises."

60

KATE DECIDED THAT GETTING AWAY FROM EVERYONE AND stretching her legs a bit was a good idea.

Terry had made the strategic error of leaving his keys in his car with the gate guards. "I'm off into town for a few ingredients I need for lunch," proved sufficient for Kate to steal his vehicle.

Instead of Fort William, she drove up to the base of Ben Nevis. She didn't have time for the whole climb—the tallest mountain in the British Isles rose fifteen hundred meters from sea level. Though it was tempting, it would dump lunch service wholly into Dirk's lap.

In lieu of that, Irene had provided her with a map that followed a little-used maintenance road high up onto the mountain's flank. Trees were not a major feature of the Scottish Highlands. She left the car where the road finally decayed into thick brush and found a deer path that led upward until she was above most of the brush. The top of Ben Nevis was nothing but a jumble of rock. At her present elevation, it was scattered boulders with tenacious clumps of clinging moss and lichen.

She chose a comfortable looking boulder that faced south and west. The sun had cleared the peak and warmed her back.

In the valley before her Fort William nestled in the crook of the ninety-degree bend in Loch Eil, a long arm from the sea that sliced Scotland almost in two. The Inverlochy Castle Hotel was tucked out of site from here, but its private lake marked the location.

This was about as private a spot as she could arrange. She pulled out her cell phone and dialed Rikka.

"Morning, Kate. How was breakfast?"

"Eat shit, Rikka."

"Ick!"

"Sorry, rough morning."

"No sex from T-2, huh? What is wrong with that man?"

Not much that Kate could think of. Integrity, decency, thoughtfulness, too much goddamn self-restraint. Of course, she also hadn't jumped him. They should both be taken out and slapped for foolishness.

"I need to place a secure call. An exceptionally secure call. And I'll need you to translate."

"You're talking to the right lady," a keyboard rattled in the background. "Who are we calling?"

"What time is it in North Korea?"

Rikka's string of curses covered at least three languages and lasted an impressively long time without any repeats that Kate could detect.

61

"Is this Rang Jin-ho?"

"It is," Rikka's translation echoed Jin-ho's voice.

"This is Kate Stark."

"Ms. Stark," his voice shifted from intense caution to supreme pleasure. "Are you well? Never mind. I can only presume that this is not a social call."

"Regrettably, no. I need a favor." While he was a marine Captain, Rang Jin-ho had offered to do Kate a favor in exchange for inadvertently elevating him into the leadership council of the North Korean money-laundering Office 39. Better him than the man who previously held that seat in their government's illegal activities division; for one thing, his predecessor had kept trying to kill Kate and Rikka.

"If I can do so, I shall. My wife and I are *deeply* in your debt."

Well, Kate stared out at the quiet landscape, there was an opening if she ever needed one. There were advantages to saving a man's life and helping him achieve his goals, nefarious or otherwise.

"Half-a-billion-American-dollars worth?" Then she laid it out.

She didn't need a translation of the sharp hissing as Jin-ho sucked in a breath through his teeth.

"And I would need it nearly immediately."

"Would this money," he hid his initial surprise well, "be recoverable?"

"I expect not."

"A moment please." And the phone went silent.

"Can he hear us, Rikka?"

"No, but I can hear him."

"Didn't he just mute his phone?"

"Mute is for sissies. Now hush, I'm listening."

Kate hushed and tried to admire the view of the rolling Highlands. Tried to remember that forty-eight hours ago she'd been looking forward to filming a television interview and enjoy the fine food tasting at Inverlochy. Tried—

"Apparently…"

Rikka's voice whispered out of the phone and wiped all those pleasant fantasies of how different Kate's life could have been these last forty-eight hours.

"…his wife is reminding our good Jin-ho that he has his eyes on a higher prize. Wow! He works fast. He's already head of the inner council at Office 39. We helped him climb onto the council only when, three months ago?"

"Two," Kate wondered what monster she'd unleashed inside the Democratic People's Republic of Korea. Couldn't be worse than the old one. She'd found herself liking the man and his scheming ways.

"Oooo!" Rikka sounded excited. "Kim Jong-un should not sleep peacefully just because he is the hereditary leader of the country."

"Ms. Stark," Jin-ho was back. "We would like to suggest that you consider the following account at the Bank of China." He read off a number that Kate assumed Rikka was writing down, followed by a password.

She knew better than to ask whose account it might be. She'd give herself one guess. North Korea's leader was going to be in for a rude shock the next time he went to buy another luxury car or fancy motor yacht...or someone's allegiance.

"A pleasure as always, Jin-ho."

"A favor such as this I am always glad to perform for my best American friend." His tone was politely suggestive.

"Please extend my greetings to your *wife*," who was the real brains behind Rang Jin-ho. Kate would like to meet the woman someday, if she could guarantee her own survival.

Of course, she and Rikka barely managed to escape alive from their last meeting with Jin-ho. His wife would be far more dangerous.

62

ONE THING THAT MARCUS HATED MORE THAN HAVING TO SPEAK to the Secret Service every time he called Kate Stark was having one now show up on his tail.

"No," José Osgood assured him, "I'm not here to take over your case. I'm strictly an observer to assist if I can." And he hadn't quite shoved Marcus and Leona aside, but it was close.

Now the three of them, an NYPD detective, and a garbage truck driver stood in a circle at the back of a reeking truck in midtown. The driver smelled no better than his vehicle and was grousing about who was, "gonna make sure I gets overtime for sittin' here on my ass. Got a route, buddy. They pay me by the route, not for the fuckin' sittin' around and shittin' with you fuckers. This thing was weird and I called it in, but anything else you fuckers want, you better start paying me now." His accent was thick Bronx, as were his arm muscles. Not a man Marcus wanted to tussle with.

The NYPD detective, about half the driver's size, in turn threatened to arrest his sorry ass if he didn't shut the fuck up for at least one goddamn second. His accent said Morningside Heights, which didn't bode well for the driver despite his size advantage. A disadvantage that the driver recognized and finally shut his trap for a minute.

That left Marcus, Leona, and Secret Service agent José Osgood looking down into the back of the truck. A cell phone with a wire that led up to a New York Yankees ball cap covered with a long smear of what might have once been a salami on rye with extra mustard before it had gone green.

Marcus pulled out a pen, and used it to flip the hat over and then tossed the pen in with the rest of the garbage because no way was he ever going to touch it again.

Inside the hat was nestled a spy cam. The hat matched the one they'd found on videos of the unknown audience member. The videos revealed little of the wearer's face because the hat was kept pulled low. A fake beard snagged on the soggy rye bread and sort of merged into it said that what little cameras had captured would be useless.

"God damn it," Leona's curse was low and heartfelt. But she wasn't looking at the hat anymore. She was looking up at the sky.

Marcus looked up as well and felt all the blood drain out of his face. The garbage can that had been the source of their current problem was open on the sidewalk beside them. And the building it stood in front of was the Chrysler Building.

The top three floors of which he well knew boasted perhaps the most luxurious penthouse in New York. A penthouse that belonged to Paul and Kate Stark.

63

When Kate returned to the Inverlochy, she was met at the gate by Terry and three other agents.

"Here's your car back, safe and sound. I needed to get out for a bit."

Terry didn't say a word, so she tossed the keys to the guy at the gate and headed up the drive. They grouped about her tightly, too tightly. There was a difference between a safety escort and the escort for a suspect, and she knew the latter though she had never been in the center of one before.

Halfway back to the hotel, where the driveway made a blind curve through the hedgerows, she turned to confront Terry.

Before she completed the turn, two agents grabbed her arms, and another slid a thin cord tight around her throat. Any attempt to struggle and she'd choke herself.

Despite that, she barely resisted the urge to kick Terry in the balls as he thoroughly frisked her without the least bit of friendly. All he unearthed was her cell phone and her wallet.

He riffled through her wallet before jamming it none too gently back into her pocket.

"Sir," one of her captors spoke up, "they're reporting the car is clean."

Terry stood in front of her with his arms crossed over his chest, glaring at her.

At his nod, they released her arms and the line, choke-tight around her neck, slipped away.

Kate leopard-punched Terry in the solar plexus with all the force she could muster.

With a whoosh, he collapsed to the driveway. As he went down, she slipped his service Glock out of his shoulder holster.

She placed a foot on his throat and aimed the gun at Terry's head. She didn't bother to turn as she heard the other agents draw.

"Anyone willing to bet whether or not I can shoot out his brains, *after* you shoot me?" She pressed harder with her foot and Terry grunted—quietly.

They responded with silence.

"Terry, I'm gonna ease off and the first thing you're going to do is order them to stand down or you're going to lose something you value a lot." She shifted her aim to his crotch. "We clear?"

At his microscopic nod, she eased off enough for him to speak. He managed to state the order. She could see in her peripheral vision that his people backed down, but they were slow to respond.

She took her foot off Terry's throat, but gave him a sharp toe in the ribs for good measure. "What are you teaching them these days? They never should have stood down at all, not when their commander was under duress."

Terry sent her a fulminating look from where he lay on the pavement. So much for up close and cozy.

She flipped his weapon and handed it back to him butt first, "Don't think I can't take it back if I want it. Now explain what the hell that was about."

Terry struggled back to his feet, short on breath as his body struggled to recover from the strength of her blow. He crossed his arms back over his chest once more and she had to fight the urge to hit him again.

"Well?"

"They found the hat and camera rig that filmed Max Klugman's murder."

"Where?"

"In a garbage can on the sidewalk at 42nd and Lexington. Garbage man called it in, though he'll never help a cop again."

She lived at 42nd and Lex.

"Shit!"

64

THE ONLY REASON KATE HAD BEEN ALLOWED TO COOK LUNCH WAS because she'd been in Scotland and Paul had been in Colorado at the time of Max Klugman's murder.

Rikka had been with her, as she'd pointed out to Amy Franklin several times.

Now the Secret Service was focusing in on Sam. Let them. Not only was Kate sure he was innocent, but she knew that a Marine Force Recon operator wasn't going to leave anything visible that he'd mind being found.

Kate cooked with two forensic specialists hovering over her every move. But she finished the meal without killing off the official taster.

She wasn't close to being done with agent Terrance Tyrell though.

Not one bit.

65

STEPHANIE BRONSON SOON-TO-BE-MADSEN—GEORGE WAS FAR less progressive than he thought and would want her to change her name—showered in the clubhouse after the round of golf. She'd wanted to drive her ball past the thicket on the tenth green today but hadn't wanted to arouse the golf pro's suspicions. She did what was expected, made appropriate noises, but didn't remember any of it.

On her drive to the course, the money had begun moving. She'd felt much more pleasantly inclined to the hacker as she watched her Cayman Islands accounts fly past eight figures and begin counting in increments of a hundred million. The most powerful sexual experience of her entire life slammed through her as she sat alone in the back of her gold-painted Hummer limousine and watched the numbers scroll upward on her cell phone. The golf pro's skills paled to insignificance beside that heady rush.

Bye, bye, Kate and Paul Stark. There's a new bitch in town.

Everything else was in place. It was a bit past the lunch service in Scotland.

Mid-morning here in Connecticut matched mid-afternoon

at the G-7 meeting. Right about now, everyone in Scotland would be twitching. And that's how she wanted them to be.

Kidnapping and then implicating Paul had been blind luck; luck had smugly been on her side. She'd planned to do the kidnap and sheep-trailer thing to one of the First Spouses, to instill fear. The Scottish punk girls grabbed the car when it left the hotel grounds, not realizing it was too soon.

Stephanie wasn't complaining about the results.

The slap at Paul for his jilting her in high school? A pure bonus. He'd slept with many of her friends at Chapin Prep. A young Paul Stark had swept through a large section of the exclusive all-woman's school—yet avoided her. There weren't that many dashingly handsome heirs to major fortunes running around. Yet he'd managed to slip away. She wasn't the only one in her circle to note that fact. Recovering her status had required conquering both the home and away quarterbacks during the same game.

Catching Paul up in the fray at the G-7 also aroused more suspicions against his too-fucking perfect sister. She'd been the top athlete on the green-ribbon team every year. Not once in the four years of upper school had Stephanie's gold-ribbon team taken the annual prize. Bitch was named valedictorian as well, forcing Stephanie down to salutatorian. Hell-bitch!

Well, watch who led now. Kate would remain embroiled in it right up until the last minute, her final minute of freedom before the entire Secret Service landed on her head. It wasn't a stupid team-ribbon school competition anymore; this was the real world.

Stephanie played to win.

In this game, second place included a sudden death round.

The golf course locker room was crowded with the normal well-tended mid-week ladies. That the volume dropped by half as she strode out of the showers only reinforced her power. She took her time drying her hair and refreshing her makeup while wearing only her underwear in front of the mirrors.

It paid to remind the other women *who* ruled the New York and Connecticut social scene; and the soon-to-be Washington, DC, scene. Most of them couldn't afford her body and didn't have the necessary drive to maintain it.

They also could never claim the list of conquests it so easily earned for her; including a wide selection of their husbands— she encouraged the spread of rumors, though she never confirmed any of them.

Yet, some of these total-failures-in-keeping-their-man had the temerity to look down on her. Blonde, brunette, buxom, or blah, every one of them could kiss her well-toned ass.

The ones with Wall Street husbands and two children already placed in the proper schools thought she was a social-wannabe airhead. She could feel them whispering to each other about college-tracks and who was throwing the next important party.

How little they knew.

The most important social event of the decade was happening in a few hours and none of them were invited.

Two nights ago, she'd become engaged to the US Senate Majority Whip. It would go public today, though that news would be momentarily buried due to the death of the President at the hands of primetime-bitch Kate Stark.

Unlike the thousands of death threats that constantly flooded in, Stephanie would absolutely be delivering on hers.

She knew this because she already had.

She slipped into a custom Siriano to make the other women green with envy. The golden top and jacket, she never ever wore green, accented her figure and coloring, turning her red hair to fire. The flared skirt was that perfect inch too short to shift it from professional to flirty. *I'll be flirting with every one of your husbands,* it said, *and it will work.* But their precious, mundane, everyday banker husbands no longer mattered either, not with where she was headed.

Though the look on Nancy T. Reynolds' face was priceless. The woman knew her husband had slipped the tight reins Nancy tried to keep on him. Though she didn't know who with, Stephanie was the prime suspect. Stephanie made a note to let him bed her again at the first opportunity. The Harper Collins vice president had proven to be a creative lover and able to keep a secret. She'd figure out how to rub it in Nancy T.'s face later, after the biography of Stephanie's own rise to power was written and published as a Number One release.

But today Stephanie would make sure that US Vice President David Morgan cemented her path to the leadership of the nation. With the President dead, it would only be natural, and expected, when Morgan selected his newly engaged best friend and the nation's most popular senator as the nominee for his own replacement. She was going to make sure he stayed on that path.

After today, these locker-room ladies would look at her in a whole different way. The shark in their midst would suddenly thrash and consume them all.

She strolled out the door and could feel the heat focused on her back. Their nattering volume soared as the door swung shut behind her perfectly toned ass.

It didn't matter, her shields were bullet-proof.

66

"Something's not right in Bedrock tonight."

Dino made the top two levels inside the northern column that supported Sealand his empire. The southern column had been fixed up by the Prince of Sealand as the royal family's living quarters when they were in residence. There were no windows or doors in the two pillars that rose from the sunken barge to support the old fort high in the air. The only access into the legs was to climb down a ladderway from the platform above.

For privacy, the ladder areas were boxed in, but the rest of the twenty-two-foot diameter circular rooms were his.

The lower of his two levels was a near impassable server farm, a truly Fred Flintstone-sized array of gear. No way could John Goodman, the real Fred Flintstone, could squeeze into the place. He kept the room cooled with a seawater heat exchanger that pumped chill English Channel waters through thick sleeves built into the equipment racks. Cables snaked up the ladderways to the platform for the multiply redundant generators, satellite uplinks, and microwave sea-to-shore backbone.

The upper level inside the column included all his control consoles, a cot, and a well-stocked fridge and microwave so that he never had to leave. He knew, once they got into the endgame, he wouldn't dare leave until it was finished.

However...

Something wasn't right, but he couldn't tell what.

Maybe it was that he'd expected more from the notorious US Secret Service. He'd delivered the three messages like the client asked—though the President's private line had been his idea—and the Service hadn't seen him coming.

Yet there'd been no serious attempt to backtrace his location. Nothing but the lamest pingbacks against his firewalls in Australia and Malaysia, which was only his second line of defense. He'd hoped for more of a challenge after making a death threat against the President of the US of A.

Stephanie Bronson had thought to send: *Death...Waits...in the Dark.* She figured that would stir things up.

He'd decided to spice it up with something that would cast more suspicion onto Kate Stark's team since the client seriously had the hots for them. Stark's butcher had been Marine Force Recon, so Dino had altered the death threat to take advantage of that. He'd added on the 160th SOAR's Night Stalkers emblem to honor Stephanie's original idea, though it was clear she'd never heard of them despite wanting to use their motto.

She'd said that *Death* and *Dark* were a crucial pairing having to do with sunset. Local sunset was about six hours away. Who knew what the woman was up to.

Stephanie Bronson might be vicious, but not the smartest bitch in the world. Thankfully Dino had plenty of smarts for both of them. He'd let her decide the course, but he did the fine steering.

For a moment he wondered if she was going to try to snuff the American President, but that didn't make any sense. Everything he'd scraped up on Stephanie Bronson implied a simple revenge routine against Kate Stark for killing her brother.

None of it affected him any. And he was about to earn serious bragging rights. Yes, he finally decided, he would go to Black Hat this year. Then he could show all of those hacktavists impressive real-world code breaks. Walking over the backs of the US Secret Service was major; moving a half billion, well maybe he'd keep that quiet.

He'd have to remember not to piss off Ms. Redhead Bitch Bronson though. Her ideas on payback were nasty, regardless that he was invulnerable—but not worth the hassle.

It wasn't enough for Ms. RBB that Kate, her brother, and the entire team ended up in prison for threatening to kill the American President. She also wanted to devastate the sister and brother.

Strip them to the bone and fuck them hard, had been her instruction.

She'd pointed him toward where to find their pocketbooks, 'cause that's how you hurt rich people.

He'd sent a trio of worms, aimed them at the banking and investment accounts of the two Starks and Cooks Network. And damn if the money hadn't flowed. Not as smoothly as he'd expected, that had started to worry him, but then the moolah had bubbled up like Kuwaiti oil and just kept coming.

He'd slid a quick hundred million sideways that RBB would never miss and still the account had spilled out six hundred million after that and wasn't done yet.

That's what power looks like, you Black Hat dumbasses. His only question was how many women should he buy to hover at his side when he made his entrance at the conference.

Dino sat back, cranked up Bullet for My Valentine's latest tracks until the heavy metal shook and echoed about the circular steel chamber, and watched the worms keep digging. They were bad-ass worms.

67

LUNCHEON PREPARATIONS AT STEPHANIE BRONSON'S UPPER EAST Side condo overlooking the Metropolitan Museum of Art were close to complete by the time she returned from her Connecticut golf lesson.

The catering staff from Per Se were deeply entrenched in her kitchen. She'd tried to arrange for Thomas Keller to cater the meal personally, but he claimed some prior commitment at his other restaurant in California, The French Laundry. After today, he'd reconsider his choices, still, she'd serve a grand luncheon.

The first to arrive were Vice President David Morgan's Secret Service advance team. With nothing to hide, she gave them the run of the place, including her private office.

The only incriminating evidence was the burner phone she'd used to contact the hacker, presently at the bottom of the water hazard on the fourteenth fairway out in Connecticut. She'd buy another one if she ever needed to contact him again —there should never be one. And if all went to plan, she'd never be able to reach him again after midnight.

She left the agents to their inspection.

Keller's people were handling all the plating—on their exclusive fine, bone-white china—but she'd insisted on providing her own gold-plated flatware. For this one meal, she wanted to know exactly where her utensils came from.

68

CECILIA BARSTOWE MOVED AROUND THE RED DINING ROOM AT Inverlochy Castle Hotel. They were going all out for the final dinner of the G-7 meeting. The tables were a stunning array of fine linens and shining Wedgwood china in an abstract red-on-gold pattern that alluded to the Lion Rampant of Scotland without quite throwing the Scottish Royal Banner in the British PM's face; not quite. She liked that the Inverlochy had a sense of humor.

Each plate bore a hand-calligraphed card with the appropriate leader's name. The Royal Scot Crystal champagne flutes were keepsakes engraved with *G-7*, the date, and *Inverlochy Castle Hotel, Scotland.* She reached out to move one for a better photograph and almost had her knuckles rapped.

"Don't touch!" Irene Watson wore white gloves and was working along the length of the table with a ruler checking the exact positioning of every knife, fork, and plate.

"Yes, ma'am!"

Once admonished, Irene was pleasant enough about moving the piece for her to get the photograph, then she moved it back and checked the measurement twice. Cecilia was the only photographer who'd come to admire Irene's careful work, and the attention seemed to be appreciated.

There was something about the care that showed. There was a perfection to the setting that lent an air of confidence in the quality of the meal; a degree of anticipation she tried to capture in the images. All in all, a definite step up from the Chinese takeout in paper containers that was her own normal fare when she dragged a man into her bed.

Each plate sported an immense array of silverware. The dessert spoon that lay on the table sideways above the plate was a particularly elegant piece, each lavishly engraved with the leader's or spouse's name.

"Nice touch, Irene."

The woman smiled warmly as Cecilia snapped a close-up of the President's place setting.

69

STEPHANIE HADN'T INVITED ANY MEN THAT SHE'D SLEPT WITH TO this luncheon, other than George. That only two of the dozen guests were women told how men misunderstood who was the true power behind their thrones. These were the political and the food elite of the city.

She needed the latter for two reasons. First was so that they could let the political guests know that this was Thomas Keller's catering and quite how big a deal it was. The second reason was that she intended to recruit the Food Network's program director to take over as president of Cooks Network after Dino left the Starks destitute. At this luncheon the program director would see the power she wielded so easily and would not turn down her invitation; he wouldn't dare by the time she finished with him.

The political guests were Morgan and George's inner circle within the national committee. She wanted to make sure that when the news of David Morgan's unexpected ascension to the Presidency arrived at the end of the meal, that everyone moved as she needed them to.

Stephanie wanted to leave three empty place settings at her

table. One each for the symbolic ghosts of Kate and Paul Stark and the third for the soon-to-be actual ghost of Madame President Cheryl Kennelly.

She had timed her New York meal service to coincide with the dinner in Scotland that was going to shatter the G-7 meeting and kill President Kennelly.

Her appetizer of a simple shrimp cocktail with prosciutto-wrapped cantaloupe would coincide with the final emptying of the Starks' personal accounts.

The summer salad would match the emptying of the Cooks Network coffers.

The main entrée would mark the release of Kate and Paul's final death threat against the President.

And for dessert...

70

"Hɪ, Kᴀᴛᴇ. Mᴀʀᴄᴜꜱ Rᴇʏɴᴏʟᴅꜱ ʜᴇʀᴇ."

"That's a damn sight better greeting than 'Ms. Stark'. "

"Yeah, sorry about cutting up stiff on you there." He'd been pretty freaked out that she'd had the Secret Service on the phone each previous time he'd called, and then one of his own after that.

This time she hadn't said anything about being on speakerphone and the background was quiet. Besides, after dealing with José Osgood, he had more of a handle on what to do with them.

"No problem."

"I *do* have you on speaker for Leona." They sat knee-to-knee at his desk. It was hard to resist playing footsie with her. They'd managed to shed Osgood by saying they were stopping for lunch. Apparently Secret Service agents didn't eat lunch.

"Same here for Agent Tyrell."

Crap, you couldn't get away from these guys.

"What have you got for me? I'm currently plating the main entrée of morel mushroom-stuffed lamb chops for the G-7, so could you make it snappy?"

"Well, you said to call with good or bad. Sorry to say, this is in the bad column."

"Oh joy. Last one of those, I had to punch out a Secret Service agent."

Marcus glanced at Leona, but she shrugged as if that was only to be expected from someone like Kate Stark.

"At least it's not in the someone-else-is-dead column," Leona rested her hand on Marcus' knee under the desk as she leaned forward to speak into his phone more clearly. Her white blouse sagged open enough to reveal the start of what he knew from experience was a bountiful cleavage. Any circulation that once serviced his brain raced elsewhere in that instant.

"Okay," Kate's voice was tinged with chagrin, "I'll try to be thankful for small favors. What's the news?"

Marcus looked up to clear his head and was confronted by Leona's dark, knowing gaze. A deep breath, and he managed to speak—he was getting better at this.

"I think we've hit another dead end. The bomb squad finally opened that stupid box attached to the bottom of Maxwell Klugman's table. It's an SPL, a Sound Pressure Level meter. This model is high end and was an online sale from a theater equipment supply house in Seattle, Washington. Apparently, these things are used for setting up and balancing theater sound systems."

"Uh-huh."

Okay, Leona hadn't thought it was especially cool either, but he did.

"It was sent to a dead PO box. It has a registry that goes back years, but the clerk can't remember ever putting any mail into it and she's been there two years. She was surprised enough at having to put a pickup key in the box, to remember that it was a package that arrived."

"A pickup key?"

Leona leaned forward again, but she kept her hands to herself this time so Marcus had a chance of remaining in the conversation.

"Oversize package. Instead of handing it over the counter, she put it in one of the single-use larger boxes and then put the key in the smaller, regular P.O. box. That means no one saw who picked it up. We tried scanning the security cameras and got an image of a woman's floppy hat and a dress. Nice one. Designer."

Marcus made a mental note to buy Leona a nice designer dress, or at least a good knock-off, and take her out dancing in it. A nice short one.

"Any name on the box?"

"Sure. We tried to trace it, but it disappears into a holding company that no longer exists, though someone is paying the yearly fee on the box. Go back far enough and it's in the name of Earl Bronson, there are none in the New York phone book."

The silence on the other end of the phone was complete.

"Kate?"

More silence.

"You there?" Leona leaned in close enough that the heat of her skin started to overwhelm him. Together they looked down at the phone.

Still connected.

"The woman who picked up the package," Kate's voice was cold and flat. "Anything else on her?"

"Long hair halfway down her back," Leona filled in. "Well-tenced would be a guess, but a good guess by the way she walked and the hair moved."

Marcus agreed. The woman had walked like a she-lion. Not the raw punch of power that Leona packed stalking naked across the bedroom but strong and confident.

"Hair color?"

"Sorry, Kate. Black-and-white feed on the security cams."

"Any chance that it was red?"

Marcus looked at Leona. Now she revealed a different look. Still pure she-lion.

But now with the feral smile of one on the hunt.

71

Rikka answered the phone. Kate didn't bother to say hello.

"We've got the source figured out. Don't tip the hacker until we have her nailed, then take him down. All the way down."

Kate hung up before Rikka could start cheering.

She grabbed Sam for a celebratory kiss. At least it started out that way. All that power and safety in his arms, all that self-confidence that only came from deep experience, was nothing compared to the way the man kissed.

What in the world had she been waiting for? For a man to prove that he was as steady and trustworthy as Kate Stark? Well, Sam Fierro embodied that. Someone who kissed her as if she were both precious and would take on an entire wing of the Taliban himself if she asked? Sam again.

Damn!

Well, she was done waiting, but first she had work to do!

With a last hug, a small squeal of delight on her part, and a self-satisfied grin on Sam's, she dove back to her consoles.

Rikka rubbed her hands together and began pulling up her armor and weapons.

She and the pirate queen Madam Deal were about to go marauding.

72

PAUL HAD BEEN FORBIDDEN FROM THE GREAT HALL AND RED Dining Room by the Secret Service. And from the kitchen by Kate—pretty much the whole of the Ground Floor. He wanted to get his hands back on Cecilia's long form but been stymied finding the proper place and enough privacy. Last night he'd had the opportunity of undressing her. He'd done so, except for her cowboy boots, and it had been a glorious ride.

Cecilia, flaunting a degree of freedom he no longer possessed, breezed into the room in a summer blouse and dark slacks. Imagining her on horseback, riding over the summer heath was quite evocative. Or in a near-nothing string bikini on a beach far warmer than any they'd find in Scotland.

But now, he couldn't shed the Secret Service escort. So, he let his gaze wander, even if his hands didn't get to.

This room could offer interesting possibilities. He'd discovered the Billiard Room up on the First Floor. The snooker slate was perfect, the room precisely large enough to allow the stroke of a stick, but no more. It was a comfortable space done in ornate spring-green wallpaper, if one ignored the circle of many-antlered stag heads glaring down at him from near the ceiling. Perhaps not the best location for a tryst after all.

"Look at this, Paul. Look at how perfect everything is," she was bringing up images on her camera's viewfinder.

He looked over her shoulder to inspect the images as they flickered by. The men's style button-down shirt she wore offered a lovely distraction. As she was slender enough that she didn't have to wear a bra with her open black blazer, he'd have had a perfect view himself—if not for the straps of her cameras pinning the blouse to her body.

"Personally engraved silver," he whispered against the base of her neck. He wasn't above multi-tasking. And he'd seen those dessert spoons earlier in the pantry after the first night of the meetings. The one for the President with her name and an image of the Brooklyn Bridge—Kennelly's home town—engraved in the bowl.

"This one didn't come out as clearly as I'd hoped. Like someone didn't polish the silver thoroughly. That doesn't sound like Irene or her staff."

"The next picture came out fine." The place setting for the Japanese leader shone with an image of one of their swoopy-roofed feudal castles. "Use that one."

"No," she slid out of his arms. "I'll go back down and reshoot it. I'm selling these to an American magazine. Besides, the final dinner service begins any minute. I need to be in place."

"Later at my place?"

"Do you have a place?"

Paul didn't know anymore. He'd had a suitcase, but it might be in the back of the helicopter. If it had been, he'd bet Rikka enjoyed chucking it overboard high above the Irish Sea.

"Later at your place?"

She smiled at him and headed out with her cameras.

He tried to engage his own personal Secret Service escort in a game of snooker...without success. So, he worked his way around the table playing against himself right- vs. left-handed. He'd hustled enough pool for it to be a contest—left hand winning this time.

The Secret Service agent remained passively neutral in the corner of the room throughout his game.

It was hard to imagine that Kate used to do that for a living. This guy practically blended into the wallpaper. Kate would shine forth like...

Paul dropped the cue stick on the table and headed for the door fast enough that all he heard was a quick, "Hey!" as his escort fell in behind.

"Cecilia!" he called and raced for the stairs.

73

SEVEN HUNDRED AND THIRTEEN MILLION, THREE HUNDRED AND fifty-two thousand, one hundred and nineteen dollars and forty-nine cents. And that wasn't counting the hundred million that Dino skimmed for himself.

Damn! That was a hell of a lot of zeros, though none of the digits were literally zeros.

Redhead Bitch Bronson was now set to do serious damage. Not his problem.

With his cash, he'd never have dared to lift so much from a bank himself, he could—

A trace pinged at him.

Hard!

It blew through from the New York bank firewall that he'd spent most of the day cracking open. It bypassed his outer defenses in Indonesia and South Africa so fast he might as well not have put up firewalls there at all.

They slowed down when they hit Pakistan though, everything did. The Pakistani infrastructure was one of the great bogs on the cyber planet. It gave him time to cut his losses and drop his outer six layers of defense clean.

He sent a backtrace out of Japan and cut off the tail so it couldn't come back on him. It would go out, find who'd attacked him, and post it in the Help Wanted section of *The New York Times* where anyone could read it.

Dino waited twenty minutes and went and looked at the ad. It was waiting for him, along with a signature.

Shǔ. Rat.

Why in the hell was China's heaviest hacker suddenly looking to burn his ass? Dino had been picking pockets in New York.

Hadn't he?

Didn't matter.

The man was isolated, but damn he was fast. Dino would need a month to rebuild the damage Rat did to his defenses.

He sent out the final bug his client wanted, only a few minutes late.

It contained the strangest pieces of shit he'd dug up on Kate Stark. He hadn't been able to grab the entire report, but what he had of it would create mayhem aplenty.

RBB fucked her boyfriend, her trainer, and her maid twice on the day he'd showed her that piece from the FBI files. All the nervous, avaricious energy had needed some receptacle and no one person had been enough to chill her to anything even *close* to her normal level of madness.

With the last bug launched, it was time he got out of the way for a while. Way out of the way. Somewhere *Shǔ* couldn't find him. The guy had blasted a serious wake coming after him. One that made no sense.

Dino called for the Sealand Royal Chopper to swing out and pick him up. But it would be dark in a few minutes, and the guy refused to come out now.

Well, first thing in the morning would be fine.

Maybe he'd skip Black Hat in favor of going somewhere obscure, like Qatar or Mongolia.

74

CLINT JESSUP STARED AT HIS VAN IN HORROR. SECTION BY SECTION his surveillance stations were shutting down. He managed to broadcast an alert to the Brits to take over what they could before he lost everything in the Secret Service van except basic comms.

There was only one system still operating in the truck—his own. It was isolated from all the others by design. A report filled his screen, a page of an official FBI document that he hadn't requested.

God damn Stark's private hacker to Hell. She'd said she was inside his defenses, yet he'd found no trace of her. Apparently, she was in there—in here.

Clint read the first ten lines of the report and then keyed his mike.

"All agents," Clint didn't know how many could hear him. Enough he hoped. "Crash the site! Shut down the whole hotel. Take down Paul and Kate Stark. With prejudice if required!"

He closed his eyes; he might have just signed their death warrants. He knew and liked Kate. More importantly he respected her immensely.

It didn't matter.

He opened his eyes and read the information on his screen once more.

On his screen was a list of meetings between Paul and Kate Stark and the second most powerful man in North Korea. Their meetings occurred in New York and Panama and involved a ship moving millions of dollars of UN-sanctioned contraband.

They'd met repeatedly with Rang Jin-ho, who was now the new head of Office 39.

75

KATE WAS IN THE KITCHEN WHIPPING EGG YOLKS, SUGAR, AND Marsala wine in a zabaglione pot. An Italian dessert was incongruous with rest of the meal, but they were going to serve it in a split cup with Dirk's mousse, with a hint of the chili from the first night's mole sauce, topped with a slivered apricot that would also hark all the way back to that first meal she'd cooked. It would tie these last crazy days together up in a tight culinary knot.

Neat as...too neat!

All of the pieces came together at once.

Death Waits in the Dark. The sun was indeed setting outside the tall kitchen windows.

Swift, Silent, Deadly Death. Poison. But her kitchen was clean. Between her and the official taster, every single food item they'd sent to the Great Hall had been clean.

The attacks on her and Paul: financial and accusatory.

And Stephanie Bronson was behind the murder of Maxwell Klugman in the Cooks Network studio. She'd always been the queen bitch of Chapin. Even Paul, on his deep, dark, guy-quest to bed every woman in his sister's school—making Kate's social life a living Hell all those years—had avoided Stephanie Bronson.

Someone pulling Dino-the-hacker's strings.

Stephanie Bronson...and her brother Earl.

Stephanie was coming after Kate for Earl's death, for Kate not saving his life the day he'd been elected Vice President. But it was more than that. She was setting Kate and Paul up to take the fall for the President's death.

Death Waits in the Dark. Fast, poison death.

She dropped the zabaglione and bolted for the kitchen door.

The round-bottomed pot hit the floor on dead center and a fountain of warm custard shot up into the air behind her. She heard Terry cursing.

The agent by the kitchen door froze for a moment listening to his radio and then his eyes shot wide. He scrabbled for his weapon.

Kate didn't bother slowing down. She dropped him to the floor and bolted through the door.

A sharp crack sounded behind her and she'd swear that a bullet thudded into the swinging door closing behind her.

76

Her brief delay with Paul once again placed Cecilia in the worst position behind the sideboard. At least the tail of the sunset made a nicer backdrop than the morning glare.

The meal was winding up—finishing the main course—when she heard her name shouted.

Something about the tone of it made her raise her camera as other newsies were lowering theirs to see what was happening. Her war-zone-reporter training kicked in while their civilian instincts prepared to cower.

Paul came skidding into the room, and shouted her name again startling all the leaders, spouses, and translators at the table.

Square on she caught a three-shot sequence of Paul shouting, a flying tackle by a Secret Service agent, and the two of them crashing to the floor.

Then a sound she hadn't heard since Sam hauled her out of Rajasthan.

Gunfire.

She hated thinking about the photos she must have missed by cowering in that moment so long ago.

Not this time.

She caught Kate Stark in her viewfinder as she roared into the room.

"Nobody move!" she and several of the Secret Service agents shouted at the same moment. Guns were being pulled all around the room. Mostly aimed at Kate and Paul.

Several of the agents formed a blockade between the President and the intruders.

Cecilia hit the limit of her memory card, but long practice had her second camera up and firing in moments.

Damn! was all she could think. She'd never imagined herself as a Pulitzer-winning photographer, but if she lived through this, she was going to be unimaginably popular— whether or not the President survived.

77

STEPHANIE BRONSON LIFTED HER DESSERT SPOON, HOW splendidly ironic, and tapped her Waterford crystal wine glass for attention.

"I do hope that you all enjoyed the meal."

There was a warm round of applause.

Morgan then slapped George hard on the back. "A toast to the happy couple. I *am* your best man, George? Right?"

George was reassuring him when something shifted in the room.

Stephanie could usually follow, and anticipate, any shift. She lived by spotting nuance in political tableaus, but she couldn't pin down this one. Morgan and George were exactly as she wanted them.

The members of the National Election Committee were definitely thinking that four years from now they'd found the perfect team to walk into the Oval Office at the end of Kennelly's second term, Morgan and Madsen—they'd commented that it had a good ring to it. They were precisely where she wanted them.

The Program Director from the Food Network was warming to the idea of running an *unspecified* network of his own.

Everything at the table was perfectly aligned.

It was...the Secret Service. Their eyes all turned toward her.

A knock sounded at the front door. The maid answered and protested that her mistress was busy.

"FBI, ma'am," and heavy steps came across the living room and entered the dining room. A white man, a black woman, and another Secret Service agent with the telltale coil of wire at his ear.

Stephanie was too surprised to protest as they took the spoon from her hand, pulled her hands behind her back, and cuffed them.

"You are under arrest for involvement in the murder of Maxwell Klugman at Cooks Network. You have the right to..."

78

"THE SPOON," KATE HEARD PAUL CROAK FROM WHERE THE AGENT pinned her brother's face against the carpet of the Great Hall.

Terry crashed through the door behind her, covered head-to-toe in bright yellow custard. That didn't stop him from planting his feet, double-handing his weapon and aiming it right at her face.

"Down, Stark! Now!"

She held out empty hands and raised a finger to tell him to wait for a moment. She hoped that he wouldn't shoot an unarmed woman.

Amy Franklin was lying across the President, completely blocking Cheryl Kennelly from view except for an eye peeking from under her bodyguard's arm. Leaders and spouses cowered. Only two revealed military training as they moved in front of their significant other.

Cecilia's camera shutter paused for a moment.

"What?" Kate asked her in the suddenly silent room.

"The spoon?" she looked at Paul.

He managed to squeak out a "Yes!"

"Cecilia?" Kate didn't dare move. Instead she forced Cecilia's attention back to her with her voice, using the same tone she'd used when having her write down what she remembered from Paul's kidnap video.

"I, uh, took a picture of the engraved dessert spoons earlier. The President's isn't shiny like the others."

Amy Franklin started to reach for it.

"Don't!" Kate shouted, causing every gun in the room to once more jump in her direction, except for the one jammed against Paul's temple.

She moved forward slowly, keeping her hands in plain view.

Moved in until she was close beside Amy. Only the woman's thin body separated her from the President.

Then all three of them looked down at the spoon in question.

FRIDAY

79

THE HOTEL WAS STRANGELY QUIET.

Irene Holmes had wisely refused any new bookings for two days after the G-7 meeting. Most of the rooms had emptied after the final dinner; a few were scheduled to leave anyway. Others departed the second that the security order was lifted—without dessert—which was good as Terry had still worn a major portion of it.

The British Prime Minister and his former runway-model wife stayed over in the Queen's suite and the Italian leader with his latest girlfriend in the King's suite, but otherwise the hotel stood empty. Both couples apparently were sleeping in.

Kate had thought to make breakfast for herself and the remaining guests, but Dirk shooed her over to the empty side table where Kate had started this whole adventure.

'Nellie Scott will be arriving later today to take over the kitchen. You be done, lass. So, you sit here. Old Dirk will make you a nice Scottish breakfast."

'No haggis."

'No promises," he shot back with a wink and set a large pot of tea in the middle of the table.

Paul arrived with a sleepy-eyed Cecilia Barstowe on his arm. They'd stayed in a vacated room.

Kate hadn't slept yet but was looking forward to it soon.

Her brother sipped his tea and grimaced before looking at her.

"Morning, Paul."

"Hey, Katydid. Did they figure out what was on the spoon?"

She nodded as Dirk slid a plate in front of her. Two eggs easy, bangers, bacon, a scone, and a slice of tomato. No haggis.

He grinned down at her, "We save that for the Yanks. Not for people with a palate as fine as yours, lass."

"Sodium cyanide," she told Paul, too exhausted to return Dirk's cheery mood with more than a nod. "It precipitates as a salt. Dermal absorption—the first person to handle the spoon barehanded would have been dead in minutes as their skin absorbed the salt."

"Thank goodness I was wearing my gloves, as always, when I am setting the table," Irene sat down beside Cecilia and poured herself a cup of tea and dropped in a single cube of sugar. She reached for a spoon to stir it with—but hesitated and selected a fork instead. "Though I feel awful that I didn't notice the duskiness of the handle. I would have polished it off."

"And killed yourself in the process. It was deeply embedded in the engraving and filigree. Even if you had polished it, President Cheryl Kennelly would be probably be dead by now with no one the wiser as to how." Kate pointed out as gently as she could. Civilians and thoughts of their own mortality were often a jarring combination.

Irene looked deeply chagrined and studied her tea quietly.

And there was the last piece of the puzzle. Stephanie Bronson had ruined the career of George Madsen, though he'd been an innocent dupe. Her road to the White House would have been paved over Kate's own back once she'd been locked up for the President's assassination.

"But how—" Paul started again.

"You'll never guess who was a guest here at Inverlochy the last night before the meetings. Apparently, Stephanie Bronson seduced the sportsman to get a full tour of the G-7 event preparations. She must have slipped back into the kitchen that night to leave the wine. They found a note with no prints but a handwriting match that said, 'Many thanks from a grateful guest.' Then she must have treated the President's personally engraved silverware while she was down here."

"That's not hard evidence."

"No. However, she apparently threw a serious temper tantrum when Marcus and Leona arrested her in front of the Vice President of the United States. Said a number of interesting things after being read her rights that will keep Marcus and Leona busy for a while. Best attorney on the planet won't save her from this one. Seems she owned a burner phone. Once the FBI found the number, they were able to start digging out a number of interesting conversations from their scan records. All the death threats, including Klugman's murder can be traced back to her now."

Dirk dropped another couple plates of breakfast on the table. There was a brief commotion by the door, that stopped before Kate could be bothered to see what it was about.

Rikka dropped into a chair at the table and punched Paul hard on the arm.

"Ow! Kate didn't say, 'hit me'."

"Didn't have to, she gave me an open-season license on you," she cocked her fist again and Paul put up his dukes.

"You wouldn't hit a lady," Rikka sounded shocked to the core, but wore a cheery grin.

"I don't see a lady," Paul protested and wisely kept his fists up.

"Pardon me," Irene raised her hand.

Cecilia raised hers to match, "Lady here."

Kate figured she herself wasn't any kind of a lady—between punching out two Secret Service agents and what she'd do to Stephanie Bronson if she ever saw her again, which she wouldn't. So, she kept her hand down and her thoughts to herself.

To save her brother more trouble, Kate tried to distract Rikka.

"Where's Sam?"

"He's busy. Someone dropped me off. He'll be here later."

"Busy doing what?"

"Giving someone a present."

"What kind of present?" This was the Rikka she knew and appreciated. Never make anything simple when you can make it fun.

"The kind of present," Rikka turned abruptly serious and looked Kate right in the eye, "I'd give to anyone who messes with one of my friends, Kate."

This time Kate didn't resist the urge to sniffle and rose to circle the table and give Rikka a hug.

80

DINO WATCHED HIS CODE UNRAVEL.

Hitting the power switch or killing the router wasn't going to do him any good, it was unraveling in the cloud right where every governmental sniffer on the planet was going to see it.

Code like he'd never seen before. Christ, some language where he didn't know half the commands scrolled up his screens and chewed away at every defense he'd built.

He'd kept the code-sets that he'd used on each job and a screenshot of the damage or the files he'd grabbed. Man needed a brag file, after all. But no one else was ever supposed to find it on a Johannesburg stock exchange backup server. And none of it looked like this slick shit raining down on his systems.

A good hacker could go anywhere on the web, it was easy. And, in this day and age, everything resided *somewhere* on the web—just a matter of knowing where to look. Most of his for-hire work was for corporate insider crap or advanced surveillance like the recent G-7 thing.

But way more kept dumping onto his screens.

Stuff he'd never touched. Stuff that had nothing to do with him.

There was a tap on the Russian President's cell phone personally ordering attacks on foreign governments. Dino didn't know the dude *owned* a cell, but wasn't that going to shake up some impressive shit between the Russia and the US. And full details on the Iranian nuclear material enrichment program. Oh crap, they actually were doing bombs!

Where was this all coming from?

He keyed a trace, that looped back on itself and pointed to him. He launched his heaviest finder out of a Canadian forestry company's server. It scoured back along the path and then returned, *Unknown stack error: Madam Deal.* When he did a quick search on Madam Deal, all he kept getting was a 1940s comic strip. So, dead end there.

The code screen on his right froze. There was the file header that—

The file scrolled out of sight too fast to read. And then the next file popped up, stopping again on the header.

IP codes.

Another.

Real ones.

More.

Ones associated with the machines running the next level down from where he was now sitting. Not Guyana. Not Argentina. Here in the northern leg of the Principality of Sealand.

It was hard to read the files as each froze for only a moment, scrolled, froze again, scrolled. But he began to see the patterns.

Also embedded into the headers was a signature, a unique signature.

His own.

There went *Titan Rain.* Him, rather than the Chinese—

included how he'd framed them after selling them everything he'd stolen.

This wasn't going to end in a boring community service project like it had for Samy Kankar or Bobby Morris. Nor were they going to drop his butt in luxury prison for four years like Mitnick. They weren't going to pull him into being a quasi-legal governmental hacker on covert ops.

No, every person he'd screwed over, stolen from, or destroyed had just been notified of what had been done to them and by whom.

He tried once more to unravel who was after him. He found a cross-reference on *Madam Deal*. In the comic strip she was also known as *The Dragon Lady*.

Oh shit! That was such bad news.

The Anonymous group's hack to crash Mossad's servers during the missile strikes against the Palestinians showed up, absolutely labeled as being done by him. The hidden, unchangeable code altered to prove it was his doing.

He heard the vibrations of an inbound helicopter through the steel walls of Sealand.

Thank God! He should be gathering his gear, but he couldn't stop watching the screens.

The Royal helicopter...wasn't circling.

Two helicopters. Three. All coming straight in.

If the Americans didn't waste his ass, the Russians, Iranians, or Chinese were sure as hell going to.

The next report to hit his screen froze long enough for him to see it. He thought he'd been hijacking funds out of a New York Bank. But he hadn't.

The Bank of China had lost three quarters of a billion dollars, with a big B, and were going to be so unhappy.

There was an explosion as someone blew the locked door at the top of the north leg ladder.

Another report scrolled up on the next screen, leaving the

first in place. Not the Bank of China. He'd unknowingly hit a pass-through account directly to the dictator of North Korea's personal funds. He'd bankrupted Kim Jong-un. North Korea would be hunting his ass, if there was anything left to find.

Shit!

No wonder *Shŭ* came after him. Someone had slipped him a raw deal when he'd punched through the heavy security that the New York bank's...

Double shit!

The bank in New York didn't have that kind of account security. *Madam Deal*, whoever that really was, pretending to be security, routed him through China and into North Korea. It could start a goddamn war when Kim Jong-un discovered the loss. Except it didn't look as if the New York bank had received the funds, it looked as if it had gone into a different Bank of China account before simply disappearing. North Korea wouldn't attack the US, and they probably weren't stupid enough to attack China—but Sino-DPRK relations would be a long time recovering.

A final file on the final screen.

The RBB's money—including his hundred million from this job and the nineteen more he'd stashed from past jobs—was scattered so far and wide he'd never get it back. Anonymous donations to the Red Cross and pay-down of the trade deficit of Uruguay were only a few of the snarl of routes his money followed. He and Bronson each had a final balance of seven cents—0.07. The Dragon Lady had James Bond on the team? At this moment, he'd believe anything.

All of it was gone. Oh man, the North Koreans were gonna be pissed.

Every finger pointed straight at him.

Feet pounded down the ladders.

All three screens blanked—then all showed the same image.

It was a panel from some old, like 1930s-old, comic called *Terry and the Pirates*. A single view of the Dragon Lady in her long sexy dress, looking like the merchantess of death.

This wasn't a lame NSA geek spilling a bunch of documents to the world media through Wikileaks. These were deep, deep secrets that had now been routed to the wrong intelligence agencies—ones who despised each other's mere existence—with his signature on all of them.

He should have stayed in the United States. The FBI operated by the rules.

But he hadn't. He wasn't even technically in the UK. He was in the Royal Principality of Sealand.

The Dragon Lady kept staring at him with her slanted eyes, curly hair, and prominent breasts.

Who would ever think to look for him here, seven kilometers off the English coast?

Someone nasty.

And who had they told? There were so many options, each worse than the one before. His *worst-case* scenario would be...

Israeli Mossad agents poured into the room following no gentle rules of engagement like a US or British agency would have. Someone must have tipped them off for them to arrive so tight on the heels of the data breach.

Dino felt pieces of himself break as they smashed him to the floor, bound, gagged, and dragged him from the room and back up the ladders toward the waiting helicopters.

He heard the rumble and felt the whoosh of hot air of explosives as it roared up the ladder-well. The best computer equipment ten million euros could buy vaporized on the lower story of Sealand's northern leg.

Dino knew one thing for sure.

He'd pissed off the wrong person and there wouldn't be a shred of proof of it anywhere. Just a cartoon drawing staring at him out of a now-destroyed screen.

One of the last thoughts he ever managed was that he hadn't seen The Bitch coming.

One minute all normal.

The next, wiped off the face of the Earth.

The Dragon Bitch hacker team burned him down but good.

He also didn't see the big man standing silently on the upper deck of Sealand. His bare arms crossed in front of his chest. One emblazoned in Marine Corps blue with the words: *Celer, Silens, Mortalis.* The other bore the tattoo of Recon—a skull with wings and wearing a SCUBA rebreather, over crossed oars.

81

KATE PREPARED HERSELF TO UTTERLY WALLOW IN THE *GLEN NEVIS* room of the Inverlochy Castle Hotel.

Irene had offered her exclusive use whenever she cared to visit. That was too much but, as it was empty for the rest of this week, she'd accepted that much. Her grand master plan? Lose herself for a few days in the luxury that Irene and her staff made look so effortless.

Recent events—the pointless threats and deaths over revenge, greed, and avarice—left her chilled to the core despite the lovely weather.

Glen Nevis matched her taste and was what she most needed. It was the smallest room in the castle, not significantly larger than the generous bed, but it sat alone, away from all the others. Atop a private stairwell in a turret—the turret was the entire third floor.

Rikka would have teased her about her being the lone princess locked in a tower. But she'd flown home with Sam, sparing Kate that much at least.

The west-facing windows offered a sweeping view of the dark green forest and rocky peak of Ben Nevis reaching above it all. She'd have to see if she found the motivation to hike to the top while she was here. Somehow...she doubted it.

Whatever she did, she needed to start with a long, hot bath with a cheap novel. She looked forward to it, though she doubted it would melt the ice that encased her heart.

Paul was off with Cecilia Barstowe somewhere, Lake Como in northern Italy or were they in Bermuda? Either way, the Stark private jet was gone again. Didn't matter; it wouldn't last but they'd both have fun.

Cecilia had certainly been flying high when she left; a glance at the morning headlines revealed why. She'd sold her photos and exclusive story far and wide.

Chef Saves President's Life at G-7!

Kate saw it glaring from the front of the *London Times* on the carpet when she'd opened her door this morning. She'd carefully nudged it aside with her shoe, like toxic waste or half-dried dog poop. Yes, hiding away in this remote corner of Scotland for a week had definite advantages. At the top of that list was avoiding all the newsies late to the game lumbering about as they sought fodder for their feeding frenzy.

Rikka and Sam had flown back to the States. At Kate's insistence, they'd both been kept out of Cecilia's stories—it wouldn't be good for either of them to have their faces splashed across the international news. Though her friend would remain plenty busy behind the scenes. Rikka said she'd dumped Dino's massive files onto Marcus and Leona's desks, which might take years to unravel. She'd count on Mac Olson to repair the studio before she returned.

Kate closed her eyes in momentary pain.

Rikka...and Mac. Together.

The former had taken the camera with her. Kate could feel the two of them across an entire ocean, collaborating at this moment on the first episode of *Kate's Kitchen Rescue*. Well, they'd ignore her order to stop, if she was naive enough to issue one. Maybe she'd take Irene up on her offer and never leave this sanctuary—ever.

Lock the door, throw away the key. Someone...please!

Bath and a novel. Bath and a novel. She kept repeating it like a mantra as she turned on the taps extra hot.

Terry had followed President Kennelly to the airport. Who knew when she'd see him again.

Kate pictured herself enjoying egg-and-cress sandwiches, proper tea, and a good book in the gentle atmosphere of a Scottish afternoon in the Grand Hall. Though knowing herself, she'd eat the meals with the kitchen crew and Irene. Yes, far preferable to joining the more formal service in the dining rooms.

She had the tub mostly filled when there was a knock on her door.

Now what?

Wasn't she done with goddamn interruptions of death and vicious attacks over old wrongs?

Stephanie Bronson might end up in a psychiatric ward for her ongoing vituperative outbursts against Kate, Paul, and every man she'd ever bedded, by name. Going to be a lot of divorces and spouse swapping in New York society this year. Her newspaper wasn't broke; it was busted. The courts would be folding it up for good in the next few days. Every penny of the Bronson estate couldn't pay off the financial disaster Stephanie created there.

Kate yanked on a thick terrycloth robe provided by the hotel and didn't bother to tie the belt. Clutching the robe closed against the sudden chill up her spine, she braced herself, then stalked over to answer the door.

There, on the small landing at the head of her turret's private stairs, leaned Secret Service agent Terrance Tyrell. He wore his charcoal black suit, but he'd lost the tie and opened the collar on his white shirt. She had this brief image of undressing the man the rest of the way, but he'd made it clear he wasn't ready for that.

"What? Who's dead this time?"

"Do you always have such a dark view of the world, Stark?"

Kate looked up at his amused expression. Okay, no new body count; that was a good thing.

"Aren't you supposed to be with the President? On Air Force One? Flitting off to somewhere far, far away?"

"Delivered her to Air Force One. When they took off, that closed this assignment. I put in for a couple days off. Thought I'd stop by and see if you were interested."

"If I was interested?" Kate was interested in the world leaving her alone long enough to regain some slivers of her internal equilibrium. She wasn't particularly interested in going anywhere with anyone.

But Terry looked so damn good.

"Interested in what? Where were you thinking of going?"

"I don't know," he opened his mouth, then closed it again after glancing down at the newspaper on the top landing still trumpeting her sudden notoriety. The he smiled and leaned against the door jamb as if he had all the time in the world. "How does nowhere at all sound to you?"

How did it sound?

Her body practically hummed with her answer.

"What about..." She trailed off. He'd been the one who said he wasn't ready and that it was too soon after his divorce.

"Can you do me a favor and mark me down as realizing I was being an idiot?"

Kate knew Terry was many things.

An idiot wasn't one of them.

Well, neither was she.

She turned her back on Terry and walked toward the bath without closing the door.

Kate let go of the front of her robe then, after another step, allowed it to slide off her shoulders.

There was a quiet click as the door to her room closed.

She settled into the steaming water, closed her eyes, and waited for the man to remove more than his tie and come join her.

Terry Tyrell was exactly what she needed to burn away the ice that had shrouded her heart.

Go nowhere? Absolutely perfect.

AFTERWORD

If you enjoyed Ice Burn
please consider leaving a review.
They really help.

More Kate Stark coming soon.
Keep reading for an exciting excerpt from:
Kate Stark #3, Knife's Edge

A list of characters and locations may be found at:
https://mlbuchman.com/people-places-planes#KS
And return afterward for a free bonus story
and a recipe from the book.

KATE STARK #3 (EXCERPT)

IF YOU ENJOYED THAT, YOU'LL LOVE...

KNIFE'S EDGE (EXCERPT)

HE STEPPED INTO HEAVEN. OR AS CLOSE AS HE'D EVER IMAGINED while still walking upon this mortal Earth.

Bad boys don't go to Heaven, Raymond Chandler! He could hear Mama's favorite saying. He'd prove her wrong yet.

This moment was all pre-arranged, of course, but he cruised into the Brass Sheep Pub as if he'd randomly pulled off the road in his Ford Ranger. Not a tough-guy, I-own-the-freaking-road black F150 or Dodge Ram that lived to terrorize normal drivers on New England's narrow, twisted streets. But neither was it some suburban sedan and definitely not imported.

Just an average Joe in a deep-red pickup.

Shari had picked the color because it popped on video when parked near the inevitable forest green and dark wood that defined most pub exteriors—especially the Irish ones he intended to highlight as much as the television network would let him.

Shari and the camerawoman slipped in behind him.

The Brass Sheep was decorated in classic Irish style, right down to the painted board of a sheep swilling beer from a brass flagon dangling from above the entry door. Inside it sported old wood, comfortable booths, plenty of tables for groups both big and small, and a corner stage for three-nights-a-week bands. Twinkle lights and dried hops dangled from the rafters.

"Mr. O'Conner?" He greeted the portly gentleman wiping down the bar—for probably the fiftieth time anticipating their scheduled arrival. "I'm Ray Chandler. I heard that you have the best Irish pub 'round these parts."

"Best north" pronounced *nawth* "of Boston 'til you cross the wide Atlantic. Welcome to Gloucester" pronounced *Glosta.* "And call me Mike." They clasped hands over the bar.

The place was perfect. Gloucester, Massachusetts, was a small town—about twice the size of MIT's student body. *No, think middle America, Ray.* "So, Mike, what made you open a pub in a town that's a chunk smaller than the student body of BU?" Boston University had been his own alma mater, but Mama never let him forget his sister getting into MIT.

They chatted over that for a bit.

"That's quite a collection, Mike." Ray pointed at the wall Shari had already briefed him on. It was covered with hundreds of beer coasters, perhaps thousands—without a single repeat showing. There were plenty in Gaelic, but Shari's research said they came from over ninety countries and sixty-five languages.

"Every one of them are Irish pubs, Ray," his lifelong Gloucesterman accent shifted from North Shore, Mass. to Irish with pride. And the man relaxed as he started talking about something so familiar. "If we're missing one from Ireland herself, it's not from lack of trying."

Ray stayed attentive as Mike pointed out a few favorites that patrons had collected and brought back from various travels.

"The Irish Pub in Nepal, that's the most remote one there is by most reckoning, along the trekking route to Everest. The Dublin is a common last stop before leaving Tierra del Fuego for the Antarctic ice. There's Uganda, Cambodia, and Dessie O'Dowds is up to the top of Western Australia. Not much else there except crocodiles and red sand. Fetched that one myself."

Ray added that to his dreams, growing into such a media sensation that he'd be paid to travel to the world's most remote pubs. He filed that idea away to discuss with Shari and prompted Mike along on the pub's background and origins. Most of it wouldn't make it into the show, but that wasn't the point. He let his own Irish gift o' the gab prepare the opening of other doors.

Ignoring the camera and the woman behind it, yet leaving the best angles open for it, had been drilled into him by Shari during infinite practice until it became second nature. His producer was tougher. Shari stayed in the background, but she was the one who had found him. He'd been hustling as a sous chef at The Dubliner, the best Irish pub in Boston. She'd convinced him there was a whole vast world beyond Boston that he'd never really considered, then groomed and trained him enough to pass the toughest test in the industry.

At Shari's insistence, they'd started at the top and pitched to the largest food television network of them all. The actual owner of Cooks Network, Kate Stark, vetted every show personally. Five-ten, black Irish—fair-skin, jet black hair, and the bluest eyes he'd ever seen—she ruled as the uncontested queen of the media-driven side of the food world. And somehow, without crapping his pants, they'd pitched the show to her.

She ran the craziest interview process.

He and Shari never even had a chance to sit down in her office. *I watched your audition tape and read your prospectus and pitch,* Kate had said as she rose and shook their hands. *Nice enough. Let's go. This is Rikka, ignore her if you can. Something I've never managed.* She'd waved a negligent hand at a tiny slip of a

Japanese woman holding a camera far too big for her and an even bigger smile that could only be read as evil.

Without any other explanation, Ms. Stark had led them from her skyscraper office in Rockefeller Plaza in the heart of Manhattan, out onto the New York streets, and a block south to the Pig 'N' Whistle. *It's a casual place. I didn't give them any warning.* Her idea of casual needed a serious downgrade. This was an upscale watering hole of the broadcast elite in the heart of the city.

They'd called out Kate's name in greeting as she stepped in. *Hey Clive. I haven't had lunch; would love a bowl of your stew. And would you mind showing Ray here what you do?* And that was it. Kate Stark sat at the bar, ordered a pint, and looked at him for what appeared to be the last time. *One tip: it's not about you. Make them look good. You have until I finish lunch to capture enough film for a solid fifteen-minutes spot.*

He and Shari hadn't even needed to trade a panicked look, no matter how much they'd felt it. He'd plunged in. Shari orchestrated everything, including getting interview releases from some patrons also dining at the bar by the time he'd left the kitchen. Through some form of voodoo magic, the little camerawoman had always been right where he needed her.

Back at the studio, Cooks' head of production might have been cliché flamboyant but Mac Olson knew his shit. He'd taken the footage he and Shari had shot and polished off all the rough spots that neither of them had even imagined. The first shoot of *A Brew and a Bite* was beautiful and Ms. Stark's nod confirmed it good enough with only one note: *The history. These pubs often have deep history, add that element going forward.*

Shari had said that was part of the plan but this was only a fifteen-minute segment. It hadn't been, but it would be now. *Flexibility!* He and Shari were willing to flex however needed to rocket into the network's firmament. At the moment that was a pilot with an option on ten episodes in the full-hour format, way more than he'd ever dreamt of. Well, maybe Shari had when she fished him out of the Dubliner. No, by the look on her face, it was more than she'd ever expected as well. Ms. Stark had laughed at them both, but it had been a good-natured one that was easy to join.

After the pressure of that shoot, today's felt easy; anything would out from under Ms. Stark's watchful eye.

At the Brass Sheep's taps, he'd thankfully long since learned to pour and pull a Black and Tan, his favorite beer. Mike nodded his approval at the clean line he'd achieved between the heavier Harp lager filling the bottom half of the pint and the dark Guiness he'd floated on the top by using patience and dribbling the latter over the back of a soup spoon to make it land easier in the glass.

Shari gave him a smile, then shifted out of his peripheral vision. She'd be ten steps ahead of him, making sure the kitchen was prepped, the owner's friends and favorite patrons were ready, and anything else he'd never think of. Damn but that woman twisted him around. Six months ago it had taken her a single luncheon to fill his head with images of cracking into network television, and every day since she'd remade him in his own image. Polishing off his rough edges just as Mac Olson had done with that audition video—Raymond Chandler had never shone like this in his life.

Highlighting Irish pubs was only the start. He and Shari had sat at the Pig 'N' Whistle straight through to closing after Kate Stark had approved the show. They'd scribbled down structures for three other shows on the bar napkins. Then they'd gone back to their hotel room and fleshed them out into full proposals. They hadn't even stopped for sex until they had it down. Damn but they were perfect together.

Mama was gonna freak. Not because of Shari's mostly African-American heritage and coloring—except for the bleached blonde hair that looked so good on the tall, slender woman who positively vibrated with her high energy and inner vision. No, Mama would freak because that he'd fallen for a lapsed Baptist rather than a staunch Roman Catholic. The way Shari felt in his arms or making the shoot flow around him as she did now? *Deal with it, Mama.*

Mike O'Connor wasn't only the Brass Sheep's founder, it fast became clear that he was mostly the back room man. The camerawoman, Dana something, filmed him and Mike making a Full Irish together—bacon, sausages, eggs, beans, black-and-white pudding, home fries, toast, and roasted tomato slices. Then Mike's secret recipe for a curry chicken over jasmine rice.

"Ireland isn't all boiled potatoes, anymore. They welcome all types of decent folks. It's in our nature, Ray, isn't it?"

He couldn't agree more. That was how Shari hooked him, uncovering his love of just sitting in an Irish pub. A single beer could see him through a whole night; it was being there that felt most like home—especially when Mama was on a tear.

Mike was so perfect that he wanted to ask if Kate Stark had been here to prep him but knew she hadn't. It was true Irish hospitality, with a heavy slice of Shari's scouting work.

"Now, tell me about that." Ray pointed to the glass wall that backed the kitchen. "That is one serious setup. How did that happen?"

In a narrow room on the other side was a range of shining steel tanks, intricate weavings of connecting pipes, and all the other paraphernalia of small batch beer brewing. He knew the gear already from Shari's notes, it was built for a hundred and fifty-gallon batches, about ten kegs. But at Kate's reminder that it was about *them* not *him,* he let Mike tell his story.

Ray had already noted that six of the bar's taps were for Irish beers but that six more had strictly local names, Mike's own brews. Fisherman's Fancy was an IPA. Old Pear was an Irish red but an homage to the oldest cultivated fruit tree in the United States, the Endicott Pear Tree not ten miles away—

Shari had known and they'd visited it for a photo on the way here. Rockport Bitter might point to an old rivalry from the township breaking away in 1840, but the bite was good and the malt sweet and hop bitter were well balanced. There was even a Ledge Hard cider; ledge was what they called granite bedrock in this town made world-famous in the 1800s by its granite quarries.

"It took a big grant from Irish Pubs, Inc."

Ray knew about them. They rescued ailing pubs and helped launch new ones. He'd have to ask Shari where they got their money—Mike had said *grant* not *loan.* Time to dig into that later, for now Mike's was leading them into the brewery and he didn't want to break the rhythm of the shoot. The history would be better discussed when they sat in a booth together and shared a pint.

"Must have taken a bit to learn the brewing trade," Ray teased Mike as they faced all of the gleaming equipment that filled almost every inch of the small space. There was barely room to maneuver between the various tanks and piping.

"That it did, laddie. But, time and patience brings a snail to County Cork. Come let me show you." Mike sighed happily as he led them along the brewery line. His descriptions of each stage blew past Ray's studied knowledge. Where he'd been awkward at the front of the house, Mike turned erudite on the subject. Ray knew they could make an extra episode special of its own on the basics of brewing from this without any additional shooting costs, just editing and his own studio voiceover.

With that in mind, he focused of asking leading questions.

The questions.

Like the one he wanted to ask Shari about the ring burning a hole in his pocket.

"That's fascinating, Mike." How would she answer? Shari had been many things, but predictable wasn't one of them. But he knew it was right; he'd never been in such sync with a woman in his life. The sex rated spectacular, but the wonder of the woman made that fade into being a mere bonus. Nobody had ever believed in him so hard, definitely not his Mama.

She reappeared beside the camerawoman, who had suggested that she be allowed some time to get good shots down the whole line without any people in the way. While she did that, he, Shari, and Mike had simply sat together over the good food they'd made while she did her job. Dana wasn't as exceptional as that Rikka woman had been, but Cooks' people were definitely top grade. He wished for a second camera, but there hadn't been one available, so they often repeated one step or another to be shot from different angles.

When she joined them in the brewery, Shari had squinted abruptly.

Something going wrong? But it all seemed so smooth.

Then he spotted the direction of her gaze. Not the camera or their host. No, she stared at his right front thigh, where the lump of the ring box in his pocket made a bulge he hadn't thought to hide.

Her eyes opened wide and her gaze shot up to his.

One heartbeat.

Two.

Three...

And her smile blasted brighter than radiant.

In turn, Ray—

"That's odd," Mike was tapping a dial.

It didn't change.

He thumped it harder.

Still no change.

"What is this tank?" The stainless steel vessel stood seven feet high and as big as a shower stall that would fit two if they wanted to be as close as he and Shari usually were when washing each other down.

"It's the Brite tank, the finisher. We use a method here called Forced CO_2. Rather than adding more yeast to create the carbonation, I can do a multi-week process in hours with far more control by forcing the carbon dioxide into the finished beer under pressure."

Ray focused on the dial. "Is it supposed to be that high?" It was graded: white, green, yellow, and red. Even as he watched, the needle shifted into the red headed for the pin stop at the end.

Mike shook his head as he looked up at the top of the tank. "Pressure relief should have popped."

Shari edged closer.

Stepping to the control panel, Mike pressed a valve control.

The wire to transmit the electrical impulse to the valve that would stop the CO_2 had been cut. The tall supply bottles could provide one thousand and seventy-one pounds per square inch of pressure. The tank was designed to operate at fifteen psi and be safe to thirty.

It held to sixty-seven—

Then it detonated.

The first seam to fail was to the tank's side. The sideways blast of beer didn't touch any of them. But a piece of stainless steel shrapnel clipped the valve off the top of the closest CO_2 bottle. This turned the tank from a resource into a high-pressure rocket. The chains designed to keep the tanks from falling over weren't up to the task of stopping one with a missing valve.

It broke free and fell to the lie on the floor.

Mike was the first victim as the tank ricocheted off the back wall, shot beneath the tank still spewing a hundred and forty-six gallons of Shoebert the Seal Porter, and the bottle's butt end took him out below the knees. He landed face down in the dark brew had been named for a grey seal who had become a favorite of the neighboring town of Beverly when he spent a few weeks trapped in a freshwater pond, then crawled to the police station's back door for help in returning to sea. Knocked out cold, Mike lay awash in his own beer.

With the safety chain broken, the four other CO_2 tanks toppled to the floor. Another valve broke after it clipped a pipe. This tank skipped twice before going airborne and punching into the side of the brewing tank. A hundred and fifty gallons of boiling wort poured onto the floor as well. Forensics would never be able to later determine if Mike fully drowned before he was cooked to death.

The first cylinder, still ricocheting about the floor, severed the propane gas line to the wort boiler ahead of the step-down pressure regulator. The bolt of flame killed Shari instantly, not by burning her, but by the pressure wave that slammed her against the five-hundred-liter beer serving tank, freshly filled with the very popular Swordfish Stout. It was Mike's bestseller and had earned him his first contact by a national brewer wanting to license the recipe for a decently obscene amount of money.

Unaware of Shari's demise, Ray Chandler stood in the sea of unfinished brew, so far spared by the perfect storm of sloshing liquid, flying objects, and fire as the disaster wrecked the small Gloucester brewery. The CO_2 gas cylinders had run empty and come to rest, the beer flood had retreated from apocalyptic to ankle deep, and he stood well clear of the continuing flare from the broken propane pipe.

"Ha!" Ray pumped a fist in the air. The combination of three separate storm systems coming to form *The Perfect Storm* might have killed the Glosta swordfish boat *Andrea Gail* and turned the town into the setting of a major George Clooney motion picture, but he was still standing, by God. He'd always been a survivor. *Take that, Mama.*

But Ray didn't realize that a fourth element had been generated by this particular storm. The two cylinders had released two thousand cubic feet of pure CO_2 into the brewery's limited air supply as they emptied. The overpressure had blown much of the normal air mix out of swinging doors and ventilation shafts. The fire erupting at the snapped propane line continued consuming the remaining oxygen in the room at a prodigious rate.

Ray's balance wavered. He reached out a hand to regain his balance, barely noticing as his palm was sliced open by the torn steel of the tank that had initially detonated.

Instead, he stood there, weaving like a leaf on the wind. No longer able to find the oxygen to breathe, he suffocated standing up.

His knees folded first.

As he flopped onto the hard concrete, the last pain he felt was the ring box tucked safely in his pocket being driven into his thigh. His last thought was one of Mama's favorite admonitions, *Bad boys don't go to heaven.*

The camera operator was nowhere to be seen.

———

Three Days Later
Off Reykjavik, Iceland

So first-class! Exactly how she wanted everything to run all the way through.

Bert's hand rested over hers as Savannah laid the big knife on the icing of their wedding cake's lowest tier.

All hundred passengers and several of the expedition-class cruise ship's crew crowded together on the after deck. She'd arranged to have the captain turn the boat for the cake cutting so that the low sun of the Icelandic summer evening caught her best profile.

The only awkward aspect about the whole setup was that

Bert was lefthanded and she was righthanded. But because of the camera's angle, he had to stand to her left, forcing them both to use their off hands. Bert didn't seem to mind, but she always felt awkward and clumsy using her left land. She was sure it would show in the film. However, she took a deep breath to fortify herself, there was no choice. Kate Stark, the owner of Cooks Network had decided to film the wedding, and the camera had to be positioned to her right—it was only proper that the bride be front and center.

Because she and Bret were both using their off hands on the knife, neither one felt the additional resistance as the long blade snagged the thin wire hidden beneath the icing.

The knife tip connected to the metal base plate of the tier.

The circuit was closed: wire, knife, base plate.

A small battery buried in the cake's bottom layer sent a pulse of electricity through the circuit.

Neither Savannah nor Bert felt anything as they held the insulated handle.

But that's when things started to go very, *very* wrong.

———

Coming soon
Sign up for M. L. Buchman's newsletter to not miss a thing.
https://free-book.mlbuchman.com

ABOUT THE AUTHOR

USA Today and Amazon #1 Bestseller M. L. "Matt" Buchman started writing on a flight south from Japan to ride his bicycle across the Australian Outback. Just part of a solo around-the-world trip that ultimately launched his writing career.

From the very beginning, his powerful female heroines insisted on putting character first, *then* a great adventure. He's since written over 75 action-adventure thrillers and military romantic suspense novels. And more than 200 short stories, and a fast-growing pile of read-by-author audiobooks.

PW declares of his Miranda Chase action-adventure thrillers: "Tom Clancy fans open to a strong female lead will clamor for more." About his military romantic thrillers: "Like Robert Ludlum and Nora Roberts had a book baby."

His fans say: "I want more now...of everything!" That his characters are even more insistent than his fans is a hoot.

As a 30-year project manager with a geophysics degree who has designed and built houses, flown and jumped out of planes, and solo-sailed a 50' ketch, he is awed by what is possible. He and his wife presently live on the North Shore of Massachusetts. More at: www.mlbuchman.com.

Other works by M. L. Buchman: *(* - also in audio)*

Action-Adventure Thrillers

Kate Stark
Final Taste
Ice Burn
Knife's Edge

Miranda Chase
*Drone**
*Thunderbolt**
*Condor**
*Ghostrider**
*Raider**
*Chinook**
*Havoc**
*White Top**
*Start the Chase**
*Lightning**
*Skibird**
*Nightwatch**
*Osprey**
*Gryphon**
*Wedgetail**

Science Fiction / Fantasy

Deities Anonymous
Cookbook from Hell: Reheated
Saviors 101

Contemporary Romance

Eagle Cove
Return to Eagle Cove
Recipe for Eagle Cove
Longing for Eagle Cove
Keepsake for Eagle Cove

Love Abroad
Heart of the Cotswolds: England
Path of Love: Cinque Terre, Italy

Where Dreams
Where Dreams are Born
Where Dreams Reside
*Where Dreams Are of Christmas**
Where Dreams Unfold
Where Dreams Are Written
Where Dreams Continue

Non-Fiction

Strategies for Success
Managing Your Inner Artist/Writer
*Estate Planning for Authors**
Character Voice
*Narrate and Record Your Own Audiobook**
Beyond Prince Charming: One Guy's Guide to Writing Men in Romance

Short Story Series by M. L. Buchman:

Action-Adventure Thrillers

Kate Stark
Miranda Chase Stories

Romantic Suspense

Antarctic Ice Fliers
US Coast Guard

Contemporary Romance

Eagle Cove

Other

Deities Anonymous (fantasy)
Single Titles

The Emily Beale Universe
(military romantic suspense)

The Night Stalkers
MAIN FLIGHT
The Night Is Mine
I Own the Dawn
Wait Until Dark
Take Over at Midnight
Light Up the Night
Bring On the Dusk
By Break of Day
Target of the Heart
Target Lock on Love
Target of Mine
Target of One's Own
NIGHT STALKERS HOLIDAYS
*Daniel's Christmas**
*Frank's Independence Day**
*Peter's Christmas**
Christmas at Steel Beach
*Zachary's Christmas**
*Roy's Independence Day**
*Damien's Christmas**
Christmas at Peleliu Cove

Henderson's Ranch
*Nathan's Big Sky**
*Big Sky, Loyal Heart**
*Big Sky Dog Whisperer**
*Tales of Henderson's Ranch**

Shadow Force: Psi
*At the Slightest Sound**
*At the Quietest Word**
*At the Merest Glance**
*At the Clearest Sensation**

White House Protection Force
*Off the Leash**
*On Your Mark**
*In the Weeds**

Firehawks
Pure Heat
Full Blaze
*Hot Point**
*Flash of Fire**
Wild Fire
SMOKEJUMPERS
*Wildfire at Dawn**
*Wildfire at Larch Creek**
*Wildfire on the Skagit**

Delta Force
*Target Engaged**
*Heart Strike**
*Wild Justice**
*Midnight Trust**

Night Stalkers Reload
*Guard the East Flank**

Emily Beale Universe Short Story Series
The Night Stalkers
The Night Stalkers Stories
The Night Stalkers CSAR
The Night Stalkers Wedding Stories
The Future Night Stalkers

Delta Force
Th Delta Force Shooters
The Delta Force Warriors

Firehawks
The Firehawks Lookouts
The Firehawks Hotshots
The Firebirds

White House Protection Force
Stories

Future Night Stalkers
Stories (Science Fiction)

SIGN UP FOR M. L. BUCHMAN'S NEWSLETTER TODAY

and receive:
Release News
Free Short Stories
a Free Book

Get your free book today. Do it now.
free-book.mlbuchman.com

www.ingramcontent.com/pod-product-compliance
Lightning Source LLC
Chambersburg PA
CBHW021458110726
47899CB00001BA/208